"What ar

"I thought that obvious, *Luca*."

Involuntarily, he shuddered slightly, her use of his name having the intended effect.

She slid her other hand along around his waist, pulling herself closer, and he sucked in a breath, eyes fluttering closed as he attempted to keep control.

"I didn't come here for an assignation," he gritted out, eyes opening, and in them, she saw a resoluteness, an honesty, clouded with desire, that surprised her.

"You came to lift my spirits," she breathed, rising on her toes to reach his smooth jaw with her lips, trailing fluttering kisses along it. "Or would you tell me you don't want this?" One of his hands clasped a handful of her skirts, and she smiled, the rush of nearing victory flooding her veins, chasing the rest away. "Would you pretend you don't want me? That you haven't since we met? Tell me you don't want me," she challenged, ceasing her exploration of his jaw, tilting her head back to meet his gaze again. "Tell me you don't want this, and that will be the end of it."

"That isn't the point."

"The point is you came here to make me feel better. So make me feel better."

Author Note

Initially introduced in *The Housekeeper of Thornhallow Hall*, through reworking, Mary Spencer became a mere mention, though she remained with me, appearing in both *The Marquess of Yew Park House* and *The Gentleman of Holly Street.*

As she appeared in others' stories, she shared her own, and as she did, I wondered if I would ever be ready to tell it, all the while knowing I couldn't deny her her happy ending—or beginning. So here it is at last. Mary and Luca's story.

After finishing my Gentlemen of Mystery series, I wanted to remain in the world I'd created, explore it and the multifaceted genre of gothic romance further. It's fitting that hopefully what will be a new series begins with *A Lady on the Edge of Ruin*—both an ending and a beginning. A continuation and a departure.

As a note, I don't believe we are doing anything we weren't at the dawn of time. Our lives, societies, rules may have changed, and it's tempting to look back and paint a specific view of history; however, one look at the history books, and you'll see. We are, and have always been, human.

Finally, there are aspects to this book some might find distressing. If you or anyone you know has been affected by such matter as is within these pages, please be aware there is help out there. Numerous charities and organizations worldwide exist to provide support and guidance, and I urge you to seek them out if you are in need. You are not alone.

LOTTE R. JAMES

A Lady on the Edge of Ruin

ISBN-13: 978-1-335-59585-0

A Lady on the Edge of Ruin

For questions and comments about the quality of this book, please contact us at CustomerService@Harlequin.com.

Harlequin Enterprises ULC
22 Adelaide St. West, 41st Floor
Toronto, Ontario M5H 4E3, Canada
www.Harlequin.com

Printed in U.S.A.

Lotte R. James trained as an actor and theater director but spent most of her life working day jobs crunching numbers while dreaming up stories of love and adventure. She's thrilled to finally be writing those stories, and when she's not scribbling on tiny pieces of paper, she can usually be found wandering the countryside for inspiration, or nestling with coffee and a book.

Books by Lotte R. James

Harlequin Historical

The Viscount's Daring Miss
A Lady on the Edge of Ruin

Gentlemen of Mystery miniseries

The Housekeeper of Thornhallow Hall
The Marquess of Yew Park House
The Gentleman of Holly Street

Look out for more books from Lotte R. James coming soon.

To anyone needing some love to light a new path.
And always, to my mother, Brigitte.

Prologue

New Year's Eve, 1831

Harsh little balls of snow still pelted down from the night sky, nearly a curtain of white glistening in the lights of the theatre. Here, beneath the awning, they were somewhat sheltered from the blistering cold, but now that all the patrons had made their way inside, the warmth their bodies, tightly pressed together as they chatted and greeted each other, had provided was gone.

Only two of them remained now—beyond the attendants at the doors, and the various passers-by. Even most of the drivers had made themselves scarce, gone to discover the warmth of a nearby pub, whilst their masters were delighted by their theatrical New Year's Eve treats.

Luca was alone this evening—Deirdre was unwell, though she'd insisted he enjoy his evening and told him not to visit until she was cleared of whatever cold she suffered from. So to the theatre he'd come—after delivering flowers to Deirdre's home—and he'd gone inside, drunk a glass of champagne, even gone to see his seat. Only…then he'd found himself drawn back outside. Something…had urged him to…check on a woman he had no business… checking on.

Lady Mary Spencer.

Sister of the Marquess of Clairborne, part of one of the most respectable and powerful—albeit recently scandalous—families, Lady Mary was—despite being unmarried at past thirty—one of the *ton's* favoured. An unblemished rose of England, a paragon. Intelligent, powerful, wealthy, she was everything she was meant to be.

Luca had met her nearly two years ago now, when he'd first come to London with Deirdre. They'd been introduced at a ball, and yes, he like so many others, had been struck by her beauty, elegance, and grace. Also by…something else he couldn't quite name, but which commanded his attention whenever they found themselves in each other's vicinity.

Something which called him like a moth to a flame, and though he had no illusions of ever being worthy of her attention, Luca found himself over the years sharing snippets of conversation—or rather, banter and quips—with her. Though she seemed to be…annoyed by him most of the time, she also never sent him away. In fact, she seemed to welcome their bouts, begrudgingly, but with an eagerness which kept him returning, though he was mindful to never force his presence on her. It wasn't that he thought himself special, but with him, she was so different to the lady she was otherwise, and it intrigued him.

As did the rumours he'd heard over the years, the tales, the gossip, though he was always careful to take any such talk with a large grain of salt. He'd heard of her perfection, her glory, her sweetness, her influence and power in Society—to make, or break, even those in the loftiest of seats. He'd heard of doors being closed to those with blacker hearts than they had seemed to possess; of doors being opened again to kind hearts stained by scandal or disrepute.

He'd heard of how she and her brother had supported an old family friend—William Reid, Earl of Thornhallow—when the man had reappeared after a decade of exile, and not only married his housekeeper, but also fought to have a viscount punished for his crimes—including those against the Earl and newly minted Countess. The Clairbornes—Mary specifically—had been instrumental in having Viscount Mellors transported, the Earl and Countess being received back in polite company, and the others having suffered the Viscount's violence, being…given help.

Then, there had been the business with her own brother in the summer of 1830. The Marquess had disappeared from Society rather abruptly, and Lady Mary, along with the Dowager Countess, and another friend of the family—Freddie Walton, shipping magnate—had chased him to Scotland. When they'd returned, the Marquess of Clairborne had married a divorced woman—once known as *The Great Whore of Hadley Hall*—making her young daughter Elizabeth his own in all but law. Then again, Mary's—*Lady Mary's*—power and influence had ensured the family was not cast away from the highest rungs of Society. Then again, Lady Mary had quietly whispered and needled until her family name was restored, and her new sister-in-law and niece were welcome at even the grandest occasions. He'd found her…somewhat changed after that, and—

It is none of your concern.

Indeed.

Luca had also heard tell of her charitable work involving a place called Nichols House—not officially open, yet already full from what he heard. It was an endeavour started by a woman working for Walton, which from what he'd heard was a place of refuge, of learning, and enterprise, open to anyone in need; a place ruled by no moralists or zealots, but by someone who had herself once had nothing, until Freddie Walton had opened his door to her.

Yes, he'd heard so much of Lady Mary—good and ill. Even the rumours and wagers which purported she would marry Freddie Walton—whom Luca had never met, merely glimpsed on occasion at…lesser gatherings—before spring bloomed. Which was another reason he shouldn't be…getting involved.

Only…

Well, she was alone just now. No family—from what he'd heard they were all up North for the holidays, which made him feel…not sorry for her, but something akin to it—and there was no Walton either. No friends. No one.

And there she was, looking…cold, and anxious, her eyes darting across the busy streets, searching for…whoever she was meeting.

The call sounded for the beginning of the performance, and the attendant at the door gave them a perfunctory glance. Luca shook his head, glancing inside to see the last of the trailing audience move inside the auditorium.

Che fai? What are you doing? Staying or leaving...her?

Well, it wouldn't be gentlemanly to *leave* her without ensuring she was all right.

Emerging from his station by the doors, he closed the slight distance between them, and she turned, her eyes still anxious and unsettled, just as he arrived at her side.

'Lady Mary,' he greeted with a perfunctory bow.

'I haven't the time for you, Signor Guaro,' she bit back, waving him off, and returning to her search of the city just beyond the curtain of blistering snow.

Something is definitely wrong, Luca thought as he followed her, trailing a step behind as she paced the protected section of the pavement.

Banter, jests and jibes were one thing… Her harsh dismissal, barely concealing fear and concern, was another entirely.

'Besides, you should be inside with your mistress. I believe the performance has begun.'

'You'll forgive my impertinence, Lady Mary,' he said steadily. 'However, I cannot fail to notice… Well, you seem distressed, my lady, and I wondered if I might be of assistance.'

Lady Mary froze, slowly turning back to study him, frowning.

Her gaze flicked to the theatre's doors, then back at him, hesitation which was most…unusual, telling him she was, in fact, in need of assistance.

And perhaps she might even admit it.

'I am alone this evening. If she were here, Deirdre—that is, Lady Granville—would never allow me to leave a lady in need, without aid.'

'Mr Walton was meant to be accompanying me this evening,' she admitted quietly, after another moment of hesitation.

So the rumours are true, Luca thought.

A lady, attending a popular theatre with only a gentleman to accompany her…

He was happy for her, for *them*, yet at the same time, well, a pang of regret he had no right to feel twisted his heart.

'Freddie is never late. He's been… Behaving rather strangely, and I am concerned.'

The honesty, her rare vulnerability, lanced through him.

'Then I will fetch my driver, and we shall go find out what has happened to Mr Walton.'

'I—'

'Will tell me where we'll be going,' he said, before she could protest.

'Holly Street,' she nodded, grateful, but somehow… almost ashamed of accepting his help. 'To Freddie's shop in Holly Street—he lives there with—well, we need to see if he is there, and if he isn't, we shall speak to Mena. *Miss Nichols*, his…shopkeeper,' she specified, rather cryptically.

'Then to Holly Street we shall go.'

And so they did, once Luca had tracked down his driver

and carriage—a luxury he'd allowed himself considering the weather—though their journey did not end there.

A New Year's to remember...

Chapter One

London, March 1832

No one would ever even think to describe Lady Mary Evangeline Grace Spencer as an angry person. In fact, no one—living nor dead—could ever have even testified that they had seen her angry. A few customs and excise men in Sussex could perhaps testify that on January the first, in the year of our Lord 1832, they had witnessed her...being *frustrated*, and coldly authoritative, and many in Society had heard, or unfortunately, *felt*, Mary's frosty...*bite*, but they'd never seen her *angry*. Yet, it was what Mary was most days.

Electrifying, crackling rage thrummed incessantly through her veins; her very lifeblood. Quickening her heart-beat, shallowing her breath, making her clothes feel inordinately tight. Giving rise to the most unladylike, indecent urges, such as hurtling trays of priceless crystal at walls, or launching knees into gentlemen's most intimate places.

Anger's brothers—frustration, bitterness, and yes, fear—had also made their home in her; bubbling, brewing, and at times, threatening to boil over. They were her constant companions; the oldest friends she had. She viewed them thus—as friends—for she'd learned long ago that it was…useful to see them in that light, rather than as enemies. They had served her well; helped her withstand the trials of her life. Allowing herself to be fuelled by them, to accept they were a great part of her true spirit, gave her freedom, and power.

No one knew of her true disposition, her true emotions. Her mother perhaps, could lay claim to knowing not all was as it appeared with Mary; perhaps she could sense the turmoil within—but not even she knew the true extent of it. Nor did her brother, the great Henry Spencer, Marquess of Clairborne, too involved with his own life as he was, which was only natural. And there had always been a…distance between them; though in his defence, in the past years, he had *tried* to shrink it best any of them knew how to.

Her friend, Freddie Walton, could perhaps lay claim to knowing there was something *not quite right*, though he believed it to be sadness, or loneliness. And he too was now preoccupied with his own life—newly wed and off with Spencer to Scotland—to investigate any further. Beyond that… Mary didn't have many *friends*. She had…acquaintances she called friends when it served her. Once, there had been friends—daughters of Society like her—but when bonds of communal…*trial*, had been forged, the bonds of friendship had… Well, they'd all been forced to, if not *part ways*, then maintain a certain distance. The only one she still saw regularly was Frances, and though they met outside of Society, Mary was always careful to ensure her mask was firmly affixed when they…met.

It suited Mary, to be so unknown. In fact, it was…her greatest success. Her *raison d'être*—to be seen only as she wished to be. As she *had* to be, in order to have the life, but more importantly, the power she required to survive.

Everyone had a driving force. For some, it was love. Others, a need to care for their fellow man. Desperation. Survival. Ambition. Greed. Lust. Knowledge. Mary's driving force—even before she could articulate or understand it—had always been a quest for power. Not the certified power of kings, lords, or lawmakers. She'd never been so naive as to believe that was within her reach; no matter what hopeful intellectuals in certain circles posited. No… The power she sought was a quiet power, which granted the wielder safety, and freedom. The power to rule over their own destiny; and that of others.

It was an ancient, undefinable power, which struck instinctual fear in the hearts of men for millennia. It was subtle, and if properly wielded, invisible, it was the power of secrets, whispers, and intangible influence. The power to ruin, or raise up. The power wielded by those dubbed not *kings*, but *kingmakers*.

The power—its nature, its vital importance—was revealed to Mary in tangible form, when she was seventeen. She'd witnessed her mother wielding it, like some ancient sorceress bending armies of foes to her will—using secrets, promises of support, exchanging favours…whatever was necessary, using every weapon in her arsenal to have her will be done—and that was the moment Mary had found, or rather, articulated her purpose.

To master and wield that power; to become a greater sorceress even than her mother.

The first necessity was to craft a perfect, beautiful disguise. Which wasn't difficult, considering she'd already begun the journey from birth. Encouraged, taught, to become the perfect daughter of a peer of the realm. A daughter of England, and above all, *Society*. Which is what she'd become.

Hence why no one truly knowing who she *actually* was, wasn't sad, but heartening. Why it made her feel triumphant.

However, there was a problem; *had been* for some time now.

It was getting harder with each passing day—*Hell, with each passing second*—for Mary to keep her emotions in check. To keep control of those friends inside her heart, and if she lost control…she would launch a tray of priceless crystal against a wall, or knee a gentleman's bollocks, and then… The image she'd spent a lifetime crafting would disappear like smoke in the wind, as would the power she'd mastered and wielded for nearly as long.

And then, her life would be over.

It wasn't merely one thing which had prompted this… *discountenancing*, but years of things. And years spent in Society—even if her power came *from* Society. Everything which had fed her for years, now wrenched and racked her stomach. A parasite, growing sick of its host, yet unable to survive without it.

As her…*sickening* worsened, so did the emotional storm within. Anger and its brothers had children. Doubt, hesitation, uncertainty. She *wondered* now. If perhaps she'd been wrong, to become what she had. If she'd erred, finding not purpose, but instead ensuring she had *no* purpose. If accepting, and nurturing, the darkest parts of herself, had transformed her into something grotesque; if it had transformed her into the same manner of monster she used her power to vanquish. She wondered if the greatest monstrosity of all was that she wasn't so bothered about becoming a monster, but deeply concerned with the potential lessening, and loss, of her power. She wondered if holding onto to others' darkest secrets—for later use—was poisoning her, and she'd be better off exposing them all to the world rather than quietly punishing them. She wondered why she wondered so much, and how she was to stop it.

Before I lose everything.

'What a perfect day,' the Countess of Sailsham exclaimed excitedly, pulling Mary from her thoughts; a place she'd been lost all too often lately.

Thankfully, an automatic, polite smile appeared on her lips, and she forced her hand to loosen its perilous grip on the champagne coupe, as she returned to her surroundings.

A bright blue sky, peppered with fluffy white clouds loomed above the manicured lawn and gardens belonging to the Marquess and Marchioness of Forthan. Perfectly positioned oaks and alders stood watch, and provided ample shade, but just in case, a myriad of white tents, trimmed with gold, were set up strategically across the lawn, while more tables and chairs were artfully arranged on the terrace.

The very best of Society milled about, dressed in their most luxurious, and *à la mode* fashions—bright colours of the elders mixing with the pastels of the newest arrivals to the circus—sampling from the ostentatious and overflowing tables and trays of food and drink, laughing, gossiping—*naturally*—scheming, and playing; and not only the wide variety of games set up across the expanse with not one blade of grass out of place.

And here she was—*naturally*—in the middle of it, surrounded by pillars of this great Society; their tittering voices, the swish of silks and linen, the flapping of fans and parasols, even the tinkling of their dripping jewels, a strange music to underscore it, not least of all for it clashed discordantly with the actual music provided—unsurprisingly a light tune from the quartet set upon the stairs to the terrace.

'Absolutely splendid, as though God himself smiled upon us today,' the Countess droned on, whilst the others in their circle nodded and tweeted like the brainless birds they were. 'Blessing us all with His grace.'

Mary doubted that if God were to choose a place to bestow His grace, it would be this ridiculous garden party; still, she widened her smile.

Let the Countess believe what she wished. Perhaps it

was all she could do to avoid seeing the foul truth of this party. To avoid admitting that it was a meat market as surely as the one near old Saint Bartholomew's; that the meat in question paraded about today for potential buyers—like so many others—was her own daughter.

No need to shatter the Countess's illusions.

Though were it ever to serve a greater purpose, Mary wouldn't hesitate.

'Lady Forthan must be delighted,' the Marchioness of Dalton purred. 'Though this party has always been exceptional, even last year, when we were forced indoors by rain.'

'Arguably, it was even more successful *because* of the rain,' Viscountess Learst grinned slyly. 'Why, I can think of three couples who came to be as a direct result of the gentlemen's quick thinking—shielding maidens with coats, or shepherding them to safety before any muslin or silk could be ruined.'

Ah yes, that great plague that is rain for silk or muslin.

'I find myself wishing for rain,' the Countess laughed, the other women—Mary included—offering conspiratorial chuckles.

'Oh dear,' the Marchioness sighed suddenly, her eyes affixed somewhere over Mary's shoulder. 'My daughter has contrived to find herself somewhere even less appealing than ballroom chairs.'

They all looked in the direction of the Marchioness's gaze, and immediately understood the veracity of her statement, though the emotion that swelled within *them* was very different to what swelled within Mary—not that she would ever admit it.

Instead, she would pretend the spectacle elicited the same blended emotion as the others: disappointment and concern; anything else would be ludicrous.

One should only be disappointed and concerned when one of this Season's *most eligible*—Lady Lilian—wasted her time, efforts, and charm, on a *fancy man* rather than an *eligible* man. When she, and a gaggle of the new crop of marriageable misses, congregated around the Dowager Countess of Granville's *kept man.*

Signor Luca Guaro.

Lady Granville had brought him to England two years ago, after a long sojourn in Italy enjoying her widowhood, intent on continuing to enjoy it—not that anyone begrudged her that considering Lord Granville had been a hard man, and far from the *best of them.*

Since his arrival, Signor Guaro had become a staple of Society, attached to Lady Granville's side as he was. And since their own introduction at a ball two years ago, Luca—*Signor Guaro*—popped up in Mary's presence at every possible occasion, determined to…*engage* with her, though they only really engaged in verbal sparring.

To Mary's eternal woe, it had only worsened since she'd made the unfortunate mistake of accepting his help in a moment of…urgent need this past New Year's. Freddie had failed to meet her at the theatre, and Luca had not only seen her to Holly Street, but upon learning that her friend had been taken, he had accompanied her and the woman Freddie would eventually marry—Philomena 'Mena' Nichols—to Sussex. Together, they had saved Freddie from a vengeful uncle, past sins, and himself, and she couldn't deny having Luca there, for *her*, had been…really nice. However, as soon as they'd returned to the city, she'd put the distance which should remain between them…back. The…little expedition outside of time and place—outside of rules and Society—was over.

And you would do well to remember it.

Just as those little lambs should remember why they are at this forsaken party.

Which was *not* cavorting with Signor Guaro. It mattered not that he was charming—or so Mary was told; she preferred *annoying* or *impertinent*—and pretty. He was far beyond handsome, and she refused to call him beautiful—*far too complimentary*—so yes, pretty.

Tall, and slender—though nonetheless imposing by some trick of the light no doubt—Signor Guaro was always dressed in sumptuous clothes, never failing to be at the height of fashion, and complimentary of his rich olive, Mediterranean complexion. His dark brown—*yes, with hints of silver and auburn, though others at a glance mistake it for black*—artfully longish strands were as if constantly caught in the wind, framing his perfectly oval face, with its ridiculously square jaw. His features were sharp, and fine—well, except for his nose, which, when examined closely, was larger than it looked. As was his wide mouth, with its full lips—*full, not plump*—comically defined with its exaggerated bow. His deep-set almond-shaped eyes were arrestingly bright, though they too were the dark brown of chocolate having been melted into coffee. If that were something people did. Melt chocolate into coffee.

As she said, *pretty*.

Still, all that *prettiness*, and charm, shouldn't have swayed the little idiots from their purpose. They'd been warned against such distractions, *trained* against falling prey to such silliness. So yes. There was nothing but disappointment and concern to be felt.

Precisely.

'Rather distasteful of Deirdre to bring him,' Viscountess Learst commented in the worst *stage whisper* in the history of stage whispers.

Everyone tittered and tutted in agreement.

'We cannot begrudge her,' the Countess countered. 'He is entertaining enough, and she deserves every amusement she can afford.'

Sage nods followed, though Mary refrained, instead sipping her champagne.

'Well, I should attend to Lilian,' the Marchioness declared. 'If you would excuse me.'

'Nonsense, Octavia,' Viscountess Learst said. 'We shall come with you; there are others who require our aid, and swiftly, if I do say so.'

Heads bobbed, nodding, and then the women were off. Mary accompanied them—it would not do to remain planted there like arboreal decoration—though halfway across the lawn, she excused herself. Not that anyone noticed—too invested were they in their rescue—and slowly she meandered towards the tables set beneath a mighty oak likely two centuries old, all occupied by viscountesses, countesses, earls, dukes…all the best this land had to offer of *nobility.*

Attempting to focus, to lessen the tightening of her clothes and seemingly her own skin, she gazed at them all, trying to determine which gaggle would be most useful to join, though that was tricky since today she had no defined purpose beyond seeing, and being seen. Information gathering was *always* essential, but then one must determine the *type* of information one wished to gather—affairs, politics, financial turmoil—in order to make an informed decision.

For some reason, she couldn't choose, and she refused to admit it was connected to that strange feeling which most certainly *was not* jealousy or *envy* or anything akin to either. What reason would she have to be jealous of those little geese, batting their eyelashes at the most infuriating, annoying man ever?

None, to be sure.

Taking as deep a breath as she could manage, Mary's gaze drifted across glittering diamonds, embroidered silks, and a hundred faces she knew too well. Their voices and laughter melded into melodic chatter, which she needn't hear to decipher. She'd heard the same conversations, the same scheming for years and years.

Take the Duchess of Fanshawe, for instance—there, a sharp-eyed eagle, keeping watch over her table of cronies. Though barely fifty, she comported herself like some great aged matron, down to the stiff-necked gowns and walking stick she didn't need. Mary would bet a fair few pounds that she was chastising Lady Gladstone just now for allowing her boy to play badminton when it made him look both uncoordinated, and sweaty.

Most unappealing.

And there, the Countess of Warton—the sly, porcelain beauty—Mary would wager she and her sycophantic, drunk husband, alone as they were, were trying to find new friends; though considering the sizeable loss of assets they'd suffered, it was a wonder they'd been invited today. Lord and Lady Forthan were *very* careful to only invite those at the very top of Society's echelons.

Such as Lady Kielhurst, *there*, likely regaling her retinue of devotees with her adventures returning from the country, which involved a broken carriage wheel, a runaway cow, and ended with two daughters married.

Most fortuitous, she would say.

To have them wed before it could be known one was ruined in a tryst with a stable boy, she would certainly not say.

Yes, Mary could hear it all from her vantage point; said and unsaid.

How tragic that he died without an heir since the title will go to a man of trade.

Have you heard about her appearance at the ball last Saturday? Why, she wore a gown two seasons out of fashion! No wonder she wasn't invited today.

There are large sums in the books—we shall see how long it takes the Farrow boy to win the affections of that actress.

The French disease they say; no wonder at all that Hilary retired to the seaside.

Pain thumped behind Mary's eyes, dizzying, and constricting. She ground her teeth tightly, trying to force herself to relish it as she once had; still, the headache and accompanying nausea worsened, and she wished she could tear off her stifling clothes, and scream at them, or merely scream until she could no more.

Such a modern Cassandra I would be...

'Walton was her last chance, truly,' some high-pitched voice sighed, pulling Mary from her daydreams. She stilled, as the voice droned on, and she recognised it as that of Viscountess Porens, who, to avoid the consequences of being *enceinte* following an ill-advised tumble with a sailor, had contrived to be publicly compromised by a resentful Viscount Porens not two months ago. 'One would've thought she would try harder to secure the match. Particularly since the tradesmen are increasingly eager to breach the walls of our Society, it could not have been so daunting a task. But then, with age, everything becomes more trying.'

Icy fury flooded Mary's veins, settling her for a moment as nothing else might've.

Turning, she did not have to look hard to find the vicious viscountess—along with a bevy of other vipers—not even pretending to keep her voice conspiratorial, as she discussed Mary's private affairs.

It wasn't the first time she'd heard such comments since Freddie had married a month ago—after all, for years people were convinced Mary would wed him—and typically, she pretended to neither notice nor care, for she didn't care. It was no damage to her reputation that they thought her and Freddie *more* than friends, or even that he'd spurned her. It would take a great deal more than something so trifling to damage *her* reputation. If anything, it made people pity her, and that was inordinately useful.

Only *this* wasn't pity, but viciousness. It was proof...

Mary's power was...wavering, if *this* viscountess thought she could so easily, *inconsequentially*, be vicious. No...

Besides, Mary had never liked the Viscountess—or her band of hangers-on, not since they'd all made their debuts a couple years ago—and only interacted with them when it served. Which wasn't often; they barely made the cut for this lauded company—by way of marriages, not breeding.

It took less than a few seconds for Mary to settle on how she would deal with this harpy; to find the perfect *coup de grâce*.

'Lady Porens,' Mary smiled, her tone even, and chilling. 'How well you look. Such a remarkable gown; you must share the name of your *modiste*. It does wonders for your figure, and emphasises your...*curves*.'

With a pointed look, and raised eyebrow, Mary cast her eyes towards the Viscountess's belly; the condition which had prompted her to snare the title was far beyond what it should be considering *when* she'd been found *in a scandalous position* with the Viscount.

She did not remain to see the effect of her words—beyond the Viscountess's paling, and the horrified gasps of her circle. Instead she marched on, straight through the marquesses, dukes, earls, and countesses, into the house.

It wasn't until she was alone, ensconced in a small, darkened library far away from everyone—even servants—that she felt as if she could breathe.

Somewhat.

Leaning back against the door, Mary drew in breath, after breath, trying to stop the tumult inside from taking over—though her hands shook, even flat as they were against the cool wood.

In less than an hour, rumours surrounding the Viscountess's yet unborn child would swirl in every circle, though few would remember from whose lips the truth had sprung. A truth—or rumour of truth, for one never said *truly* what they meant—that would reach the Viscount's ears in likely less than five minutes. Even if he did not seek…legal remedies, Viscountess Porens's life would never be the same. She would be cast out from this blessed upper echelon, and if she remained in Society, it would be one of the very lowest rungs. *If* she were that lucky. Whatever happened to her, it would be Mary's doing.

Not mine. It was her choices, her treachery and trickery, which led her here.

Precisely.

Only, it didn't feel so simple.

Pushing away from the door, she removed her hat, tossing it on a table before wandering to the window. Mary tried to push aside…the *guilt*; an unwelcome, unfamiliar emotion she'd only recently become acquainted with.

For guilt brings nothing but weakness. And I can never be weak again.

This is the power you sought. You have it, and wielded it. Never regret it.

Chapter Two

Something was amiss with Mary. *Lady* Mary, he reminded himself; though Luca only mentally allowed himself the transgression. Well, except for New Year's, when she'd granted him permission to call her Mary for a grand total of two days. Regardless of what he called her, it didn't change the fact that something wasn't…*right*, and truth be told, Luca was worried. Though he had no business being worried.

Technically.

Publicly, he could claim only that she was an acquaintance. Privately, he liked to think they were some manner of friends—even if she would likely scoff at the designation. Publicly. Privately she might not, considering she *had* allowed him to assist her in a most dangerous time; but then since, she'd barely spoken to him—not even at the Waltons' wedding breakfast. So perhaps the circumstances had merely led to a temporary…*dégel*. Thawing.

Whatever her feelings towards him—and despite the utter stupidity of it—he cared for her. About her. Both. Either. He cared that she was…*out of sorts*, as she left the garden party—swiftly, but gracefully. And as no one else batted even an eyelid, nor stopped or followed her, apparently he was alone in noticing.

Perhaps I am merely imagining it...

'Go on, Luca,' Deirdre whispered. He turned, and her effervescent green gaze met his own, the edges crinkling as she smiled. 'You've seen me refreshed with tea and pastries, and if you tarry any longer, you shall attract all manner of unwelcome creatures,' she finished, glancing pointedly at a group of ladies eyeing them—ever *so* indiscreetly behind their fluttering fans.

Luca grinned, though he didn't rise.

After all, he was here for her—*always*—and he'd barely returned to her side after being waylaid by a group of fluttering debutantes on his way from fetching refreshments.

Luckily, mothers and matrons knew as well as he the mistake those young ladies had made, and though they came to save the misses, they'd saved him too.

'Who will protect you from such creatures should I leave?'

Deirdre turned to him, an indulgent smile on her lips.

'Go, Luca.'

He nodded gratefully and rose, taking her hand, and gently kissing the knuckles.

Then, careful to appear purposeful enough to avoid being hailed, yet mindful not to seem eager to follow one of the *ton's* most prized members, Luca made his way into the Marquess and Marchioness of Forthan's grand home.

He took a moment to get his bearings once inside the decadent maze, filled to dizzying heights with the most exquisite furnishings and art. *People too*—servants, and guests looking to refresh themselves; or for a private enclave to conduct *all* manner of business. Too many people for Mary to have tarried long, and since her position afforded her every privilege as a guest, Luca posited she must've found somewhere not so easily discoverable. As he made his way through the house—*casually*—Luca tried not to think on what he was doing, and why.

I am merely looking in on...a friend.

It wasn't as if he was searching Lady Mary out for a tryst. Though if anyone discovered them alone together, that was undoubtedly what they would put about. And despite the fact that Lady Mary was unattached, and firmly, as the saying went, *on the shelf*, it would be an utter scandal. No matter that she was beyond certain rules and requirements merely by her age, it would ruin her good standing—her *perfect* standing, Luca corrected—because of *him*.

Yes, *he* was the problem. His station…limited him in so many ways. He supposed it was the same for everyone—one's role in society, it defined them. Defined what their life had to be. He'd never resented his own position, or the requirements of it; until he met Mary. Then, he'd begun to feel their restriction; their bitterness. Though he could never be ashamed, or regret his choices.

He certainly could never be ashamed, or regretful, of his relationship with Deirdre. Lady Granville had been good to him, and though Society believed otherwise, theirs had long been a platonic relationship, rather than romantic. Shifting from lovers to friends; though her support—pecuniary, emotional, advisory, and so much more—had never wavered. Deirdre encouraging him to seek out Mary—though he'd never spoken of his…*tendre* for the lady, even if his escapade with her this past winter might've been proof enough of one—was testament to Deirdre's exceptional and surprising nature. She was a kind, generous, beautiful woman, and he adored her. That would never change.

Still, he felt the…weight of what he was the first time he met Lady Mary Spencer. Regretted, for the first time, that he was not some dashing hero, clever man of business, or wealthy prince, but a *kept man*. One who had not acquired wealth, status, or even his own survival by his own hands and wits, but instead by being a *companion*. Now, with Deirdre, merely providing company; but previously by providing *company* as well.

Some respected his...*profession.* Those who did were more often than not Continental. Here, he may be *somewhat* acknowledged, and accepted, but he would always be looked down upon, as a necessary evil. And Deirdre would always be viewed with pity and envy.

I do detest England for that, he thought, his jaw clenching as he shut the door to another blessedly empty room. *Blessedly,* for it didn't contain couples *in flagrante*, or disapproving lords making deals to sell the fruit of their loins.

This really was a terrible idea. He should turn back, go to Deirdre where he was meant to be, and cease chasing after a woman—friend or not, noble reasons notwithstanding—and...

Learn my place.

Just one more door, he promised, and whether he would've kept it, none would ever know, for finally, he had found her.

Luca let himself into the library, which was certainly not the primary library of this residence, considering its intimate size, though it was nonetheless imposing with its vaulted ceilings, walls of books, and rich, sumptuous furnishings, from the plush rug to the leather armchairs set by the dark hearth of swirling marble.

Not that he saw much, as he closed the door with a quiet snick, for all he saw was *her.* Stood at the ostentatiously grand windows, overlooking the very park they'd just left, nothing more than an outline in the gloom, she was still the most glorious sight.

He knew it was utterly foolish to harbour such...*appreciation,* yet it was impossible to chase away; and he should know, having attempted the feat many times since they'd begun their acquaintance. Only his feelings were as vital as breathing now—not that he'd ever speak of them, or presume to believe his could ever be anything but a distant, and lonesome appreciation.

Mary turned slightly as he traversed the room, the outline of her profile a shadow portrait.

'Signor Guaro,' she sighed, turning back to the glass. 'After being detained by the debutantes, I would've thought your mistress would've summoned you swiftly back to her lap.'

Luca frowned as he came to stand beside her, the bite in her tone unfamiliar.

He studied her, not merely to appreciate the living art that she was, but also to understand her current mood. He'd sensed her being...*out of sorts*, but he'd been half a lawn away from her all day, unable to note specific markers to support his...instincts. Looking—*gazing*—at her now...

Her hat was gone; her long golden locks tightly curled into fashionable ringlets—though her hair was naturally softly curled—and pinned around her head, tiny dried blossoms of blue sage tucked into them near the front. Barely a hair was out of place, as if God himself had forbidden any strands to disobey their call to perfection. Just as He'd forbidden her gown—which was of the finest silk stripes, the colour of cherry blossoms and silver, framing her collarbone, and emphasising her perfectly rounded shoulders with its voluminous sleeves, bordered with the most intricate lace he'd seen in a long time—to droop or wrinkle. Not a speck of dust marred the pure white of her gloves, covering her tightly clasped hands, and the few rays of sun which made it to this side of the house had been ordered to catch in the rubies hanging at the dip of her throat, and from her perfect ears.

It wasn't merely her ears, or her dress, which were perfect; the rest of her appeared so too. From her form—something akin to Botticelli's infamous Venus—to her features. Sharp, symmetrical—as if etched by an artist. Long straight nose. Neither thin nor plump lips, drawn in a perfect shape. High, rounded, but sharp cheekbones. Eyebrows a darker shade of gold—as if the nuggets had only just been torn from a river—and gently arched, as if they too had been drawn. And beneath them, her rounded, almond eyes, lined with long, brown lashes. The most vibrant blue—that of the thickest ice—speckled with shards of silver—three in each eye. All so beautiful; the near-perfection aching.

Only, Luca knew it wasn't—*she* wasn't perfect—and it was those tiny details others might view as imperfections that made her even more achingly spellbinding. How her hands turned shades of blue and purple when she was cold. The freckles across her chest. The strange way her straight white teeth curved inwards. The fact that one eye was infinitesimally larger. Her lightly crooked smile—tending towards the right. And naturally, the lines on her face which told the tales of her life, if only one could read that language.

All Luca could read was that they had deepened; multiplied in the years he'd known her. Those by and beneath her eyes; those that ran from her nose to the dimples nearly always in view—she was nearly always smiling—and those between her brows. But the lines, like the dark shadows beneath her eyes, were not from smiling. They were born of sadness, and…

That reminded him of his purpose, her words, and *that* tone. Cold, lethal, and disdainful—meant to wound, like the words, though they didn't.

In a strange turn, they fascinated him, and gave him… the opportunity to say something he dearly wished her to know.

'It isn't like that,' he said, facing the window, his own hands clasped behind his back lest he do something beyond the pale such as try and smooth all that sorrow away. 'I'm not a pet. Certainly not Lady Granville's. I am her companion, and her friend, unquestionably, but not in the manner you nor Society believe. I have a duty, to be sure, but I am not some manner of leashed lap dog.'

'There is a leash tied about your neck, Signor Guaro,' Mary retorted, mockery lacing her tone. 'A shiny, golden one, to be sure. Denial doesn't negate its existence, plain for us to see. But I care not about your relationship to your mistress,' she sighed. 'What I wish to know is why you're here, intruding on my solitude.'

'I don't believe you,' Luca mused.

He felt Mary turn to him, and looked at her as her brow raised.

It was the oddest thing. The more she pushed him away, attacked, the more he felt…*drawn*. Only once before had he felt her nearly as unguarded as now—devoid of her visage of sweet gentility—but even then, others were present, and now…

There is only us.

'I don't believe you seek solitude.'

'Why do men always refuse to heed a woman's plain words?' she muttered, overtly exasperated, rolling her eyes, and turning from him again. 'Why is it they are always so utterly convinced they know us better than we know ourselves?'

'I don't pretend to know you better than you do yourself. I don't pretend to know you at all.' *Though to know you is my dearest wish.* 'If you wish me to leave, say the words. I only sought to…ensure you were well. You seemed… troubled.'

'Why? Because my smile is missing?'

'You rarely smile in my company.'

'Because you annoy me,' Mary replied, the bite disappearing with every passing moment. And she hadn't said: *leave me*. So he wouldn't. If he could lift her spirits—even by verbally sparring—well, he would. 'But you already know that, and have apparently made it your purpose to hound and exasperate me.'

'I don't hound you.' *I seek you out.* 'And I do not think you annoyed just now.'

'You're right,' she shrugged. 'I'm bored. Bored of this endless farce. Bored of watching the lambs go to slaughter, year after year.'

The bitter sadness and viciousness caught him off guard again, rendering him speechless.

He'd never heard her speak thus—but then he doubted anyone had. It worried him, and he couldn't but wonder where such vehement feelings stemmed from, yet he also felt… Hypnotised, and honoured in a twisted sense, to be privy to this side of Mary he doubted few—if any—had seen before. He wondered if she meant to shock him, drive him away, or provoke him into an argument, but he couldn't quite believe it, for this Mary felt…

Brutally unguarded. Honest. Vulnerability laced with viciousness.

'Then why do it?' he asked, quietly and gently.

'Only a stranger to this world would ask that,' she remarked wistfully. 'I am witness to it all, for I must be. It is part of my function.'

'Your function.'

'We all have one. Yours is to be pretty, and charming; to help women forget their mortality and sorrows. My brother, for example, his function is to uphold our good name, and ensure the title never leaves our bloodline, which he has accomplished, despite his chosen wife. And as for my sister-in-law… Her function is to breed those heirs, which, as you know, she is well on her way to doing.'

Luca's heart twisted, not because of the harsh cruelty of the words, but because of what it said of Mary's view of the world.

He wasn't sure what he'd thought her before; perhaps realistic, but never...*jaded*. No...

Cynical, maybe.

'What is your function, then?' he asked, welcoming each insight into this newfound version of her. Not the truest—but another facet. 'Beyond bearing witness to the rituals of this farce, as you call it.'

'I am at once a beacon; a paragon, meant to inspire,' she smiled, only this was not a smile he'd seen before. This one held an edge of sadness, and disdain. 'And a cautionary tale.'

'What would you be, if you could choose?'

'Who said I didn't?' That look again—he did not turn to witness it, but he felt it. *Challenging.* 'What would you have me be instead? A scholar, like many of my sisters? Sharpening my mind, so that I may know the universe, yet always be forced to remain in the shadows lest I be metaphorically burned as a witch by this society who deems intelligent women a mortal peril greater than any other? Or should I be an explorer, perhaps? Travelling the world... Studying all manner of exotic locales and civilisations, only to return here, satisfied in the superiority of my own? Something more gentile, perhaps, Signor Guaro? An artist, who paints pretty pictures, pretends they mean something, and lives in charmed hedonism.'

As she spoke, Mary turned towards him fully, arms crossed, and Luca slowly faced her, allowing himself to study her again.

Though she bore it with no trace of discomfort, he did notice she breathed...quicker; as if she were holding herself tightly together, to avoid unravelling.

'I would see you do something you were passionate about,' he said simply, and her jaw tightened, teeth clicking nearly loud enough for him to hear. 'Something that made you happy.'

'I am passionate about nothing, Signor Guaro,' she told him flatly. 'Passion wasn't woven into my fabric whence I was made, and even had it been, it isn't a luxury I'm afforded. Or have you learned nothing of us cold Englishmen?'

'I don't believe you devoid of passion for one moment.'

He hadn't meant it to sound so…suggestive, and Lady Mary would've been well within her rights to strike him, and call him out for his impertinence, only she didn't.

She merely quirked her head in the slightest degree, while her eyes flared with something…not unwelcome, but impossible.

Desire.

Swallowing hard, Luca cleared his throat, and turned back to the window.

It should've given him hope, that desire, for there was no denying part of his interest in her was…of a *baser* nature, only that wasn't why he'd come. He couldn't quite recall *why* he'd come, or how any of their conversation achieved whatever aim he'd had, but he knew indulging in flirtation would…

Distract them both.

'Your work at Nichols House,' he offered. 'You are passionate about that.'

'Charity is expected of me,' Mary bit back. 'And Mena should be given her due for creating a place not run by simpering hypocrites and odious moralists.'

Luca didn't believe her; not for one moment.

Oh, he agreed with Mary's summation of Nichols House—though it sounded begrudging, it was a compliment—however he didn't believe she went there merely to be seen doing *good charity work*, as yes, ladies were meant to. Not that he was about to tell her he didn't believe her again. No, this time, he would do much worse.

Turning to her, he saw her eyes widen ever so slightly when she glimpsed his seriousness.

'What is it really, Mary? Bothering you?'

Chapter Three

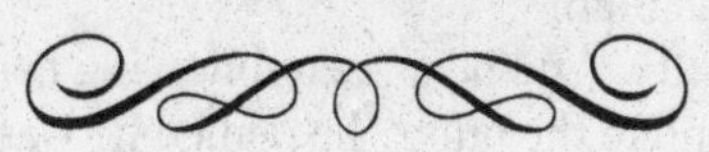

Everything, Mary wished to say. *This world, my life, myself...it's all bothering me. I feel I am cracking inside, and I don't know how to stop it, to return to what I once was, and most of all what bothers me is that I cannot stop myself from showing you all I have already.*

This whole conversation…was a mistake, from beginning to end. She'd come here for solitude, and a moment to…pull herself together, and instead, she'd been plagued by a vexatious Italian. She'd certainly never meant to say all she had, *how* she had, revealing a side she'd never shown *anyone*; hoping to be rid of him, yet praying he wouldn't turn away from her ugliness. Somehow, he, by his mere infuriating presence, had torn down her defences, rendered her speechless, and left her…unsteady. Every question, every retort, chipped further away at her, leaving her feeling as if her skin were on fire, and she was restless, yet also—

No. I'm merely tired, frustrated, and I need...

To release some of what's inside. To feel something... other.

Eyeing the man before her, she concentrated on *him*, rather than his stupid words and irritating perspicacity.

The words she'd pretended not to care about returned to the forefront of her mind.

'I am her companion...but not in the manner you nor Society believe.'

If he was to be believed—and for some inexplicable reason she believed every word coming from his mouth; most distressing and confusing—he may be a *kept* man, but he was also a *free* man.

He was pretty. And he'd been following her around for months not unlike the puppy he denied he was. When she got like this—overwhelmed by all that lived inside her—well, there was only one thing which helped restore her natural state of apathetic solidity.

A tumble.

Society believed that because she was unmarried, and they never saw nor heard evidence of indiscretions, that she was pure as a babe. Like so much else, they were wrong. Since her second Season—since she'd decided…all she had—she'd been a busy bee. Always careful, always discreet; always choosing *company* who didn't know her, or who could easily be cast away, lest they get fanciful notions, or threaten her reputation.

Luca…

Was perfect. Seemingly attached to another. Far beneath her. Someone whose word would never be taken over hers should he decide to be idiotic and speak of this. Mary resolutely ignored the whispers arguing that she didn't believe half of that; that she merely wanted him.

And? I shall have him, and he shall have what he's been chasing, and then I'll have peace. For a time. In this matter, for ever.

Precisely.

Decision made, Mary felt once again on solid ground. Stepping into the invisible circle of Luca's being, she slid her hand under his coat, slowly, along the decadent silk brocade lapel to his shoulder.

Smiling her most infallibly seductive smile, she slowly raised her gaze to his.

'This talking is bothering me,' she whispered, her hand travelling inch by inch towards his neck, fingers tangling in the ends of the loose strands.

'What are you doing?'

'I thought that obvious, *Luca*.'

Involuntarily, he shuddered slightly, her use of his name having the intended effect.

She slid her other hand along around his waist, pulling herself closer, and he sucked in a breath, eyes fluttering closed as he attempted to keep control.

'I didn't come here for an assignation,' he gritted out, eyes opening, and in them, she saw a resoluteness, an honesty, clouded with desire, which surprised her.

'You came to lift my spirits,' she breathed, rising on her toes to reach his smooth jaw with her lips, trailing fluttering kisses along it. 'Or would you tell me you don't want this?' One of his hands clasped a handful of her skirts, and she smiled, the rush of nearing victory flooding her veins, chasing the rest away. 'Would you pretend you don't want me? That you haven't since we met? Tell me you don't want me,' she challenged, ceasing her exploration of his jaw, tilting her head back to meet his gaze again. 'Tell me you don't want this, and that will be the end of it.'

'That isn't the point.'

'The point is you came here to make me feel better. So make me feel better.'

She'd meant to make it a very firm…*suggestion*.

Fine, an order.

She'd meant for it to sound inviting, seductive…and she failed; the utterly desperate part of her slipping through, and revealing itself by making it a plea.

Unable to take it back, to hide again, she did the only thing she could. Stood strong, and kept her gaze affixed on his, breathing as steadily as possible though she felt she was gasping for air.

His eyes flicked across her face, searching hers in that way that…exposed her. As if he could see the cracking inside; the tumult, even the secrets. It made her…more restless, but still she refused to break, even though every second stole more of the ground beneath her feet; like the ocean scratching away at the bottom of a cliff, unseen. She couldn't read him, nor the decision he made just before he strode away from her, leaving her cold and stunned.

At least, until she heard the snick and scratch of the door being *locked.*

Satisfaction, and relief—at having *won*, certainly not at having time with him—washed over her, drowning the rest, as she'd hoped something might. Glancing over, she found him posted by the door, stowing his gloves away, not hesitant, but…thoughtful. Only thoughtful wouldn't do. How long already had they been missing from the party? No, they couldn't tarry much longer, so this tumble needed to happen sooner, rather than later.

Clutching to those thoughts as a drowning man would straw-like reeds, rather than admit the ache for *him* drove her, Mary strode over, until she stood toe to toe with him, the door at his back still.

Raising her hand, she reached for the bottom of his waistcoat, intending to begin her work on his trouser buttons, but he stopped her, his hand encircling her wrist with a careful, gentle firmness that stayed her with exciting ease. There was an assertiveness she'd not felt from him before, and it intrigued her. Looking up, she found him…*changed*, really. No longer was he the youthful, pup-like creature she'd known. No…

Now, he was a serious, determined and resolute man who…stole her breath.

Once again, he knocked her off balance, and she may well have tumbled backwards, except his touch kept her grounded. Slowly, he leaned down—eyes never leaving hers, as if wanting to watch every detail, and ensure she still wanted *him*, every step of the way—then finally, just as her mind began to process the deliciousness of his scent—*lavender, wild skies, and warm sunsets*—which she'd never allowed herself to, for fear of wanting to wrap herself in it and die happily, he touched his lips to hers.

Her eyes closed against her will at the achingly tender touch, underscored by the brush of his hair against her cheeks. It was not a hesitant kiss; it was a slow, soft thing, full of intent, and care, and it…

Hurts.

It glided against the cracks within, amplifying them, encouraging them to shatter, and Mary couldn't…endure it. Inhaling sharply, she pressed herself closer, her lips demanding something more. *Else.*

The only passion she was allowed—and then, only in such stolen moments—drove her to fervently explore his mouth, demanding, *begging* him to change the pace. With a groan that vibrated within her, he acquiesced, his mouth opening to her, as he dropped her wrist, clasping her waist, pulling her to him with both hands. She could feel his arousal, and she smiled against his mouth—the reassurance that he wanted her grounding too.

Relaxing, the hurt of his care fading under the haze of fiery passion, she wound her arms around his neck, and let herself be swept away by the fierce dance of their tongues, lips, and teeth. By his decadent taste—*sweet plums and the sating warmth of cinnamon*—and his solidness which supported her as nothing ever had. They remained thus for an unacceptably, and terrifyingly long time, until finally they broke apart, panting. There was a sort of awed wonder in Luca's gaze…and Mary hated it.

Thankfully, she didn't have to endure it long—perhaps he sensed it—for then he was dropping his hands, and sliding away, taking her hand as if to guide her somewhere more comfortable or suitable, only that terrified her too. She could imagine him taking his time, being careful, offering more than a tumble…and *that* she couldn't have, so she turned and leaned against the door, tugging him back with his own momentum.

His eyes narrowed, questioning, but she raised a brow, and he nodded. They stood…*pausing*, and he changed again before her eyes; transformed, as surely as some prince in a fairy story, bewitched by an evil sorceress.

In this tale, I am the evil sorceress.

Something shuttered away within him; an openness, or gentleness. His eyes lost warmth—not making him chilling, or cold, merely…*removed.* Someone else might've been bothered, but Mary welcomed it. Welcomed Luca back into her own circle as he stepped forth, dropping her hand. From there, it was…just as she wanted. As she'd always preferred this sort of thing. What she'd expected from a man like him. Well, what she told herself she *should.*

All business.

Mary took care of releasing him from the confines of his trousers whilst he expertly—she had to admit—rolled and bunched her skirts until they were out of the way, and preserved from such handling. All was done without a glance at their own actions, with hurried, skilled haste. Their gazes never wandered from the other's, and Mary couldn't deny the fascination—discomfiting though this shuttering away of…part of his soul, *for her*, was—of this new Luca. Challenging, purposeful, and un…breakable.

Both unhindered by their garments, Luca stepped forth, bracing one hand on the door, and another around her waist, demonstrating a graceful power she'd suspected, but never *felt*, as he lifted her so she could wrap her legs around his waist.

The pleasure of that simple gesture flooded her veins, making her dizzy, but she had no time to revel in it, nor in the sweet brush of his manhood against her most private self, for then, sure she was braced against the wood, he removed his own hold from the door, and reached between them to place himself where she wanted, and needed him most.

A strangled cry she didn't hold back—nor could've had she wanted to—escaped as he slid into her already slick, throbbing channel, and a groan escaped him. They held still, Luca's forehead dropping to hers as he bit his lip, trying to centre and control himself, and Mary slid her hands from his shoulders, back to that lovely spot at the base of his neck, tangling her fingers in the silky strands again. They breathed together, Mary falling into the warm delicacy of that splinter of time, when she held him within herself; satisfied, complete, yet restless, and pulsing with need.

And then finally, he was moving again, a hand returning to the door beside her head, as his hips ground, swayed, and moved in ways she could only admire as he held her tightly, safely, and worked her into a…*frenzy*.

The raw, slick, sweaty, gritty, and intoxicating passion was unlike anything she'd ever felt. It was *meant* to feel functional—a drive towards utmost pleasure—only it still felt too intentional. She felt too hot, and breathless, and the way his body moved, the way *they* moved and fit together… his beauty up close, it was all too…*dizzying*. It didn't feel animal, and impersonal—not when he looked at her as he did now, studying every speck, watching, and learning with incoherent ease the pace, length, and strength of the strokes which sent her flying further, from the room, and the world, and…

Myself.

Her lungs refused to fill beyond the barest amount as he ruthlessly drove in and out of her, every nerve and muscle clenching, and melting all at once. The spot behind her lower belly where he reached effortlessly, sent waves of delectation through her, until she was a clutching, clawing mess, glued to him, chasing that elusive, wonderful peak.

Still, he looked at her with that intent, and she needed… to kiss him. To look away, to break the connection she'd thought he'd silently promised wouldn't be created, and she gasped, searching his mouth with her own, but he refused her, his eyes darkening beyond what she thought possible as he finished his work. And finish it he did, mercilessly.

Everything within her broke in seconds, clenching him so tightly with every part of herself as she squeaked a cry out, her inner muscles holding him so firmly within herself it felt as if they were no longer *two* beings. Her head fell forward, nestling under his chin, and he held himself just as tightly while she rode the crashing waves of pleasure; of lightning coursing through every fibre, every nerve, until she was spent. A heaving, sweaty mess of mush. A settled, safe, warm, and *happy* mess that—

Luca removed himself with a grunt, disentangling himself from her, and setting her down on *very* shaky legs. Her eyes flew open at the brutality of that separation; the coldness, and regret she felt shocking her back to reality more efficiently than ice water topped over her head might've.

That was all far too...

Calming.

Glorious.

Intimate.

She stood there like a ninny, watching him suck in deep breaths, still leaning against the door, his jaw set as he tried to…

Oh.

Understanding *what* he was breathing through, and what he'd been avoiding—without her even asking, because she'd…*trusted* him, which was reckless, stupid, and to be examined *later*—she reached out, only then realising she still wore her gloves, which angered her, for she'd not touched his skin with her own fingertips. Removing the right one quickly, she reached out, taking him in hand, whilst she also pulled a handkerchief from her bodice.

His eyes flew open when her fingers encircled his admittedly *impressive* self—something she'd *felt*, but not rationally recognised until now, and that look of surprised wonder crossed his features for a blissfully short few seconds before his own release hit.

Mary quickly prevented it going anywhere but her already sticky fingers with the handkerchief, as Luca nearly fell into her, straining to keep himself upright as the most beautiful and entrancing look of ecstasy came upon him.

When he'd finished, she wiped him clean—she would clean herself in the retiring room after leaving this place—folded up the handkerchief, and slipped it into his pocket. Luca wavered as he straightened, fighting the urge to kiss her, but his sentimentality was just the reminder *she* required to tear her from…whatever *that* interlude was, for it certainly *wasn't* a tumble.

It was far more than I bargained for. Far more than I can...handle.

Straightening, she turned away before he could indulge his…desires, and smoothed down her skirts. Luca nodded, a flash of bitterness sparkling in his gaze, and she welcomed it.

Go on. Hate me, Luca.

He put himself together as best he could, while she put her glove back on, and fetched the hat she'd left…*oh yes, before the hearth.*

The air was tight, taut, and charged, and she knew what needed to be done without delay.

I had him. He got what he wanted. Now we can be done with each other.

'I'll leave first,' she said, putting her hat on.

She was still slick with sweat, rumpled, and likely her lips were…well-kissed, but hopefully by the time she made it to the retiring room, it wouldn't be so apparent.

She would just be mindful not to encounter many people. Thinking on it, perhaps she would find another place to tidy herself, before cleaning herself up properly in the public rooms.

An excellent plan.

'You should wait a few moments before returning to the party,' she continued, her voice blessedly even and strong. *I am myself again. Who I must be to...do this.* She purposefully didn't look at Luca, busy…fixing herself. 'Do find a glass before you do. You are slightly more…*crinkled* than I meant you to be.'

Finally, she looked at him, straight in the eye, forcing down the remorse, and regret.

The hurt, the confusion on his face…

Like a damned downtrodden puppy.

Don't let it affect you. Get it done.

'Don't look at me thus, Luca,' she admonished sharply, striding to him on blessedly steady feet. 'I feel much better, so thank you,' she smiled sweetly, patting his chest. He blinked at the offending hand as though it were tentacles instead. 'Now, now. You knew what this was, and wasn't. We both had an itch, we scratched it, and now we shall return to our lives, and that will be the end of it. I promise, whatever sting you feel now, within a day you shall feel it no more. In less than a week, your sights will be set on another. I did us both a favour today.'

Mary drew on all her reserves of strength, and the last

lingering bliss of ecstasy, and smiled at him like the sweet young pup he was.

She held his gaze, and guarded herself against the desire to kiss him, and tell him she meant none of it, and would he please hold her.

'Good day, Signor Guaro,' she said firmly, meaning it as, if not *farewell*—for inevitably they would meet again—then as…*may we never be so dangerously close again.*

'Goodbye, Mary,' he whispered gently, and it pierced her heart—*damn him*—as she strode to the door, and let herself out.

Just walk on.

Clean up.

And move on.

So she did, appearing at the party—which had become even more of an intolerable pit—for a short time before finally climbing into her carriage and returning home, feeling somehow worse than she had before. Instead of settling her, and restoring her nerves, the interlude with Luca had worsened the cracks within.

And she'd just cast away one of the few people who made her feel…

Less.

Of everything ugly.

Chapter Four

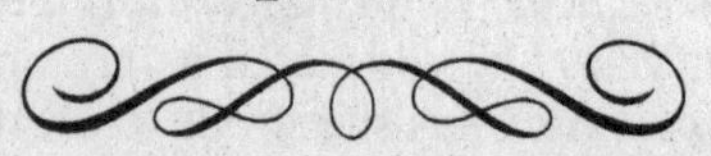

'Luca? Have you a preference for Norfolk or Hampshire this summer?' Deirdre said, obviously repeating herself, which was good, considering he hadn't heard the first time. It was inexcusable, and he forced his mind from its melancholic wanderings, turning from the painting which had set him off on his wanderings.

Smiling, he looked at the woman who *should* have his attention, because she was here, and so he should be present too. Common courtesy, really.

Not that spending time with Deirdre was ever a chore, particularly not when they indulged in their common love of art—such as today, when they wandered about a gallery, admiring paintings, sculptures, etchings… All of it should bolster him, soothe, and restore his soul. And Deirdre's company was always restorative; she had a delightful and incongruous sense of humour, and a passionate, empathetic soul.

All things which had originally attracted him—well, perhaps not originally; he'd first been drawn to her physically, and if that made him superficial, then so be it. Ironically, it was his physical attraction which had initiated their acquaintance, as Deirdre had refused to believe the—granted, *many*—compliments he'd given. *Luminous* had been the first, after she'd caught him staring for nigh on a good quarter of an hour, while she sketched the ruins of a villa outside Rome.

Only she *had* been luminous; still was. There was an eagerness, a dedication to the manner in which she put ink to paper, loyally reproducing the view in the barest strokes, which fascinated him. She'd been sporting a serviceable brown gown, which unpretentiously complimented her generous curves and small height. Her long strands of thick, impossibly straight hair—a sun-catching mix of pine-brown, silver, grey, and pure white—had been unceremoniously piled beneath a large straw hat, strands escaping here and there. Tiny fingers had been smudged with charcoal, and her defiant chin, and button nose, had bobbed up and down as she went from the view to the paper. Slowly, he'd approached, and then he'd glimpsed the rest. The sharp lines of brow, cheeks, and lips, dividing her square face—which would've looked harsh on another, but which suited Deirdre's determined air. The magnetic round emerald eyes—so soft and yes, *luminous.* A contrast to the lines of her, but which opened her to the world, and vice-versa.

He'd said something similar—after she'd quizzed him on *why he was dawdling, staring at her* and he'd told her she was luminous—not the poetic part, but the part about her eyes being magnetic, and she'd stared for a full minute, before laughing for a good three, her laugh so full and deep-bellied, he'd just had to join in the mirth.

When they'd finished laughing, they'd begun talking. Of her journey, of art. A little of himself, though he was careful what he shared. That had been before he'd known he could trust all he was to Deirdre—as she could trust all to him. Though he'd never dissimulated *why* he was wandering about places which attracted tourists of her sort. Wealthy, unattached foreign women who enjoyed the company of men such as he. Lying to Deirdre…lying to *anyone*, it was repulsive.

Besides, she wouldn't have borne it. After half a lifetime in Society, married to a wastrel who had done nothing but taught her to hate herself, Deirdre had no tolerance for liars—and her clever mind, and empathetic soul, meant she knew very well when someone wasn't truthful. Another thing he liked about her.

The list was long after three years together.

A very good three years.

Chasing the memories away—though he was grateful for them as they lifted his spirits—he patted Deirdre's hand reassuringly where it lay in the crook of his elbow, and moved them along.

'Norfolk,' he said decidedly, as they passed a grim, pedestrian version of Judith and Holofernes. 'Less crowded, and the seaside can be enjoyed comfortably. Besides, you prefer the company of Lord and Lady Grevest to that of Lady Blanford,' he added.

Widowed six years ago, with a very comfortable portion, Deirdre also had properties—from her mother, her husband, and shrewd investing—across the country.

Choosing where to go in summer then depended not only on whether a house was let, but equally who their neighbours would be. Though never was there question of visiting her family, as she, her sons, and *their* new families were…estranged.

Choosing their summer locale therefore depended on which *friends* she wished to spend time with, for despite years of difficulty dealing with Society, Deirdre had made many good friends. The choice often came down to who lived a more active summer lifestyle; who preferred walks and reading to balls and parties.

As both he and Deirdre did.

'Norfolk it is,' Deirdre nodded. 'Luca… Have you

thought any more about sharing something at Clarissa's salon tomorrow?'

Luca sighed, his glance darting to the right, where a statue of Themis was doing her damnedest to judge *him*, as he struggled to find the words to answer.

This was only the latest of her attempts to have him show his art at the lady's exclusive and often revolutionary *salon*—a gathering of the best and brightest London had to offer at any given time. To get him to show it anywhere, if truth be told.

And his reluctance stemmed not from self-doubt, but something which he'd never discussed with Deirdre, he realised then, for she was always so proud and eager to vaunt his merits. In some way, he'd never wanted to tell her *no*, for he never wished to…disappoint her.

Such as tumbling a lady in a library might.

'I appreciate your championing, Deirdre,' he said, shaking his head of the unwelcome, intrusive thought. He would tell her what he'd done eventually—honesty was paramount in their relationship. Besides, he wouldn't say no to her counsel on *that* matter. *First things first, however.* 'I should've told you this when you first encouraged me to bring my work into such circles. I… Well, I don't see the point, if I'm honest. My art is for myself, and for you,' he added with a complicit grin, as they continued their wandering through the rather packed gallery, nodding to anyone they recognised. 'I don't seek to make it my occupation, nor am I searching for commissions. I don't even really care to have others' opinions on it; merely to create.'

Deirdre nodded, and they fell into silence, their steps—despite the surrounding cacophony—loud against the wooden boards.

Luca was at once relieved to have admitted the truth, yet apprehensive of what she would think of him.

'Admittedly, I thought you might like to make a profession of it,' she said finally, neither disapproving nor judgemental, which was…a relief. 'You have the talent, though now I realise it isn't doubt which has stopped you—as I thought. I understand your decision, and respect it, however I would say this: art is meant to be appreciated, as we do now. We may have thoughts, opinions, about these works which surround us, yet that is not what we seek by coming here. We seek to enjoy others' views of the world, their interpretation of tales which have captured the imagination of mankind. Clarissa's salon can be a place of *critique*, however, if you were to share your work, and clarify that you seek nothing *but* to share, I'm certain everyone would understand. It is, in my own opinion, a shame for your art to be reserved solely for the enjoyment of a select *two*.'

Luca couldn't help but smile broadly, his heart warming, and he leaned down to kiss her cheek, pleased he could still make her blush.

'You will have the gossipmongers buzzing,' Deirdre chided, playfully swatting his arm.

'There is barely anyone here we know,' he reminded her, waggling his brows, and making her laugh that delightful laugh. 'Those who do will be positively jealous.'

'Quite so. What is it you wish to do with your life, Luca?' she asked suddenly, after a few moments of companionable silence.

Reeling slightly, he paused, and looked over into those green eyes able to cut through to the very heart of him.

And others too.

'I don't know,' he managed, his voice quiet and sombre.

With a slight tug, Deirdre prompted him onwards, allowing him time to sort through the mired thoughts and emotions her question prompted.

It felt…somewhat shameful, not having a proper answer. Made him feel unworthy, to not have some grand—if impossible and unfeasible—dream that he pursued without reserve whilst acquiring the means to realise it with his current…*occupation.*

Only, he'd never had the opportunity, nor the inducement, to dream of what he could *do*, of who he could become. He'd been taught from a young age to become something…he would never be. His *mamma*—though he loved her dearly—had been lost, and still was, in daydreams of her own. Where their family was what it had been in centuries past: pillars of the highest society. People with land, titles, and wealth, who had no need of something so base as *an occupation.* To her, Luca was destined to become a courtier, a politician. He was to marry a woman with a large dowry, and live a life of leisure.

None of it was real, only he hadn't realised until it was too late.

There were no titles. There was no land. There wasn't enough money to put food on the table. There were no connections. No women of fortune to marry. No use for his languages, education, knowledge of the rites of Society, conversation…and there certainly wouldn't be a life of leisure.

Although he'd realised the extent of the fantastical daydream he, Mamma, and his sister Sofia had been living in, ironically, he'd actually not become something so very different to what he'd been prepared for. He'd used his education, charm, knowledge of how to live among those more fortunate, to support his family. And lived now, to some degree, a life of luxurious leisure, relying on the open purses of those he charmed.

No, he didn't regret his choices, wasn't ashamed, but shouldn't there be more? He and his family were no longer in the destitute, desperate circumstances they'd been when he'd begun his…*work*, so could he now become something…else?

Or shall I do this for ever? Is this what I want?

'You wouldn't be the first to thrive as you do now well into your old age,' Deirdre remarked, shockingly following the thread of his thoughts. 'To retire someday with a handsome bounty. There is no dishonour or ignominy in that, if it's what you wish for. But, I do not think that it is.'

'It isn't a terrible existence,' he grinned, lighter, for being able to speak of this, grateful to her for challenging him out of comfortable stupor. If she hadn't, how long might he have dwelled there? *Considering you already felt the strain, perhaps not so long...* 'Yet… I don't think I would be…fulfilled, were that to be *all* I ever did. Not that everyone is lucky enough to live fulfilled lives. And I don't even know what I *do* wish to do.'

'You are young, Luca,' Deirdre said comfortingly. 'You have time. Not everyone is lucky enough to live a fulfilled life, however, you have the opportunities and freedom to do so. It is a worthy endeavour, to seek such fulfilment, and I should know, having waited long enough to do so.'

'Thank you,' he smiled, pulling her closer.

'Will you tell me now what mesmerised you so about Orpheus and Eurydice? Masterful though it was, it wasn't so hypnotising as your inattention suggested.'

You miss nothing, Luca thought ruefully, reminding himself he had wished for counsel on this—and now was his chance.

'Correct, as always,' he sighed. 'I lost myself…in the myth. Wondering…if Orpheus was always doomed to look back as he led Eurydice from Hades. To break that one rule, and lose his only chance of saving her, because he couldn't maintain his faith in the gods. If that was their punishment for what they saw lurking in the depths of his heart.'

'You wander into the philosophical depths of free will, and the existence of God… However, I think… What you truly fear is that you've made an irreparable mistake, and artist that you are, you've fallen into the romance of tragedy to soothe, and explain the hurt.' Luca chuckled, and Deirdre led him towards the windows, overlooking the busy courtyard below. 'Considering you've been pensive since the garden party, would I be correct in surmising this mistake is regarding a certain lady, for whom you've had a *tendre* for some time?' He nodded, not surprised about Deirdre's deductions, considering he'd realised his inclinations supremely transparent since she'd told him to seek out Lady Mary there. 'Dare I ask what passed between you?'

'A great deal more than expected. Enough for her to decide I served my purpose.'

'Hm.'

From the corner of his eye, Luca watched as Deirdre pondered all of it.

Again, she didn't judge, merely examined the problem as his friend. Not many people he knew, in a relationship such as they had, and *had* had, would be so open to discussing the, if not intricacies then barest details, of his relationship to another.

Or lack thereof. The desire for.

'Hear this as it is meant, Luca, please,' Deirdre said finally, and he nodded. 'Often, we cannot see the faults of those we…*appreciate*, and I never wish to see you hurt. I never said anything before, for I thought your interest a passing thing, if I'm honest. Even after that…trip to Sussex at New Year's. Now, I think it important to caution you, that Lady Mary is a creature of Society. As firmly, as deeply, as one can be. Appearances can be deceiving.'

'I know there is more to her than what she appears,' he reassured her. 'That is precisely what I find…*intriguing.* Even those parts of her less than…charitable.'

'There is more to us all than the world can ever see. I don't know what you wish to find with her, but I do hope you know she will never abandon all she has worked to build—her name, her reputation—in the name of something intangible, like romance. Rumours swirled around the party after you stepped away, about Viscountess Porens. Rumours which could be the end of her, see her cast not only from Society, but from her house, and family. I have it on good authority that Lady Mary was the one to utter the words which may see it all done, and not by accident. I would hate for such craft to be used against you, Luca.'

He frowned, the revelation surprising, yet also…

Resounding truthfully.

He wouldn't condemn Mary for her actions before he knew the truth of them, however he did know he would ask her for it. Not that he didn't heed Deirdre's warning, but this piece—as all the others he'd collected—added to a puzzling picture of Mary. He couldn't fully believe Mary cruel or with a heart as black as others he knew in this world, though he certainly didn't dismiss that parts of her could be less than…kind. As for furthering his acquaintance with her…he couldn't say what he aimed to achieve.

He knew as surely as anyone, that ideas of happily ever afters would be pure fantasy, but perhaps he could…get to know her better.

'I'll be mindful, Deirdre. And of the consequences my choices have on you, always. But I cannot shake this feeling… Well, I am a moth to flame, really. Still, I'll be careful not to get burned.'

'That's all I ask,' Deirdre nodded. 'As for the initial problem… If your experience of any encounter with the lady differs from hers, I suggest you tell her plainly. You've always been a truth-sayer, Luca. Don't let fear, or hurt, temper that, for it's one of your most endearing qualities. If she casts you away again, I would suggest you have the grace to respect that. And count yourself lucky that you wasted no more time on someone who couldn't see your true worth.'

Unable to find the words to express his gratitude—for

all Deirdre said, and was—he kissed her cheek again. She didn't blush this time, only wrapped her arm in his, and ordered him to *lead on.*

So he did.

Chapter Five

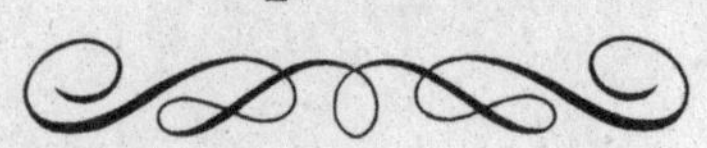

Mary sucked in a breath to avoid crying out in pain as the girl tugged her hair in an effort to make the braid perfect. It wouldn't do to frighten the sprout or make her feel bad. Her, or the other two working on different sections of Mary's hair. After all, Mary had been subjected to many more painful tonsorial experiences and suffered through them silently; though none had for an outcome both arranged hair, and the satisfied looks of children.

It wasn't that she *loved* children—most days, she found them unappealing creatures leaking too many fluids, cries, and questions—and even before…everything, she'd never really wanted any, though she'd known her duty to provide some to a potential husband. Only, these children creating art of her hair were endearing, and not so annoying as others, and it wasn't sporting to hurt their fragile feelings.

Too easy, she thought, though she knew making *them* happy, and giving them confidence, actually pleased her.

And beyond some eager tugs, the experience wasn't *so* trying. They were doing a good job, actually, given that the girls were barely five, and the young chap was six. It was relaxing, really, and God knew she sorely needed relaxation.

Hence why she was here, at Nichols House. She hadn't *entirely* lied to Luca in the library. A lady like her must be seen doing charitable work, and this place didn't have a parcel of hypocrites and moralists running it, which Mary admired. It was what had originally made her donate to the project. And what kept her coming after her first visits, to help where she could—be it teaching a new stitch in embroidery class, or boiling linens for the unwell and injured—though often her help was…*unnecessary*, this place being a well-oiled machine now.

Really, Mary came here out of pure selfishness. It made her feel better. Not because of *all the good* she did, but because here, she was herself as much as she could be. There were no prying Society eyes, and the atmosphere was truly one of goodwill, acceptance, and simplicity. Here, was one of the few places she'd ever felt…*relaxed.*

Considering she'd felt *unrelaxed* since her encounter with Luca four days ago—*not counting*—well, since that entire fiasco of a party, she sorely needed something to restore a semblance of calm and tranquillity. If not, she wouldn't survive the next week, let alone longer, without…

Cracking. More than I already am...

It didn't help that she'd received a letter from Scotland this morning. From Yew Park House, to be exact, where her family had retired whilst they awaited the birth of Spencer and Genevieve's child; their friends all retiring there with them. The Reids of Thornhallow, as well as Freddie and Mena—the latter conquering deeply held anxiousness at being anywhere beyond a five-mile radius of her home to do so. Meanwhile, Mary hadn't joined because…someone needed to be *here*. In Society. Upholding—

Excuses...

Excuses which Genevieve—*the damned letter-writer*—incessantly picked apart, along with the others who regularly *apprised* her of news—even Spencer, though his letters were less regular—despite knowing well the true reason Mary had no desire to be at Yew Park House for a birth of all things. A birth expected in June, so close to her own birthday…

They are driving me to murder, or insanity, Genevieve wrote, as if they were old chums. Her sister-in-law had tried to make them thus; in fact she'd tried the hardest to…get Mary talking. But Genevieve could never know *all* of it, so it was… A doomed endeavour.

> *Mena, Freddie, Rebecca and Reid, even Elizabeth, they are keeping Spencer and your mama busy, and away from me when they are in a state, but I am concerned about this worrying. If you were here, perhaps—*

Perhaps we'll never know.

Spencer's and Mama's *concerning* worry—and over-attentiveness, and somewhat *overbearing* attitudes, had been worsening since Genevieve had got with child—and it was no wonder *why* considering their…family history. No one who knew it would fault them—and anyone who knew it would question *why* they'd thought it a good idea to go to Yew Park for this.

Healing, they purported.

For the McKennas, they said.

Nothing but an aggravation of old wounds you are all content to ignore, Mary thought.

And she wasn't entirely sure what Genevieve thought but… Let their friends, be there for them. She…could not. No matter what Genevieve seemed to think, there was nothing… Mary could do the others couldn't.

So yes, she'd come here, and found herself in yet another library. This one was thankfully devoid of pesky Italian puppies; instead it was populated with tiny truants eager for entertainment. A better woman would've chastised them for dodging their scholarly pursuits, but Mary was no such woman.

If she reminded herself of that often enough, the…guilt and ill ease would lessen. The self-loathing and doubt regarding Viscountess Porens—who'd been summarily sent to the country—would lessen. She would feel better about how she'd treated Luca, and not…as if she'd kicked a puppy. Ill-treated one of the few she trusted to some degree; someone who'd been there when no one else had. She would feel less like she'd missed out on something…extraordinary.

Surely. It's just a strange, turbulent time.

Moments such as this, removed from Society, along with a constant reassurance that she wasn't a good person—and there was nothing but honour that recognition—would see her right again.

Forthwith.

'*Ich bin fertig*,' one of the girls declared. Gerda, who rose with a contented smile on her freckled face. 'I am done.'

'And you tied it?' Gerda nodded fiercely, and Mary winked. 'How about you two?'

'Almost,' the boy, David, said; judging by his enunciation, his tongue was between his teeth as he concentrated.

'I am done also!' Ingrid cried, leaping up.

'There you are!' Another voice—not so young—said, and the sprouts gasped in unison. *Oops. Caught.* 'I thought I'd find you here, though I expected better of you, Lady Mary.'

'I cannot imagine why,' Mary grumbled back.

'Off you go,' Susie ordered the mites. 'To class with you.'

They didn't even mutter a single protest, scuttling to where they should be, and Mary rose from the floor where she'd been sitting, running her fingers along the three braids, a gentle hum of satisfaction escaping when she felt their near perfection—though David's remained unfastened.

Taking a ribbon from her pocket, she tied it off, and slowly turned to face Susie.

Short, but strong in stature, with chestnut curls and amber eyes, the young woman was fetching in a simple way—at least she was when she wasn't scowling, tapping her foot, arms crossed in disapproval, such as now. Originally from Belgium, she'd befriended Mena, who'd then offered her a position working in Freddie's shop—his first endeavour before he'd built his shipping empire—and eventually, enlisted her help building Nichols House. With Mena in Scotland, Susie was running Nichols House with an iron fist, a symptom of her innate dedication to…everything. Something which made Susie…tolerable. That, and her talent of speaking unreservedly.

Grinning ruefully, Mary picked up the cushions she and the children had set beneath the window, replacing them on the chairs.

'Don't you come to *help*?' Susie asked. 'Not encourage children who don't know better to shirk their lessons?'

'I was teaching them to arrange a lady's hair. I would've thought it a valuable lesson.'

'If they were to arrange a lady's hair *thus*, they would be promptly dismissed.'

'I like it. Perhaps I'll start a new fashion.'

'Wouldn't be the worst I've seen.'

The two women stared at each other, before Mary grinned widely, a chuckle escaping her.

Susie lasted barely a second before she too was laughing, shaking her head.

'We weren't aware you were visiting today, Lady Mary,' she said once they'd settled.

'I wasn't aware I needed to announce my visits. I thought this place open to anyone, any time.'

'Indeed it is.'

'And I believe I asked you to call me Mary,' she said,

raising a brow. 'I did come to *help*, however, there wasn't much for me to do today, hence how I found myself here. Though I wonder if people are reluctant to enlist my help for the same reason you refuse to use my Christian name. Because I'm a *lady*.'

'People are used to you now,' Susie shrugged. 'It's quiet, that's all, and everything is well in hand. *Mary*.' Mary smiled, and Susie came to stand beside her, looking out of the window at the inner courtyard, full of play and industry. 'I've had a letter from Mena. She says they are having a pleasant time, though apparently she and the others have been focused on…keeping your mother and brother busy to avoid them, well, driving the Marchioness mad.'

'I'm sure they're all doing a commendable job,' she said, not offering anything about her own letter.

None of Susie's business.

'When will you be travelling? You must be eager to meet the new member of your family.'

'Indeed,' she said, meaning it. For she was eager to meet the babe whenever it came—it was all the rest which was… complicated. 'Though I likely won't make it for the birth; too much for me to attend to here.'

And being there, seeing the child born so near to my own birthday would be...

A test of strength I cannot meet.

'Of course,' Susie said, not pointing out the oddness of Mary's priorities. Parties, teas, calls, and balls over *family*. But then Susie wasn't of the same world. 'Forgive my impertinence, but are you well, Mary?' she asked, and Mary started at the gentle concern.

What is it with everyone asking me how I fare?

Am I losing my skill to conceal it all?

'Perfectly well,' she replied, hoping the lie wasn't obvious. 'Thank you. How are you, Susie?' she asked congenially. 'Enjoying having the run of this place, and Holly Street?'

'I am. It is quite the responsibility, and I worry that I'm not as good at it as Mena, but I try my best to keep it running smoothly. The financial, and administrative side of things here is rather complex, but I'm making my way through it. The rest…takes care of itself. Rather, everyone takes care of each other, ensuring it does.'

'Mena trusting you with everything is a testament to you. And if you require assistance with the trust, or administration, you need only ask.'

'Thank you,' Susie smiled. 'I might just do that.'

Mary turned to the window, though she felt the other woman studying her closely.

I should leave.

'Why are you here, Lady Mary?'

The question wasn't reproachful, merely direct, and cutting for the tender complicity it was filled with.

Mary schooled her expression lest her shock appear—at the woman's perspicacity—and turned, one challenging brow raised.

'I'm unsure of what you mean,' she said evenly, schooling her expression lest her shock at the woman's perspicacity appear. 'Charity work is an essential component of a lady's life.'

'I've been in my fair share of *charitable institutions*. To help, or to seek help. I've seen wealthy patrons come to *do charity*. How they behave; that look in their eyes when they leave. The superior satisfaction about them. You… I've never seen that. I think your reasons for coming here are very…personal. Most come to places like this to be seen. Not to hide.'

There was no concealing her shock this time, not at the woman's impertinence, but again, at her perspicacity.

Not that you should indulge perspicacity—insolence—with truth.

'You're not wrong, Susie,' Mary smiled, feeling the tightness undermining her words. 'This place is my refuge too. A life in Society can be…trying.'

'Yet you choose to remain, rather than escape to the country with your family and friends.'

'Do you have a family, Susie?' Mary asked bitterly, knowing very well the answer before the woman shook her head. 'Then you could never understand what it means to shoulder the responsibility one does when part of one, particularly a family such as mine. And unless you've been hiding patents of nobility, I don't think you could ever understand what it means to be part of Society.'

Head held high, Mary strode over to the table and snatched up her bonnet and gloves.

The effrontery—

'We low-borns have thicker skins than those of your ilk,' Susie said flatly, stopping Mary in her tracks. 'Best you try harder if you wish to make an enemy of me. You forget I've seen the lengths you go to, not only for your friends, but also those you know nothing of. And I know it isn't all just…pretence.'

Mary sucked in a breath.

She'd come here for peace, and instead she was getting a lecture from an impertinent—*I should avoid all libraries in future.*

'We aren't friends, Lady Mary. Barely acquaintances. Don't think me so foolish as to forget that. Still, it's not in my nature to remain silent when I see something amiss. And here, far from Society life, you should know you'll only ever find understanding, should you care to unburden yourself of whatever weighs upon you so.'

Not confident in her ability to face the woman again without…

Bursting into tears. Unburdening myself. Asking for help...

Mary angrily plopped her bonnet back on, and strode from the room, then from Nichols House entirely.

Once safely ensconced in her carriage, she leaned against the squabs with a heavy sigh, exhaustion cutting bone-deep. Susie's words may have appeared kind, but to Mary, they only highlighted her increasing inability to mask her feelings, growing weakness, and turmoil. They only seemed to make it clearer that she was on the edge of a great precipice. One wrong move, and everything she'd spent a lifetime acquiring—*reputation, power, control*—would be gone.

Though for the first time, she wondered if that would be a blessing, rather than a curse.

Chapter Six

Readjusting his gloves for the five hundred and sixty-fifth time that evening, Luca shook a strand of hair from his eyes, and surveyed the room of swirling silks, excitedly fluttering feathers, and blinding precious metals and jewels. Though he'd never particularly *enjoyed* such grand affairs—too many people, too much frippery and noise, too many nauseating smells—he'd never been as nervous to attend one.

Not even his first four years ago, though it felt a lifetime. Oh, he'd been nervous, anxious to ensure he played his role, and made no missteps, however he'd been able to control it then, with sheer, blind confidence. Trusting in his own education, and charm, to get him through it. And it had. That night, he'd learned the key to admittance into places he didn't belong: *never pretend to belong*. He'd found over the years that the novelty of him not attempting to claw and scrape his way into his *betters'* good graces in fact made them eager to include him in their lives, schemes, or secrets.

Tonight was no different. He wasn't here to cement himself a place in Society. He had no true place here, at this celebration of some marquess's birthday. He was *welcome*; though decadent and formal, it wasn't *so formal*, and therefore *the more the merrier*, particularly if the *more* entertained and gave guests a pleasant view.

Only, he wasn't really doing a good job of that—even providing a pleasant view, ensconced in an alcove as he was—and he couldn't even blame Deirdre, for she'd escaped into a card room, ordering him to enjoy *his* evening. She was being kind, as always, though Luca wouldn't have been surprised if her dismissal of his services—beyond seeing her home—had to do with his inability to cease fidgeting, ever since he'd heard Lady Mary would be in attendance.

It had been a week since the garden party—four days since his and Deirdre's discussion in the gallery. There had been myriad other events and business to keep him busy, including their evening at Clarissa's, during which he'd shown a charcoal portrait of Deirdre, which had garnered much appreciation from the gathering. Nothing more; Deirdre was right, as ever. It had bolstered him, settled him, and even distracted him for a short time. But as soon as they'd left, he'd returned to its recent ruminations: i.e. how and when to approach Lady Mary to…tell her his feelings on their…entanglement.

For he'd resolved to… To tell her he didn't want to be cast aside, to lose her company. Hell, he would settle for returning to, if not friends, then whatever was between *friends* and *acquaintances*. If she didn't want it—*him*—then he would…cease *hounding* her, though he would for ever deny that accusation. He merely sought out…*her company*.

Si.

Luca shuffled in his hideaway, pretending it was because some gentleman with extremely busy curls was in front of him and he couldn't see the door, not because he was *so damned nervous*. It felt as if the rest of his life depended on this potential conversation, which was absurd. He felt like he was a boy again, experiencing the first fluttering of interest in another; all bumbling words, sweaty palms, and jittery nerves at the prospect of seeing—

Mary, finally.

He'd begun to believe she wouldn't appear, but there she was, gliding through the doors, unmissable even among the crush, sporting a gown of the richest, shimmering blue, barely adorned but for trims of embroidered purple flowers, and a glittering set of sapphires and diamonds. Though nerves still plagued him—what to say, when, how—he felt able to breathe again.

He watched for a time as she laughed, and mingled, swiping a coupe from a passing tray, and making her way around the room. As always, she appeared flawless, in control, yet there was also a stiffness born of…lassitude about her. As if the slightest breeze might crack her like a twig left too long in the sun. He felt the urge to dash over there, drop to his knees, and beg her to impart unto him whatever she must to make her less…*friable*, only he knew very well that wouldn't do, and so he bided his time, slowly emerging from the alcove.

Luca wandered too, engaging in countless meaningless conversations, his mind and heart elsewhere, as he tracked Mary's progress; an opposing orbit to his own. When she stepped through to the ballroom a stroke of brilliance hit, making his steps sure again, and he made directly for her.

He approached as she made her way from one group to another, and he felt as if he'd just slid across the boards after a spirited run—though in reality, it was a graceful and seemingly casual step into her path—when he finally stood before her.

'Lady Mary,' he bowed with a bright smile—too bright to be polite, but he didn't care. 'Good evening.'

'Signor Guaro,' she nodded.

She wasn't surprised by his abrupt arrival—nor particularly displeased—merely…*resolved.*

As if she'd known she would have to face him eventually, and was waiting to plan her moves until after he'd shown his own cards.

Which I will, unreservedly, if given a chance.

'May I have the honour of the next waltz?' he asked, and a flash of relief crossed her face.

Raising a brow, she casually studied those around them, and it wasn't lost on him they had a few witnesses now.

'Why not,' she smiled, meeting his gaze again.

He'd thought she might refuse, given the tittle-tattling a dance would engender—they'd never danced together before, Luca only did so with Deirdre, and those with whom dancing would cause no indignant furore—however, apparently Mary wasn't concerned.

In fact, she looked eager to create some…*tittle-tattling.*

Or perhaps she merely believed this the best way to be rid of him again.

'As you are the first to seek my partnership tonight, you should be granted your wish, Signor Guaro.'

Luca grinned, though as they stood staring at each other, he realised he wasn't entirely sure what to do next.

There was a full dance before the waltz, Mary needed no refreshments, *he* had neither want nor need of any, and now wasn't the time to begin…*the* conversation—he would wait for the dance, when Mary couldn't run, and they could mostly escape the prying ears of the crowd. He had no real desire to make inane small talk, but neither could they just stand here, gazing…

This isn't going well.

'Signor Guaro!' a strident voice called. He and Mary turned to find the Duchess of Fanshawe approaching them determinedly. *Saved?* 'Lady Mary, good evening.'

'Your Grace,' he and Mary intoned, dropping into bows and curtseys.

'I hadn't the chance the speak to you Wednesday, however I simply *must* tell you how utterly exquisite that portrait of Deirdre was,' the Duchess said without further ado, and Luca knew he was blushing to an inordinate degree, completely thrown. He felt the weight of Mary's questioning gaze, but kept his eyes on the Duchess, and smiled gratefully. 'Deirdre has been singing your praises for months—we all thought she was exaggerating since you wouldn't show your work—but dare I say, she was right. I simply had to tell you that should you ever change your mind about commissions, I would be the first to engage you.'

'Thank you, Your Grace,' he bowed. 'I will remember that.'

'Will you be showing us more at Clarissa's next soirée?'

'I hadn't given it much thought.'

'Well, you should. I would be curious to see these sculptures of yours. Tiny things, aren't they?'

'Yes, your Grace.'

'I will look forward to that,' she said, wilfully misinterpreting his assent, and he blushed further. The Duchess turned her gaze to Mary, recalling her presence. 'How is your family, Lady Mary? Most unusual of your mother to miss the Season, however I expect she is eager to meet her first grandchild.'

'Indeed, Your Grace,' Mary smiled tightly, and though it reached her eyes, they themselves darkened with…*something*. 'Mama regrets not being in London since last autumn, however, it is much less of a trial to travel from Clairborne House to Scotland. She is enjoying doting on Lady Clairborne, to be sure.'

'To be sure.'

They were saved from anything further as the notes from the dance faded into silence, and those on the floor departed, making way for those who would waltz.

'If you'll excuse us, Your Grace,' Luca said with a bow. 'I've been granted the honour of this dance by Lady Mary.'

'Of course,' she smiled, inclining her head gently, the long ostrich feather atop it bobbing merrily.

There was a gleam of intrigue in her eyes, but Luca brushed his unease away, focusing on the task at hand.

He offered his arm to Mary, then led her onto the floor. Sucking in a steadying breath, he told himself not to make anything of how that simple touch quietened his nerves. It was merely because he'd...arrived. At his goal. Speaking to her. There was nothing about her closeness, her touch, that could affect his body so; *utter nonsense.*

Yet as the waltz's first notes rose into the air, and he and Mary took their positions, not only did the mere touch of her through layers of fabric settle him, but it also made the rest of the world fade away into a dull, quiet blur. The circle they created was so powerful, it left him able to see and hear only her with exquisite detail, and as they moved with the notes his body inherently heard and obeyed, he reminded himself not to drown in the ocean of her eyes, but rather, if he ever wished to experience this wonder again, say what he must.

He might've baulked, but gazing into her eyes, seeing the change in her, however subtle, gave him the strength to say his piece—for he wasn't the only one affected by this closeness. Mary too, was lighter, more at ease, so there may still be a chance for him yet.

Piccola. Small.

'You promised my sights would be set on another by now,' he began as they swirled across the floor, their bodies so in tune, so synchronous, that with even half the skill they possessed, they would've looked perfect.

He tried to make his voice light, *non-threatening*, though he let the strength of his feelings come through.

Mary needed to know how deeply he was drawn to her. That he *cared.* She needed to understand how serious he was—that he wasn't playing games.

Though she showed no great reaction, neither did she protest.

Avanti.

'Yet here I am, interested only in you.'

'It will wane and fade away,' she stated, more regret than heat in her voice.

'Perhaps, in time,' he agreed, though a voice whispered, *liar*. 'Until then, I should like to know you better.'

'What do you want from me, Luca?' she sighed, once they'd passed another couple closely.

'Time,' he said, telling his heart to calm itself. Just because she hadn't said *no* outright, didn't mean she wouldn't. 'I don't know what we can be—I do not forget our stations. I'm not asking for…more of what occurred in the library, merely for time. I don't want to return to being barely better than strangers. If friendship is all we can share, I will be happy. Your time, a chance to know you, that's all I ask for.'

'To what end, Luca?'

'Do you ask all your friends the purpose of their friendship?'

'I may not ask them, but I do ask myself.'

Luca frowned, only half believing it.

Then he shook away his thoughts on that—the dance was half over, and he needed to win his chance.

'I can be very useful,' he pointed out with a sly grin. 'As you know, having availed yourself of my assistance this past New Year.'

'I was desperate.'

'You should keep me around, in the event you ever are again.' Mary's laugh tinkled, and he felt his victory near. 'Until then, perhaps…a chance meeting at a park? Or I could come visit Nichols House, or…'

'Fine,' she said, sounding reluctant, yet somewhat pleased at the prospect. That one word gave him wings, carrying him across the floor with a broad smile, his feet barely touching the floor. 'Tomorrow, I *might* be riding through Hyde Park. Around eight or so.'

'Unfashionably early.'

'Typically quiet.'

'I will look forward to perchance meeting you there.'

'Be warned, Luca, that should our association ever prove to...give rise to the slightest hint of tarnishing gossip, I will end it.'

'Of course,' he nodded, reminded of the other matter he needed to speak to her about—however, he was out of time. 'Though I don't think you mind a little bit of chatter, or you wouldn't have agreed to dance with me.'

'Sometimes a little bit of chatter is needed to distract small minds from more interesting titbits,' she said flatly, as they slowly came to their ending positions. 'Thank you for the dance, Signor Guaro.'

A curtsey, a bow, and he led her back to the rest of the world, which now seemed so busy and head-splittingly noisy.

'Give my regards to Lady Granville,' she said, as he bowed yet again, taking his leave.

'Good evening, Lady Mary.'

And with that, he left her, grasping his victory tight to his heart as he went to check on Deirdre.

It may not have been much, but to Luca, she had given him the world.

Chapter Seven

The world was lavender. Thick mists hung over the landscape, covering it in a shroud. Suspending this time and place; veiling the deeds done here from the world, not that the world would ever care to see them. There was a briskness to the air, but Mary couldn't feel it, too enveloped in sickly warmth and cloying sweat.

At least she looked ill—they all did—so any witnesses to their early departure would be able to repeat the lie with confidence. She could barely stand, but had refused to be carried down, as they'd needed to carry Simone.

Simone was gone now, swept away into the mists as they soon would all be.

Frances was gone too. She'd been the first. She'd... nearly woken the house with her raging. Mary envied her.

Hushed voices echoed loudly on the shroud around them, and Mary vaguely heard Mama beckoning. She didn't move. She followed the sound of churning gravel, and saw another carriage disappearing into the mists. Eliza...

Mama called again, only Mary still refused to move. She pulled her arm away when Mama reached for her. She needed to be the last.

To be the one to see the others....

A stifled groan.

As if moving through water, she turned to find Catherine, trailing behind a group of wraiths. Tears which weren't allowed to fall glistened in her eyes.

Mary wanted...

For them all to be gone. For them to never leave. To never part.

But part they must.

And there went Catherine.

Mary moved. One step after another. Though she couldn't quite remember that.

She remembered...riding through the mist.

Lavender turning to rose-pink.

The shroud...lifting, or...being left behind.

Left behind to cover the girls who had been, and never would be again.

Old Mary. Old Simone. Old Frances. Old Eliza. Old Catherine.

And—

Enough, Mary ordered her mind. *The morning is bright blue,* she reminded it. *Not lavender.*

Perhaps she should…ride for a while longer around the streets before heading into the park to meet Luca. She needed…her mind to not be so full as it was now—*always*—in order to… Properly handle him. And herself.

To properly enjoy it.

This time of year…was always…*something.* A period when her already full-to-the-brim mind threatened to… implode. Not only did she have others' secrets, her plans, meaningless conversations to remember, but…*all the rest* too, which she habitually kept in a locked portion of her soul. So her recent…discomfiture was no surprise really. She would blame it on…*today.*

Another reason—*the* reason—she'd agreed to meet Luca. The past few days, the ticking clocks which drew her nearer to the perverse anniversary she wouldn't honour, yet could never forget, had told her that no parties, teas, shopping, or useless chatter would do the trick this time. Get her through it.

Fourteen years.

She wondered how the others fared. How they made their way through the day; if they marked it somehow. Catherine—*the Duchess of Barden*—had been at the ball last night, looking...well. They hadn't spoken—they rarely did—but Mary had longed to go over and *ask* her all those questions. But asking her, asking any of them, in person, or even in a letter...well, it was an unspoken agreement that they never speak of that night. Mary knew Frances... had difficulty—though she always refused company—and had...difficulty all year round. The others, she never saw *today*, so she never witnessed how they dealt with it.

It doesn't matter. It changes nothing.

Perhaps it was...loneliness, making her...*pensive*, and prompting her to behave uncharacteristically. Like giving in to Luca. A desperation to not feel that unwelcome, unfamiliar, and unpleasant emotion. Was it an emotion? She wasn't sure.

She'd never felt lonely. Alone, yes; her entire life. Her parents were distant though not *unloving* or neglectful, and when she'd understood her position, that of her parents, her family, she'd believed that the reason. Now, she understood the distance better, though understanding made it more... bitter. Worthy of regret, and anger. But before, she'd still believed that peers didn't raise their children, love them, pay attention to them; employees did that, which wasn't... *wrong*, so long as a child was taken care of, one way or the other.

Which Mary had been, suffering no unkindness, no neglect. Merely growing up in a cold home, alone despite the nurses, governesses, and tutors, who had all kept a respectful distance. Spencer...had been sent away to school—but even as small children they hadn't been close. Not even playmates. Then Papa had died, and Spencer had become the little lordling he was destined to be, and the distance grew. Mama had grieved her husband in a very dignified manner, and Mary had…carried on alone.

The solitude hadn't bothered her. She'd revelled in it. Especially when she joined Society, even before she was *introduced* to Society. She'd never been bored, or lonely. Quite the contrary; she'd kept her mind alive, and entertained herself.

After her first Season fourteen years ago…*then*, she'd begun feeling the desperate ache of *aloneness*, but that was easily explicable. At the very least by her removal from Society whilst she…recovered. Aloneness became isolation through silence. Though Mama had tried, Lord knew. And Spencer, well, he knew nothing of it. Never would.

Yet even then, it had been a sense of *isolation*. Not loneliness. Not as she felt now. As she had felt for…some years. Feeling alone, submerged in a sea of people, she could handle; she knew that well. Feeling all that, *and* wishing for someone to take her hand and tell her she wasn't alone… that was new.

It was a fault in the manner in which she'd been made—by God, Society, her family, and…that night. She wasn't averse to *friends*; she'd made some to varying degrees. Freddie, Mena, Genevieve, the Reids of Thornhallow, Susie even, Luca—only it always came back to the same thing. She couldn't trust anyone.

Everyone had a price for betrayal. She may never learn what that price was, yet she couldn't trust she never would. Therein lay the rub.

Still, if she didn't do something about this loneliness, it would devour her. Gobble her up surer, and quicker, than anger, pain, or hatred. She wasn't so fool as to not recognise that.

Shaking her head, she took a breath, and cast her eyes over the few people wandering the streets with her—though they did so purposefully. And she did have a purpose—*go meet Luca*—only she didn't quite feel…settled enough yet.

Luca will settle you…

Yes, that was part of the problem, wasn't it. Part of what made him *irresistible*. She meant that wholeheartedly—she was unable to resist him. Some part of her knew that was… part of his *profession*; a requirement. To charm, lure, and attract. She'd known that from the first, and it had always enabled her to maintain her distance. Reminding herself that his charm, attentiveness, and irresistibility were tools of his trade enabled her to…not be affected.

Two years ago, at the beginning, she hadn't known much of Luca, or his relationship to Lady Granville—she didn't know *that much* more now—and when he'd begun popping up everywhere, annoying her at every possible opportunity, she'd wondered if he was seeking out a new protector. After all, she satisfied the necessary criteria. Unattached—though whether that mattered, she wasn't sure—ostensibly lonely, and most importantly, incredibly wealthy. Her family also hadn't been immune to scandal these past years though they'd survived, not least of all thanks to Mary's powers. So, it would've been no great leap for Luca to believe she…wouldn't be averse to a scandal of her own, with him.

Then…time passed. Things changed.

He never alluded to wanting a new protector. He annoyed her, but never crossed a line. Never pushed her, in any way. He was just…*there*, challenging her, making her laugh, *truly* laugh. And after she'd gone to Scotland the summer before last, chasing Spencer, and learned the truth of their family…

Luca changed. He'd sensed the change in *her*, and softened. Their verbal sparring held slightly less *pique*. If she was in any way uncomfortable—alone, or with someone else—he would appear, as if by magic, and…make it better. Though he continued to pop up at every fathomable moment, he did it with more…consideration.

Then, this past winter…that whole expedition to Sussex to save Freddie… Luca had *been there*. Physically, yes, when she'd felt more alone than ever, offering her a steady presence throughout the ordeal. He'd remained by her side, every step of the rescue, then seen them all safely and quietly back to London. He'd *been there*…emotionally. A steady presence to lean on—loath as she was to do so—without her ever having to say she needed him. That… escapade had changed things too. Created an unwanted—or at least, unsought—intimacy. A friendship she neither needed—*wouldn't admit needing*—or wanted. She'd tried to dismiss every new approach he made, reassuring herself he was only…up to his old tricks, but she knew better.

It was why she'd succumbed to him in the library. Despite all she told herself to the contrary, she *wanted* him. To crawl into him, and find more of what he'd already given.

Comfort. Calm. Unwavering...affection.

It all made him *irresistible*. Dancing with him last night… Reminded her of what she'd sought to bury beneath flimsy reasoning. It wasn't only the way he awakened her body; how when she placed her hand on his arm, or felt his hand on her back…how it…*thrilled* her. Sent her heart racing, even as it slowed time. Being in his…orbit, it made her feel…a thread of inexplicable joy—which wasn't something she felt. It was foreign to her. She called it *joy* solely because it fitted the definitions of joy she'd read, or heard described.

Lightness of being.

Closing her eyes, she allowed herself to fall into that sensation, still thrumming though her being despite…the rest, as if Luca had seared it into her by his mere touch. Given her body the ability to recollect it as one would the steps of a dance learned long ago if only the tune were to play again. But it wasn't only that—the...*physical*.

It was how *comfortable* she was with him. Though her... trepidation would never go away entirely, with him it lessened more than with anyone else. And his eager tenderness, the way he respected her dismissal, while at the same time challenging it. Opening himself, revealing...if not his heart, then his desires. No games. No minced or pretty words. Merely a request, for her time.

It was reckless to agree. It endangered that reputation she'd fought so long and hard to maintain. Whatever their friendship may come to look like, there were certain things it could *never* look like. She was a lady. He was a kept man. Some lines...couldn't be crossed lest she court ruin. Not that she wanted their relationship to ever become...something which would require a choice. A sacrifice.

When she'd found Spencer in Scotland, hopelessly in love and ready to marry Genevieve... She'd told him that should she ever love someone, she would want them to be willing to risk as much as he did. Ruin, dishonour, loss of power, even potentially family. But the truth was... *She* wouldn't ever have that courage. Hell, she wouldn't have been courageous enough to support Spencer's choice if she hadn't been so sure of her power to preserve...their good standing, status, all of it. Her power alone gave her the courage to occasionally...be sentimental.

So no, she didn't want true love, or some fantastical *happily ever after* with Luca; those weren't things she could ever give another. She was far too...broken. Even if she had wanted such things, she wasn't so unrealistic as to believe them possible with *him*. At the very least because of his age—which had to be at least a decade less than hers. Though she may call him *puppy*, still, she knew his age diminished none of his maturity and intelligence—often far superior to those twice his age. Regardless. It was all moot, since that wasn't what this… What she wanted. His friendship, his time…those things he offered, however, those sounded…*nice*.

Having dallied long enough, though still…troubled, Mary set off towards the park. If she wanted the niceness, she'd better get there.

And...enjoy it.

Chapter Eight

The sun had barely risen when Luca left home, and even though he walked York so slowly they might've been travelling backwards, he and his trusty stallion arrived at the park by seven. It was only then, as he wandered around, loath to just stand there, that he realised they hadn't set a meeting point.

I'll find her.

A ludicrous notion given the size of the park, only he felt sure of it, and not because he was being *romantic*, but because he knew Mary resided in the family townhouse in Mayfair. Therefore, if he kept to the east, he would surely find her. Particularly since it wasn't very busy—though the city was waking with a vengeance—a few riders and wanderers, the only visitors.

I will find her.

Certamente. Surely.

The morning—which was lovely, the sky a disconcerting wash of blindingly bright blue and pinks—was surprisingly chilly, a brisk breeze whistling through, and he kept York at a vigorous walk; warming, but not tiring. He tried to tamp down his eagerness, if only to keep York's nerves calm, but he wasn't successful. He blamed the brisk breeze, and beauty of his surroundings for further awakening his entire being, though he knew the prospect of time with Mary was responsible.

Time, to get to know her.

Not for the first time, he wondered if her contradictions intrigued him. Amplified by her…unattainability. If combined, they sparked some desire for…discovery, and conquest. If his interest was born from years of…not having any *personal* interest.

Oh, he'd been attracted to Deirdre, and those before her, he hadn't *feigned* interest—not that he judged those who did—however he'd always known it was… There was always a recognition that the pursuit was…for business. His purpose was survival—his own, and his family's. Though the others before Deirdre hadn't expected fidelity, he'd given it, unreservedly, as they had. Deirdre had ended their sexual relationship months before they'd arrived in London, and explicitly encouraged him to find his own *interests*, yet despite the various offerings, he hadn't found anyone who prompted him to pursue a relationship of any sort. So perhaps Mary was just the first who sparked a *personal* interest, and therefore why he was so…intent on believing anything could come of it.

Not for the first time, Luca rejected the notions.

Her mystery, her contradictions… They did pique his interest, but only in the same way he longed to examine every facet of a sculpture; to see the whole. Her unattainability… That filled him with regret, not a sense of safety, or challenge. It shouldn't, as he wasn't even certain he wished to find what *attainment* in this context meant; for her to be his, and him to be hers, for all the world to see. As for her being the first he'd had a personal, *non-business* interest in making him more eager…well, that didn't *feel* right. There weren't any *reasons* countering that idea. All he knew was that the first time he'd seen—

Mary.

'Lady Mary!' he called, too loudly to be considered gentlemanly, waving as he spurred York on.

Sporting a riding costume of forest-green velvet, atop her impressive jet-black stallion, illuminated by the spring rays, the breeze catching her golden curls, she was certainly…

Magnifica. Heart-stoppingly magnificent.

Especially when she smiled—as brightly as he—when he approached, her surprise at his boisterous hailing gone.

'Well met, Lady Mary,' he said, breathless, sidling up beside her—not too closely, to avoid any enmity between their mounts.

'Well met, Signor Guaro,' she replied with a sly grin and mirth in her eyes. 'What a surprise to meet you so unfashionably early. I thought I was alone in enjoying the park at this hour.'

'A happy coincidence,' he nodded, watching as a young lord he didn't know pranced by. Once he had, Luca lowered his voice, leaning in slightly. 'How did you sleep, Mary?'

'Perfectly,' she lied. He liked to think he'd had some part in any sleeplessness—in a good way—though he… knew there was something else. 'And you, Signor Guaro?'

'I was too eager for the day to start anew to sleep very well.'

Eyes narrowing, she surveyed him, deciding if he was attempting to disarm her with platitudes, but she must've seen the truth in his gaze, for then she smiled gently.

'Shall we exercise these gentlemen properly?'

'Lead on, Lady Mary.'

A nod, and she spurred her mount onwards into a vigorous trot, Luca following suit quickly.

Together, they toured the park for at least an hour, happily trotting alongside one another, carefully avoiding any others who appeared on the paths—known or unknown—silently enjoying the morning.

It was a peaceful time, of quiet comfort. Of existing in concert, and Luca felt as settled as he'd been with her in his arms last night. Though this morning the world didn't fade away; rather, she brought it into violent definition. Colours were brighter, scents more intense. The birdsong more melodious; even the cacophony of the city beyond the green haven was a lullaby.

Eventually, they slowed to a quiet amble as they followed the Serpentine, heading eastwards. This was his chance, to *get to know her better*, and there were a myriad of things he wished to ask—*what's your favourite flower, what experiences led to your view of the world being so cynical, what makes you happy, what are your thoughts on Mendelssohn, why do you ask yourself what use a friend could be*—but he led with the one which had been troubling him.

He needed to know the answer before they went any further—though her answer wouldn't dissuade him from… continuing on, unless perhaps she said with an honesty he couldn't refute, that it was *because she wished to.*

'Why did you start that rumour about Viscountess Porens?' he asked abruptly, and the smile which had lingered at the corners of Mary's lips died.

She looked at once affronted, remorseful, and angry, though she schooled her expression instantly, lifting her nose, and appearing unaffected.

'Lady Granville gossiping? Not such a free man after all, are you, Luca?'

'Do not speak ill of Deirdre,' he warned, his seriousness surprising her. 'She doesn't gossip, as you well know; she suffered enough because of it. Though I won't deny she told me what you'd done.'

'You shouldn't be so bewildered, Luca. If you are, then you haven't been paying attention. Besides, I started no rumour,' she said flatly. 'Had you been there, you would've heard me compliment the Viscountess on her dress.'

'I have been paying attention, Mary. I know you aren't who you have painted yourself for all Society to see. So do not feign innocence, and play us both false. You knew what you were doing, and you knew what the consequences could be, though only time will tell the whole outcome.' Tightening his thighs, he sped up, moving just slightly ahead, to look at her nearly square on. Her jaw was tightly clenched, and had she not been wearing gloves, he would have seen the whites of her knuckles as she grasped the reins. 'I'm not judging, Mary. Only seeking to understand.'

'It isn't so complex, Luca,' she shrugged. 'Had you been there, you would've also heard Her Ladyship disparage me. Mock my inability to secure a match with Mr Walton.'

'I wouldn't have thought such comments would bother you. You knew very well what the *ton* thought of your and Mr Walton's relationship, and it isn't the first time someone has commented on the shock it was to see him marry another. You yourself said there was nothing romantic between you, during our escapade to Sussex,, as I recall.'

Which he did—*vividly.*

Up until then, he'd also believed an engagement lurked on the horizon for Mary and Freddie Walton, and when he'd heard her dispel those rumours—to the woman who would be Mrs Walton—as they rushed to save the man himself, he'd felt… For the first time, that perhaps his *tendre* for the lady wasn't so doomed.

Mary sighed, reining in her mount to a stop, and Luca followed suit.

Silence, but for their surroundings, and the impatient nickering of the horses.

'Why do you care, Luca?' she said finally, not meeting his gaze, her sights set on something far away—likely not even in the park. 'What difference does it make, *why*? It's done.'

'It matters to me.'

'Because you wish to determine whether or not I'm a good person? Worthy of this…juvenile infatuation you harbour?' The words should've cut, yet they didn't; he heard the pain, the defensiveness beneath them. Mary turned to him, that imperious raised brow of hers in full force. 'Let me spare you some time. Lady Granville was right, when I imagine she warned you to keep away. I'm not a good person. I'm not kind. I destroyed another woman's life because she hurt my feelings, though you are correct, I've heard her words before, and no, I wasn't aggrieved to not marry Freddie. I told the Viscountess's secret to the world because she is a mean-spirited, vicious snipe who spent two seasons doing everything in her power to destroy her competition, and who entrapped a good man because she couldn't face the consequences of her own actions. I did it without second thought, and I would do it again. She isn't the first I've ruined, and won't be the last. *That* is who I am.'

Mary turned, but not before he glimpsed a sheen in her eyes—which he doubted, despite the outburst, were tears of anger.

She made to ride off, but before she could, he uttered not the first thought he'd had during her tirade, but the last.

'I don't believe you.'

Mary froze, and he relaxed with a sigh back in his saddle, urging York on slowly.

A few moments later, she was beside him, quietly waiting for whatever he would say next.

'I don't believe you exposed her secret because of what she said about you and Walton,' he said finally. 'I believe her attack on you was the last in a long line of offences injuring others. Now, I don't know the Viscountess, and cannot pretend to understand what might've made her into what she is,' he said meaningfully, and Mary's gaze went from her saddle to some spot on the Serpentine. 'Perhaps she was desperate to escape her father's house, or she merely is mean-spirited. Regardless, I don't condone what you did, for I don't believe it is up to us to mete out judgement. Yet I cannot deny that preventing people from injuring others is…not dishonourable. I haven't yet come to any decision, as to whether or not I agree with my countryman's thoughts in *Il Principe*.' He paused, patting York as he gathered his thoughts. 'The Viscountess is responsible for her own actions. I don't know how you came to learn her secret, but having lived in both villages, and the greatest metropolises, I do know that someday, it would've come to light. All secrets do, particularly in a society where they are currency, though that doesn't diminish your culpability. However, that is for you, and you alone, to live with.'

Mary nodded, and they proceeded in silence, while he gave her time to digest his words.

They were halfway back across the park by the time he continued, knowing he must say it all before they parted, or never have another chance.

'As for you not being a good, kind person…'

Mary stiffened, awaiting his summation—which heartened him only because it meant she cared what he thought, and that meant, in some twisted way, that she cared to have his good opinion.

'Humans are composed of multitudes. We cannot be all *good* or all *kind*, no matter how hard we try. All I've ever witnessed, when Society is looking, and more importantly when it isn't, is you—reluctantly or not—helping others unreservedly. Without forethought. I've heard of how you fought to see a viscount convicted for his crimes, aided women injured by his hand, and stood by the Earl of Thornhallow when he made a wife of his housekeeper. You went in search of your brother at the first suggestion of trouble, and championed his marriage to someone Society had discarded twice over. You rushed to Walton's aide without thought for your own safety, travelled through the night, haggled with lawmen, and found the key to his haunting past, all so that he could be free, and happy. You reassured a woman you knew only little in her darkest hour, and by your own admission, you denounced a woman who had injured others in her quest for…whatever it was. *That* is all I have seen.'

Mary was all clenched again, only this time not in defence, but to prevent herself from…

Showing any emotion.

Luca wanted to dismount, tie up their horses, and just… *hold her*, but before he could, a man in livery ran towards them, and alarm overcame all the rest.

'Lady Mary!' the apparent footman called, panting as he skidded to a stop.

'Nigel? What's wrong?'

'A note. From Fenton Hill, my lady,' he choked out, handing over the letter. 'The messenger said it was urgent.'

Mary nodded, and ripped open the note whilst he and Nigel waited with bated breath, Luca attempting to think of anything he'd heard about Fenton Hill—beyond it being a small village northwest of the city.

At first sight of the few words scribbled, Mary's whole demeanour changed to a determined worry he'd witnessed once before: the night Walton had gone missing.

'Can I help?'

Mouth gaping slightly, Mary looked over at him, ready to say *no*, yet after a moment's consideration, she closed her mouth and nodded.

'I would be most grateful, and will explain on the way,' she said, before turning back to Nigel. 'Ride with Signor Guaro, if you can manage.'

A bow, and the footman approached York's side.

Luca offered the man a hand, and with only a little difficulty, Nigel mounted behind him. In a trice, they were off, racing back to Mary's townhouse. Luca had absolutely no idea what he'd agreed to, but found he didn't care. All he cared about, was helping Mary in any way he could. Easing her life, her struggles, her worries, in any way he could.

Sara fatto. And so I shall.

Chapter Nine

It was well past time Mary told Luca *something*. He'd been patient and understanding of her need for silence as they'd ridden swiftly to the townhouse, changed horses, and she'd changed into a more serviceable, *discreet* gown. She'd spoken only to give orders—including that Brooks, her butler, cancel her engagements for today, and tomorrow—and Luca had only spoken to request pen and ink to send a note to Lady Granville.

She'd nearly baulked then, said, *I'll be fine, no need to inconvenience your Deirdre*, only she hadn't, though it was imminently foolish bringing him along—the news they'd travelled in great haste together would spread like wildfire. The last thing she needed was *that sort* of gossip about her and Luca—the last time he'd assisted her the fact that it was *New Year's Eve night* had saved them. Now, in the light of day…it was an utterly careless choice, which could put a nice dent in her spotless armour called *reputation*. She would've been better off going alone, or taking Nigel, or one of the others, as she had before.

And she could tell herself that she had brought Luca along because *he was there*, and offered help, but the truth was, she'd brought him because she needed *him*. His company, friendship, support. She needed what he'd given before. The solid, reassuring, non-judgemental presence of someone who…cared for her.

Which he did, she knew now, with an utmost certainty she'd not experienced many times. When she had, too often, it had been shattered by *truth* eventually. Still, she knew the fact Luca cared for her would never change. Be it as a friend, a stranger, something more… Most importantly, she wouldn't fight it, as she had for some time. No longer would she push him away, even if… The way he made her feel—*too good, too comfortable, too safe*—was perilous.

Which was why she'd *tried* to…be done with him earlier when he'd asked about Viscountess Porens. She'd tried to warn him away—to keep herself safe—but he'd not budged, like some great lump, so determined to *know* her as no one had ever cared to, and he accepted her, *warts and all*. He'd pushed back, scraping at her walls, so gently, and it was maddening, terrifying, and also…

Liberating. Wondrous.

She'd hung on to his every word—neither condemning nor condoning—grasped every summation he made of her as though they were blessings from above.

Perhaps they were...

That was all well and good, but now, nearly finished with their hour-long journey to Fenton Hill, she owed him. More truth—the best she could give.

A warning of what you might see. But first...

'Thank you, Luca,' she said quietly, to be heard over their trotting, and the noise of the busy, though not packed, road. 'For agreeing to come, with no knowledge of what I'm dragging you into.'

Luca glanced over, studying her, before that playful, sweet grin of his made an appearance, and he nodded.

Then, he turned back to the road, content to remain in the dark. Although she appreciated that, she wouldn't let him go there entirely…unprepared.

If only for Frances's, and her own comfort.

'A friend runs a dame school in Fenton Hill. Frances. Frances Warton.' She let the name hang, though Luca, if he made the connection, didn't query it. 'We've been friends for a long time. She…'

Damnit.

Explaining without explaining was tricky. At least when she brought one of the servants, explanations were never given, nor expected. Not that Luca expected any, yet…

For some reason I wish I could tell him everything.

'There are times Frances cannot… That is, she suffers periods of…*unrest.* Dark periods, where she grapples with demons. Sometimes, she is vocal, active. Others…she cannot rise, nor feed herself. She isn't mad,' Mary added quickly, lest Luca attempt to suggest Frances might be better off in some…asylum or similar house or institution. 'Only some days are harder than others.'

Days...like today.

'What do you need from me?' Luca asked simply, and Mary let out a breath she hadn't realised she was holding.

'It depends on…how she is. Sometimes I require help moving her, or tidying the house. Once, we had to drag her in from the snow… That was not a good day.'

'I'm sorry, for whatever demons your friend battles. I will assist in any way I can.'

'Thank you.'

Luca nodded, and nothing more was said as they continued on.

Mary felt…lighter. Worried, still, about Frances, but also…freed, from having said what little she had. As if he'd taken up some of her concern, and carried it with him now so she wouldn't have to.

As friends do for each other. As...

No.

They rode in silence, passing quickly through Fenton

Hill—a small collection of low, squat brick or stone houses, shops, two half-timbered inns, and a church—before taking the first path eastwards as they left the main road. More cottages lined—or were set some way from—the lane, interspersed between the fields most of their inhabitants worked.

It was rather idyllic, pastoral, with the thick hedgerows, glorious weather, and occasional lines of grand oaks, though Mary barely saw any of it, too determined to arrive and see…what awaited them. They climbed a short hill, and turned up a muddy, somewhat gravelled drive, surrounded by apple orchards. At the top, past a small iron gate, beside another mighty oak, sat Frances's home and place of business, a plain, but once impressive grey stone, two-storey house with grand windows. The house, and small parcel it stood on, belonged to Frances—though the orchards didn't, sold some years before the house—the last thing her parents ever did for her, hence her need for an occupation.

The patches of roses and wildflowers before the house were well-enough tended—*reassuring*—and at the sound of their horses, a figure rose from the doorstep. Mary and Luca stopped before the gate, dismounting, and leading the horses through as Mrs Garrity—Frances's closest neighbour, mother of two of her oldest students, and Mary's informant—raised her hand in greeting, approaching slowly.

As always, the birdlike woman—who worked the mill a few miles away—with an abundance of freckles, and thick, straight black hair, sported a plain cap and brown gown of rough cotton.

'Mrs Garrity, good day,' Mary greeted with a small smile, as Luca tied up their horses.

'Lady Mary, thank goodness. I'm sorry to have sent for you. Only, short of asking James to beat the door down, I didn't know what to do.'

'How long?'

'She's been out of sorts for days now—the children told us—but I've managed to put it about 'tis merely an ague, and 'tis been two days without classes, though she let me in and I brought her soup, and bade her rest, only today she won't answer, and if not for the shouts and sounds of breaking things, I would've thought the worst…'

'You did right calling for me,' Mary said softly, taking the woman's hand. 'I thank you for all you've done. I shall take it from here.' Mrs Garrity's eyes flicked uncertainly from Mary to Luca, then finally, she nodded. 'For your trouble,' Mary added, sliding coins into the woman's hand, who looked about to refuse. 'And that of any others who suffer the children not having school.'

'Thank you, my lady.'

A curtsey, and the woman was gone, hurrying down the lane, casting apprehensive looks back every few yards.

Mrs Garrity out of sight, Mary turned to the house, stepping up to the portico, and raising her fist to knock.

Well, bang, more like, she thought, continuing her unladylike pounding. She should have a key made—she'd thought about it those times Frances was unable to rise from bed—only, that felt an intrusion on Frances's haven, and though she would force her way in if necessary, it would only be in the direst of circumstances.

Which isn't today.

If Mrs Garrity had heard shouts, the likelihood was that Frances was *not* abed.

'Frances, open the door this instant!' Mary shouted, anger masking the concern. 'I know you're in there, and if you don't unlock this door, I shall break it down!'

'I'd like to see you try!' a muffled, vicious, and slurred voice called back.

Not abed, and likely drunk.

'Do not test me, Frances!'

Silence.

Then, the sound of footsteps, accompanied by some short bangs as someone stumbled into furniture, and a key in the lock.

Luca, give me strength.

Chapter Ten

The irony of having had that conversation in the park—Mary declaring she wasn't a kind, good person—then witnessing what he was now, struck Luca as he watched her relentlessly bang on the door, calling out for her friend; her angry desperation masking a deep, and chilling concern.

Even if she hadn't told him what little she had—which he appreciated, if only because it meant she was beginning to, if not *trust* him, then something akin to it—he'd have known she was on a mission to help someone she cared for. As soon as she'd read that note, he'd known. Just as he'd known he would help her.

He wouldn't lie—he was curious about this friend, and what tied them together. He suspected this Ms Warton was part of the Warton family—the head of which was a viscount. Only, he wouldn't ask; it wasn't his business, and he didn't need to know in order to lend a hand. He suspected that beyond servants, and Mrs Garrity, no one had ever lent Mary a hand in this. Perhaps in any other matters either, beyond that which served them. He'd suspected that since New Year's, when she'd accepted *his* aid in finding Freddie Walton. Well, Walton perhaps had lent Mary a hand over the years, still, Luca suspected, not with this. Which meant he was privy to something…very personal. The idea filled him with an odd sense of pride, and determination—to not let Mary down after she'd trusted him.

The door swung open, revealing an angry-looking woman of about Mary's age—though she looked a decade older with the tell-tale signs of constant over-indulgence of liquor—and potentially other things—marring her elegant, patrician features. Dressed in a stained dressing gown and night dress, which both swallowed her, she swayed in the breeze, clasping the door as her matted and disarrayed mass of dark brown curls made her appear even more unsteady.

Bright brown eyes narrowed as she examined him, disgust turning her angry mouth into a moue.

'Who the bloody hell are you?'

'This is Luca, and no amount of harrying will deter him—believe me I've tried—so don't even think about,' Mary retorted, and Luca tried to appear stern and unshakeable, whilst trying to make sense of what the situation was, and what needed doing. 'Now step aside so we may see what mess you've made.'

Interesting tactic, Luca thought blithely.

No gentle hand of comfort today; those were the marching orders.

Not that he didn't believe Mary would be gentle when the situation demanded, just as it apparently required a firmer hand today.

'Ha!' Frances mocked, stepping back. 'Yes, do come in, *Lady* Mary, so that you may judge me as always. See how much better off you are than I.'

With a sigh, Mary pushed inside, and Luca wasted not a moment following.

Mustiness, the smells of food, liquor, and uncleanliness, as well as a mess of furniture, furnishings, books, and rotten flowers met them. Frances had apparently taken out her rage on the house; on top of neglecting it to begin with.

'Oh, Frances,' Mary said, taking in the view.

'You can bugger off back to the city, Mary,' Frances spat. 'I've no need for your disapproval.'

'No, you've need of a bath, food, and to sleep off that rum. You smell worse than a distillery,' Mary bit back, and Frances shrugged. 'This is how this will go,' she continued, stepping into the other woman's space, all steel and magnificent power, and not even the King would've argued then. 'We're going to get you cleaned up. We're going to get you fed. And when you have recovered a *sliver* of your wits, we're going to clean this mess. *Together.* One word of dissent, and I *will* leave, and you'll be on your own. The consequences from then on out will be yours to deal with.'

Frances said nothing, her eyes cast downwards as she hugged herself, and Luca saw tears stream down her cheeks.

Mary ignored them, though he sensed the distress they caused as she turned to him.

'I'm sorry to have dragged you into this,' she whispered. 'I…had no idea. It has been some time since it was so bad.'

'There's nothing to apologise for,' he reassured her, and the look she gave him was of pure relief. 'I'll set some water to boil, shall I?' he asked, louder, to be heard by their audience of one. 'The bath is in the kitchen?' Mary and Frances both nodded. 'I'll also see what I can find to eat. Then take care of the horses when the bath is ready.'

'Thank you.' Luca nodded, then glanced down the hall. 'Behind the stairs, to the left,' Mary told him. 'There is a trough out back, and a shed with some hay I hope will be in good enough condition. Frances and I shall fetch the necessaries for her bath.'

He nodded again, then slipped past them in the direction given, avoiding the overturned tables, vases, dead flowers, and pictures strewn about.

Also resisting the urge to grasp Mary's hand, and give it a reassuring squeeze. He wouldn't presume, especially not in front of her friend. He'd asked for time, friendship, and though he admittedly wished for more, he wasn't about to jeopardise the trust he'd won by pushing for more than Mary was able to give. Even if the gesture would only be meant to reassure, they weren't so close he could just presume to touch her.

Stepping into the kitchen—a veritable wreckage of crockery, pots, food, and detritus he didn't care to name—Luca stopped, surveying it all, forming a plan of action. It didn't take long—he was no stranger to tidying, cleaning, or cooking—and in a few minutes, he was divested of his coat, his shirtsleeves were rolled up, there was a fire in the pleasantly large hearth, above which a giant pot and kettle of fresh water from the outdoor pump bubbled merrily.

Mary and Frances hadn't descended yet—likely giving him time to get things moving—although he suspected it wouldn't be long.

He did his best to gather up as much as he could in piles—one for dirty dishes, one for detritus, another for soiled linens—whilst he also dragged the hip bath from a curtain-hidden alcove, and rooted through the pantry to find edible food.

By the time Mary and Frances appeared at the door, he'd cleared the floor, half filled the bath, put another pot of water on the fire, made tea with the dustings of leaves he found, and set up a station outside where he could wash the dishes, and prepare the meagre offering of vegetables for a soup. He'd also found a tin of oatcakes and smothered them in preserves, which he'd left out on the mostly clear table with the tea, so Frances would have something in her stomach.

He made himself scarce when they appeared—Frances hovering behind Mary, having lost any will to fight—offering Mary a reassuring smile before disappearing outside.

It was glorious, the chill of this morning's air barely lingering, and he enjoyed the warmth of the sun and clean air as he took care of the horses—the hay was useable, though barely. Then he began his work on the food and dishes, sat atop a stone bench which looked much older than the house.

The view from this vantage was stunning and picturesque—fields peppered with crops and lone trees, cut with lanes and streams. Vibrant colours, offset by the brilliant blue sky, and rolling clouds creating moving shadows on the landscape. He paused to memorise it, so he could sketch it later. Not paint—no array of colours could reproduce the view. Perhaps he could just manage to capture the tranquillity, the peace of this place.

Luca had always preferred the country—the true country, not that of fine houses and parties. Whether it be the countryside of his past, or that of his adoptive homeland—though surprisingly he had a preference for the latter. He understood others' fascination for the country of his birth—the glorious sunshine, the history etched into the rolling hills, the tall, wise cypress trees lining roads once travelled by ancient warriors. He'd never have believed the land which was…baked into his very soul could ever be replaced by another, but then he'd come here.

There was something so…breathtaking about the misty mornings, the gnarly oaks, and rain-soaked grasses. Even the grisly grey days. They soaked into him, like water into soil after a drought, and took root, deep within.

He may not know precisely *what* he wished to do with his life, but when he thought of the future, he imagined it… full of vistas like this. A quiet, fulfilled life, somewhere beyond London's business and the terrors of Society, where he could breathe. Somewhere he could…*be.* Not unlike this place, or where he'd put Mamma and Sofia. Somewhere life was…slower. More meaningful. Where one grew with the crops; where the seasons still marked the rhythm of life.

Though I don't think I could be a farmer, he mused, a smile growing. *No. I think not.*

He wondered what Mary would prefer—given the choice. It wasn't just her presence in the house which made him think he could see her here, standing atop a hill like this one, hair unbound, gown blowing in the wind, the sun reviving her like some ancient goddess. He'd seen her in various environments—in Society in various ways, and unfettered, riding across the Sussex countryside by moonlight—and he thought, city life didn't fit her, though he was sure others would disagree, since she was, as Deirdre put it, a creature of Society. A pillar of it. But given a *true* choice—to be where she would—what would she choose?

And do I merely think a quiet, removed life would suit her because that is what I wish for myself?

Considering he couldn't deny picturing her desires was linked to his impossible hope that there *could* be some sort of future for them, together...*possibly.*

Muffled, raised voices interrupted his thoughts—*good, you must stop wandering such foolish paths*—and he rose, approaching the door quietly, intent on checking all was as well as could be inside, and that no one required...his intervention.

Not eavesdropping exactly.

'It isn't so easy for the rest of us to merely carry on, as if nothing at all had happened, not even after fourteen years!' Frances shouted.

Luca stilled, knowing he'd already heard too much, and then quickly returned to his seat, the sound of Frances telling Mary to *leave her be for ever* or something such half heard—reassuring him this was merely a dispute, not something requiring his intervention.

He told himself to forget what he'd heard, and think no more on it.

Mary wouldn't appreciate that he'd heard it, and she especially wouldn't appreciate him...wondering, what happened fourteen years ago. What dark event tied Frances,

Mary, and apparently others, together—for there was no doubt whatever it was had caused lingering…*distress.*

Non sono affari tuoi. Not your business.

Indeed.

If Mary ever wished to speak of…*it*, he would listen. Until then, he would peel his potatoes, and never speak of what he'd heard.

Ever.

Chapter Eleven

Concentrating on the business at hand, Mary stared at where Luca had been, and didn't watch his progress to the kitchen. She waited until she heard footsteps on the kitchen's stone floor, then took a deep breath, steeled herself, and turned to the stairs, not looking at Frances either. Her friend's soft footsteps followed her—for now, Frances would obey, *one battle won*—and they made their way upstairs, Mary noting that no space had been spared Frances's rage.

Stepping over debris of what little decoration and furniture was peppered throughout, they went to Frances's room, and though Mary paused when they reached it—to not lose her countenance at the sights and smells therein—she proceeded on quickly inside.

Frances hovered by the door, and Mary was grateful. She just…wasn't quite ready. There was much to be said, but a hurricane of emotions raged inside, twisting, shrieking, and blending into an unrecognisable inferno. If they spoke now… Mary wasn't sure what she would say, and that could end badly. For both; or either.

Instead, she threw open the thick curtains, choking on dust, then opened the window to let in fresh air. She made her way around the room purposefully, but not as swiftly as usual—giving Luca time to get the bath ready. She didn't even want to think of what state the kitchen was in. She picked up soiled clothes, emptied chamber pots, and made piles of detritus, piles of items which belonged elsewhere or which could be restored, and stripped the bed. She wasn't sure how long Frances had been unwell, but it was certainly longer than a few days—though as usual, she'd hid it for some time.

Mary hadn't lied to Luca; it hadn't been this bad in a long time. Frances had had a…melancholic period some time before Christmas, but she'd been more…functioning. The last time things had been so bad…was three years ago, when Viscountess Warton—Frances's mother—had passed. Frances had been spotted by the old Viscount when she'd gone to set flowers on the grave—after everyone had left, not presuming to attend the funeral—and he'd chased her away.

Loathsome wretch.

Frances had fallen into a similar…period as this, only then she'd been in London, and Mary had tracked her to some dockside tavern.

At least she's home this time. A much better place to make such a mess as she wishes.

Mary continued her work, wondering if anything specific—beyond the repugnant anniversary—had set Frances on this path, though she doubted it, and so her wondering didn't keep her mind away from the twisted envy and frustration she felt.

Soon enough, she was seething, wrapping herself in the dark thoughts which covered the anger and worry. It wasn't the first time she'd felt the twisted envy and frustration when dealing with Frances, only today they danced about in her heart as merrily as revellers around a pagan bonfire. She wished…she could be as free as Frances, notably to destroy…everything. To let her rage be expelled; to have expelled it *that* morning. She wished *she* could march about the townhouse, shattering vases, ripping books to shreds. She wished she could scream, be lost in liquor, and *let go.* Instead, she was forced to remain placid, perfect, and yes, she'd learned to channel her rage, to do *some* measure of good with it, except it wasn't enough. It never was.

Never will be.

Gritting her teeth, she sucked in a breath, and tore through the chest of drawers for a clean set of under-things, and a plain gown, setting it all aside before assembling the rest of what they needed to bathe her.

As though she were a child.

The thought roused that envy and frustration again, twisting them so high they were a gleaming fire to be seen for miles. She just…wanted Frances to be better. She didn't want to come here, clean up messes, and make *her* feel better. Spend hours nursing her, reading her books, or just murmuring reassurances, and holding her when she wept. *She* wanted someone to do all that for her—even though she never showed the utter desolation inside. *She* wanted to be cared for—or better yet, she wanted them all to just move on, and forget. What good ever came from weeping anyway?

Grabbing the pack of linens, clothes, and bathing materials, Mary swept back downstairs, the patter of Frances's feet again reassuring her that she needn't say, nor do anything more for now.

What Mary wanted was her friend back. The one she knew in good times. The one who was witty, clever, and fun. She wanted to be her, yet never to be so weak, and she wanted *not* to be the strong one, the smart one, the one who *fixed* everything, for once in her life, and she…

Nearly dropped to her knees in gratitude when she saw all Luca had done. The reassuring smile he gave her before making himself scarce might've felled her too, had she not been steadied by her own putrid resentment. Nonetheless, it wrung her heart, and it took a deep breath before she could walk again.

She led Frances to the bath, and set the pack down on the clean corner of the table where a pot of tea and something resembling oatcakes smothered in jam waited. A smile nearly made its way onto her lips, but she forced it back, putting on her sternest face. Not until Frances was in the bath, sobering, could she let her touch gentle.

Good thing I'm not feeling particularly gentle just now.

'Come on then,' she ordered, and Frances obeyed, stripping, then stepping into the water.

Mary swaddled up the soiled clothes, set them on a pile of dirty linens Luca had made, then dropped oil in the water, and handed Frances a cup of tea, before she began washing her, scrubbing vigorously with an herb-filled block of soap, every so often stopping to refill the tea, or hand her a jammy oatcake.

She worked in silence, not leaving an inch un-cleaned, then rinsed her with cups of hot water from the pot over the fire, and bade Frances to stand.

Handing her clean linens to dry herself, Mary was pleased to note Frances looked much restored, her eyes no longer glassy—though Frances still refused to look at her.

Soon, it would be time for Luca to re-join them so they could begin their assault on the house.

Mary was feeling slightly more…settled, and so it was as good a time as any to say what must be.

'You were doing so well, Frances,' Mary said, as gently as she could, whilst her friend wrung and dried her hair, stepping out of the bath. 'How did it come to this again?'

'How can you ask me that?' Frances hissed. 'Today, of all days. But then it was always easier for you. Not a month later, and you were already your shining, *perfect* self again. Only you didn't suffer half of what I did.'

Mary winced.

Though she knew the words were said in anger—not for the first time—it didn't stop the unquenchable demon of guilt from clenching her heart.

Frances angrily tossed the used linen onto the soiled pile, then grabbed up drawers and a shift, throwing them on.

'It isn't so easy for the rest of us to merely carry on, as if nothing at all had happened, not even after fourteen years!' she continued, her voice louder with every word. Every word, which pierced Mary's heart; no matter that she'd heard them many times. 'You coming here, judging me, telling me how I should be, doesn't help. In fact, I wish you would leave, and never return. Go!' Frances screamed. 'Take that man, and go! Live your life, and don't worry about me any longer. Go, suffer the ugly truth of me no more!'

Frances's voice cracked on that last cry, and Mary tossed down the gown she'd been holding, strode over, tears in her own eyes, and wrapped her arms around her friend tightly.

It took a moment for Frances to accept it, then finally she did, wrapping her arms around Mary tightly. Then the sobbing began. Mary held her, letting every tear expel itself, until there were none left. For now. There would always be more—no matter how much either woman wished differently.

If only...

'I will never abandon you, Frances,' Mary whispered. 'Never. I thought you realised; you'll never be rid of me.'

'I'm sorry,' Frances rasped, pulling away, wiping her blotchy face. 'I wish I knew how to stop this. I wish I knew how to be better, how to move on.'

'You have, no matter what it seems like now,' Mary said, repeating words spoken to her once, hoping they might reassure Frances more than they had her. 'There are setbacks along every road. Despite what you think... I'm no closer to being free of that night than you are. I merely…found different ways to expel the poison of it.'

'I know.'

'Come, let's get you dressed and see what Luca is up to.'

Mary handed her the gown, and Frances slid it over her head.

'About Luca…'

'Don't ask, Frances,' Mary sighed, turning her friend to button the gown, though they were on the side, so Frances might've done it herself, but it gave Mary something to do. 'I beg you. I haven't the strength to speak of that just now.'

Nor perhaps ever. For I don't even know what I would say.

With Frances decent, Mary tossed her a soft smile, then went to fetch Luca.

No idea whatsoever.

Chapter Twelve

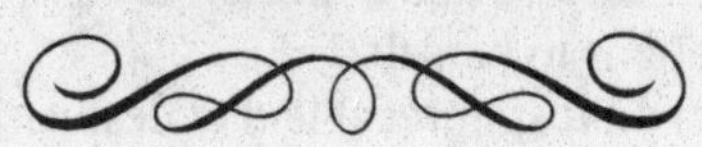

The late-afternoon sun washed the house, its surroundings, and Mary, in a radiant glow. All of it, especially *her*, had been restored as the day crept on. He liked to think he'd helped. That he'd eased the lines of concern, the dark shadows of distress, and something...*older*, behind her eyes; eased the exhausting weight she carried. That she *and* Frances carried—for by the time he'd bid her *good day* moments ago, she'd seemed strengthened too.

Despite the circumstances, even he felt invigorated by the day in all its simple industriousness.

Once Frances had her bath, tea, food, and whatever conversation needed to happen between the two women—though he suspected there would be more—happened, Luca had finished preparing his soup, upended the bath and washed the kitchen floor, then gone to Fenton Hill for supplies. When he'd returned, the women had already rolled up their sleeves and begun tackling the house, and after depositing his purchases in the kitchen—adding meat to his soup, making it stew—he'd joined them as they made their way through what once was a drawing room, but was now a destroyed schoolroom. They'd toiled in silence mostly, making quick enough work of tidying the worst of it, until breaking for food.

Then they'd set themselves outdoors, and whilst the women did laundry, he did his best to use what supplies he found to repair some of what Frances had broken. Slowly, they'd begun to converse, mainly about Frances's work, her pupils, the weather, philosophy, history, art, and life in Fenton Hill. There had been an unspoken agreement not to discuss anything personal, and though he suspected Frances was as curious about him as he was about her, she kept any questions to herself.

It had been a most agreeable day despite the circumstances, and he couldn't help but feel…he'd been given a gift. Yes, he would've preferred to meet Frances in better times, but then he suspected he mightn't have met her at all. Given the choice, he doubted Mary would allow him to be privy to anything remotely personal. She let him see only as much as she let others—unless circumstances forced her otherwise. Unless she was too weary to hold up her mask as one would at carnival. Perhaps it was...*wrong* for him to cherish the moments when her strength diminished, and she allowed him a glimpse of what lay beneath; only, it didn't feel wrong.

It felt like a privilege, and as if…he was *meant* to see what she reluctantly exposed. All he could hope, was that someday, she would reveal herself without reserve; by choice. Until then, he would…be patient. And hope.

Luca smiled, and returned his attention to Mary. They'd been standing thus—her at the door, he on the step below—for some time. Though they'd agreed he'd return to London, while Mary remained the night, they were *both* reluctant for him to actually leave. They'd been stood there a while, silently, if not *gazing*, then certainly enjoying their view of the other.

He knew he should say *goodbye*, and leave, but he also felt…they weren't quite finished.

'I always seem to be dragging you into my…personal

business,' Mary finally said, barely above a whisper, her gaze breaking from his, her fingers twisting together in her skirts. He longed to place his own on them, but again, he daren't presume. 'Calling upon you for help, though I usually manage fine.'

'I wouldn't call twice, *always*,' he replied, hoping she heard the smile in his voice. She saw it too, and returned it, when she glanced back up. 'And I would argue I *offered* assistance; you didn't ask for it. On both occasions. Though the circumstances have been…less than ideal for your friends—be it today, or this past New Year—I am… honoured that you trust me to help. Even if you only do so because I'm there when events…arise. I will never begrudge you asking me for help. Know that,' he said, with as much seriousness, and sincerity as was in his heart. 'No matter what happens, I will be there for you.'

'No one can promise that,' she breathed, with a sad certainty he didn't like.

Neanche un po. Not one bit.

'I didn't say *always*. You're right. No one can make that promise, and abide by its infinite clause. I meant that, regardless of…how we stand, my aid will never be refused.'

'Thank you, Luca.'

'If you wished… I could stay…'

'Our shared absence, after our shared departure, would be noticed, Luca,' she said firmly. 'I thank you, for everything, but I must beg you to return to London, and be seen before the night concludes.'

Luca nodded, hesitating.

Not because of what she said—she was right, it would be best for all involved if they weren't known to have spent the night, presumably together, away from town—but because he didn't want this to be *the end*. And if he knew anything about Mary, it was that at the first chance, she would attempt to sever whatever fragile ties had been created between them.

As she did earlier this year.

'We should speak, Mary,' he said, as firmly as she had. 'Properly. When your friend is better, and you've returned to London.' Reluctantly, she nodded. 'Are you certain you're well?'

Though he'd told himself to forget what he'd heard earlier, he hadn't quite managed it.

Especially not when, restored as Mary looked, he could still see a shadow of the demons her friend battled in her own eyes.

'It isn't so easy for the rest of us...'

But it isn't easy for you either, is it, Mary?

'I will be. I think it is best that I'm here today, in the end.'

He frowned enquiringly, but Mary shrugged.

Then, as if struck by genius, she stepped forward, and kissed him gently. Not on the cheek, oh no, on the lips. It was brief, chaste, and really he shouldn't make such an event of it, or feel as excited—like he could leap up, gather all the stars, the moon, and the sun itself were she to ask—only he couldn't help it. The simple feel of her lips against his, and his heart was ready to explode.

Not the worst way to die—from a kiss.

He didn't try to school his expression when she stepped back into the shadowy protection of the doorway. He stood there, grinning like a befuddled clodpoll, *wanting* Mary to see what she did to him.

Perhaps she did, for he might've sworn he saw a blush rise on her cheeks.

'Goodbye, Luca,' she said, closing the door before he could be sure.

'*Arrivederci*, Mary.'

Until we meet again. Soon, I hope.

Luca made his way back to London in a pleasant haze,

buoyed by that kiss, feeling as if he and his borrowed horse were charging through clouds, rather than dusty roads. It kept him feeling invincible, and the proudest, luckiest man alive, all evening, as he returned the horse, retrieved York—who had been excellently looked after—went home, bathed, changed, then set off again, to accompany Deirdre to the theatre.

What they saw was anyone's guess, not that Deirdre challenged him on it. In fact, all evening, she merely sported a knowing smile, which he might've quizzed her on, had he not been so distracted.

In the most remarkable possible way.

Chapter Thirteen

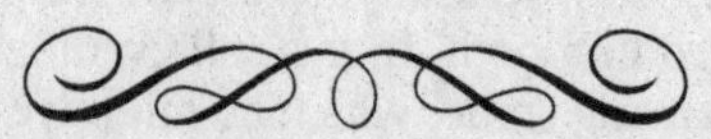

You are behaving a besotted idiot, Mary chastised herself, yet again making to return from whence she'd come, before turning back to the spot by the iron gates she'd been wearing a hole in for at least an hour. She'd watched the sun rise over Bloomsbury—her plan originally to arrive *before* sunrise so there would be no chance of being *seen.* Only, once the hack had deposited her here—well, not *here,* one street over—she'd realised the folly of this expedition. The danger.

The sheer idiocy.

Oh, this morning it had seemed a brilliant idea. The answer to her woes. She'd come here in a hazy calm, her mind, blessedly empty of doubts, thoughts, *reason,* for the first time…*ever.* So sure she'd been, that this was where she was meant to be, what she was meant to do, she'd marched all the way up to the imposing black door and raised her hand to ring the bell. Only then, reality had washed over her, and in horror at her own actions, she'd fled across the street, planting herself before the iron gates surrounding the square. Wearing a path in the pavement, glancing every so often at Luca's home.

Well, not his. Where he lives.

A sleek, brick and stone townhouse, identical to those

beside it—*nearly* identical to most in this area, prized by artists, academics, and intellectuals. Only, looking at it now, in the pale pink light of *very* early morn, Mary felt it looked different.

Only because it's his, you fanciful ninny.

Oh bother.

Why had she come? Why had she thought this so brilliant? Necessary?

Biting the skin beside her nails—having removed her gloves a while ago lest they be drenched in unladylike perspiration—Mary made another circuit, keeping her hood low as others appeared more frequently—not that any paid her much attention. Though if she kept pacing like some fretful lost girl, she *would* attract attention.

Make a decision...

Except, she felt she already had.

After Luca left Fenton Hill, she'd spent the night and most of the morning with Frances. They hadn't spoken much, beyond sharing more inane news—but that had only been over breakfast. The silence hadn't been uncomfortable, both their minds plenty occupied, and Mary had been grateful for the strangely restful interlude. By the time she'd arrived with Luca, Frances's…period of *unwellness* had reached its summum, and from there, it wasn't easy sailing, but sailing on quieter—albeit never easy—waters.

Mary had never truly believed they would all…*be well.* Be fully *healed.* Yet, the years, and yes, the willingness, the *eagerness* of so many of them to carry on, and live, if not defiantly, then with a semblance of normality—to the world at least—had dulled… Not the wound, not the sharpness of its edges in their souls, but the ache. Or maybe they'd merely grown accustomed to it.

Regardless. Passing the grim anniversary with Frances, away from the city, had…given Mary clarity. On the road back to London yesterday, she'd felt…exhausted, yes, physically, and emotionally, but also, less so than she might've been had Luca not been there. As was his way—unfailingly, unceremoniously. She'd been…profoundly, and unerringly touched, by his kindness and care. More importantly, she'd *allowed* herself to accept his kindness and care. And realised the only person she was hurting by…*hesitating*, was herself. Why shouldn't she take what he offered, for a time at least? Especially if it helped her through this…perplexing time.

By the time she'd reached home yesterday, her course was set, though she hadn't acted—needing to rest, and cancel the rest of her engagements for a few days—before she did. So she had, retiring for bed at barely seven—though she'd risen with the bells tolling four this morning. Dressed alone—as she often did—then crept out and walked until she found a delicious bun for breakfast, ate it in St James's, then took a hack here. Her absence wouldn't be noted—well, not *made an event of*, for she often went about her own business without anyone the wiser—though if she tarried here longer, her *presence* would be noted.

Make a bloody decision... Stay, or go?

What had she been thinking? That she would just march up to his door, ring the bell at some godforsaken hour, and say…what to whichever servant had drawn the short straw for duty? If indeed there was such a person, and they weren't all comfortably abed, or tending to other chores. Would Luca even welcome her…*visit*?

It was all well and good deciding she would take what he offered, but he *had* only offered friendship. Despite how he behaved…despite the way *she* felt their attraction, perhaps he didn't want to…*engage in a liaison*. Perhaps he didn't offer her more, especially since there would be no… remuneration.

Perhaps he doesn't want me as I do him.

Yes, he'd *wanted* her in the library. Yes, he'd pursued her after. Yes, she caught the unmistakable glint of desire in his eyes many times. Before their interlude in the library, and in their few meetings since. Still, he hadn't *overtly* offered. Just because she was more…attracted to him than ever—a condition not helped *in the least* by him wandering about Frances's home in his shirtsleeves, and doing all he had with an enthusiasm seldom seen—it didn't mean… *anything.*

What had she—

'*Pssst.*'

Mary whirled around, back towards the house, to find the man who'd taken up residence in her thoughts, right there, at his door.

She stopped and stared, taken aback by his sudden appearance—again in shirtsleeves, his hair dishevelled from sleep—until he smiled, and then…

Everything quietened.

Checking no one was about, she quickly crossed the street and hurried up the steps to him. He didn't ask before stepping aside, ushering her into the dimly lit corridor, and closing the door—for which she was grateful. He looked at her a long time, and she thought he might do something foolish, and entirely welcome, like take her in his arms and kiss her senseless, but then he shook his head, and stepped back.

She sucked in a much-needed breath and threw back her hood, eyes darting along the space illuminated by a mere candle and some light filtering in from adjacent rooms, noting the rich simplicity of the furnishings.

'What are you doing here?' he asked, not displeased, merely…curious.

'I wanted to thank you,' Mary told the plush runner at their feet.

A serviceable excuse, true—*somewhat*—and the easiest way to begin.

'You already did that,' Luca whispered gently, and her gaze met his. He knew that wasn't why she was here, but he didn't seem to mind. 'Come,' he said, leading her into the nearest drawing room. It was odd—all the furniture was covered with white sheets, and there were barely any decorations, beyond a few pictures set against the darkened hearth. 'Would you care for tea, or coffee? I make very good coffee.'

'You have no servants?'

He chuckled lightly, shaking his head at her uncomprehending frown.

'No need, though a woman comes weekly to tidy the few rooms I do use. And of course my driver, and those in the mews. It's Deirdre's house. I accepted it, for she wouldn't let me refuse, however, I draw the line at behaving a lord with twenty people catering to my every whim.'

'I envy you that freedom. Though I've learned to live without them being privy to every move… Some days I wish I didn't have to *evade* anyone. However, even if I wanted to, I couldn't dismiss the staff.'

'Whatever would people say?'

'Indeed,' she grinned.

Nodding absentmindedly, Luca raked his fingers through his hair, at as much of a loss as her about how to continue the conversation.

Luca, I...

'How is Frances?' he asked, not merely to say *something*, but because he truly cared.

'Well enough. Better than before, but then… She's fine, for now.'

'And you?'

Not well.

Confused.

Unsettled.

Eager.

Calm, somehow.

Yet more nervous than I've ever been.

In need of...

You.

'I am...' Mary paused, the words dancing in her mind nearly making it to her lips. Instead, she tried to find another way to say...all she wished. Without...*exposing* herself. 'I had five engagements today, and I cancelled every one. I couldn't...be around anyone.'

Luca held her gaze, daring her to break it, as he stepped closer.

Not invading her space, but softly leaning against the walls surrounding it, testing their resistance today.

'Yet you are here, with me.'

'You are not anyone,' she breathed, determined not to move.

It felt...perilous, this moment.

One of the most meaningful of her life. Another step down an unknown path she knew nothing of beyond that she wished to explore it. There were a thousand questions swirling between them, along with desire, yes, and the recognition that her words changed everything.

Let them.

'Not any more,' she added. *Not ever*, she didn't say. 'I shouldn't have presumed,' she said, reason intruding once again into the oh-too-charged moment. 'You likely have engagements of your own.'

'Not until this evening,' he replied, in a husky, seductive tone that didn't feel...*manufactured*. Merely truthful. Luca stepped closer, so that she could smell the delicious musk of his warm, sleep-filled skin. 'You are welcome here.'

Mary nodded, *feeling* welcome.

Too welcome. It was all...too much, suddenly, him, his presence, the way he looked at her as though she'd created the universe.

Needing air, she stepped aside, wandering to the hearth.

'Is this yours?' she asked, staring down at the unexceptional pastoral view of some idyllic farm, complete with incongruous gothic ruins.

'No,' he grinned, shaking his head. She wasn't *relieved*—his talent or originality wouldn't change her opinion of him—though she would've been *surprised* by the lack of emotion in the painting. 'Would you care to see my work?'

'Yes.' If asked, she would've said it was to occupy her, and relieve the tension between them. In truth, she felt privileged. To be allowed into *his* world, his inner life—especially knowing not many had been trusted with his work. 'I would. Very much.'

Without a word, but with serious acceptance of how their world was changing, Luca offered out his hand, and without hesitation, Mary took it.

There was an ending, and a beginning, all rolled into that one gesture, and for once, Mary embraced the irreparable permutation of her life.

In fact, for the first time, she welcomed it, with hope, and an open heart.

Chapter Fourteen

Luca hadn't believed his eyes when he'd opened his curtains and spied Mary there, right across the street; a mysterious beauty one might encounter in the woods in a fairy story—a beauty who would, in time, reveal herself as a powerful sorceress.

Well, a very nervous, pacing, powerful sorceress.

He chuckled to himself as he led Mary to the top floor—not the public rooms, the rooms under the eaves he'd transformed into his studio, with Deirdre's permission. There remained still two servants' rooms, but the rest he'd made his own.

He felt...*giddy* again. Mary was *here*. In his home. She'd come to him. He felt a giant again, a victorious hero, capable of the grandest feats. Had he not held her hand tightly, been able to feel her warmth seeping into him, he still might not have believed she was actually *here*.

When he'd spied her across the street... He'd believed he was still dreaming. He'd dreamt of her, and so he'd conjured her, with help from the illusions sunrises could sometimes give. Still, he'd hurriedly completed his toilette, thrown on clothes, and rushed downstairs before she—apparition or not—could disappear.

He'd spent the past day in that same daze he'd been

in since he'd left Fenton Hill—though he'd been more attentive to Deirdre on their excursions to shops, tea, and a musicale. Unable to think properly, for Mary living in his mind. He wondered where she was. If she'd returned. If Frances was well. If Mary was. When he might see her. If she would let him. If…

She needed him as much as he needed her.

To function. To breathe. To live.

Though she might not need him to *that* extent, he did know she needed him. It was there, in the unspoken words swirling beneath those spoken. She needed his company, his comfort, his affection. So she breached the gulf. Lowered the portcullis slightly. Accepted that whatever tied them together now, was best…explored. Not denied. Still, she was hesitant, reluctant, in strange territory. As was he. He had no idea what he was doing, beyond *being* with her. In whatever way she was ready.

Including sharing his work. It felt…natural to offer, despite his typical reluctance. He wanted *her* to see…part of who he was. And he thought, she did too. She'd seemed so pleased when he'd offered, and that was…

Something.

'Here we are,' he said, shyness creeping in as he opened the door, letting her into the space only one other had visited.

He hovered by the door as Mary released him, wandering in, her gaze absorbing it all, from the racks and shelves of prints and paintings, to the bookshelves lining the bare wooden walls full of materials and tools, to the various workstations set in this room and the next—everything from tables high and low for sculpting, or preparation, to easels, some with stools or chairs—each with projects in various stages of completion atop them. Mirrors—large and small, old and new—punctured the space, reflecting the light from the small windows into the cavernous and shadow filled space; the equivalent of three servants' rooms. Sliding his fingers through his hair, Luca wondered…how she saw it all.

Cluttered. Extravagant. Eccentric.

Mary straightened—she'd been staring down the length of the studio—and looked back at him, and he saw surprise—*pleasant*—and some wonder in her eyes that made him puff out his chest.

'I expected… A sketchbook, a few paintings,' she said, shaking her head, her eyes returning to her surroundings. Luca dared to approach—*not too close*—he wouldn't scare her away with his own alacrity. 'Never did I imagine…this.'

Breathless, she laughed, her arms gesturing at all there was.

'I'm…passionate,' he shrugged. 'Perhaps I did get carried away.'

'I can see why you wouldn't want servants,' she said wryly, removing her bonnet as she stepped to one of the racks of finished canvases. 'May I?'

Luca nodded, following, watching closely as she carefully looked through the unframed paintings.

Portraits, landscapes, experimentations with colour, still-lifes… Mary took her time studying them all, and he watched emotions and impressions flit across her face, telling him which she liked, and which she despised.

The lady has a preference for motion and chiaroscuro.

Having gone through the rack, she wandered to the next. Then, to a bookshelf full of charcoals and sketches. Then to his little sculpture atelier, her gaze dancing across the figures—human, animal, symbolic—in various materials.

Even if he'd wished to, he wouldn't have been able to keep his eyes off her. In the soft light, away from…watchers, with nothing to do, or somewhere to be, she was… Breathtaking, *yes*, fascinating, *naturally*, but by her unguardedness, not solely her beauty. He'd never quite seen *her* until now, every facet, as if she…no longer hid from him. Oh, there was still a profound darkness and sadness about her, an *unknown*, but it wasn't a manufactured mystery; a mask. Merely an unknown.

Her bonnet lay discarded on a table laden with research books, and her cape now hung on a chair. He was just thinking he should sketch those two images when she turned back, leaning against a table of sculpting tools. At a loss of what to do, he kept gazing, waiting for her judgement, sliding his hands up and down his braces.

Damn. No waistcoat. No coat. No stockings nor shoes, he realised bleakly.

Not that Mary seemed to mind his undress—but suddenly he felt…self-conscious.

'All this, and you don't wish to be an artist,' Mary said, the index finger of her left hand tapping against the table's edge, as a playful smile danced on her lips, and curiosity glinted in those silvery-blue eyes.

'I never said I didn't wish to be an artist.'

'You don't seek to make it your profession,' she corrected. 'No commissions, or patrons, and you've only reluctantly begun to show your work.' Luca nodded. 'Why? You have talent, and I think you know that. So why not make a living from it?'

'Art has always been my greatest pleasure,' he said softly, wandering over to her, his fingers playing over the pieces of broken pottery, wood shavings, and mounds of shapeless clay on the table. 'I was never expected to have a profession,' he admitted, and he felt her questioning gaze. 'I was expected to be part of Society once. Marry well, and have no occupation. My mother,' he explained quickly. 'She believed our family to still be part of a world we hadn't been for a very long time. By the time I understood… It was too late to try making money from my work. Even if it hadn't… Art is…one of the purest human creations,' he said, mirroring Mary's position. 'I don't judge those who live from it, but I find whenever money is involved, it corrupts. Once, art was an expression of the human condition. When it became a business…it changed. For the better some might say—one cannot deny the beauty of the Sistine Chapel—yet I think I might've felt…as if I were selling part of my soul.'

'So you sold your body instead?'

The words would've hurt someone else, but Luca knew what he was, what he'd done—and was at peace with his choices.

'I like to think I sold a service.'

'I'm sorry, Luca.'

'Don't be,' he said seriously, looking over at her, an example of *chiaroscuro* in her own right, lit from the side by the brilliant morning sun pouring in. Not a golden angel…a brittle faerie made of glass and light. 'I'm not ashamed of my choices, my life, Mary. You should know that.'

Mary nodded, battling the urge to drop her gaze.

'What *do* you wish to do with your life, Luca?'

He laughed, and she quirked her head enquiringly.

'You're the second person to ask me that recently.'

'And…? What is the answer? Or do you wish to continue…as you are?'

'The answer is I don't know,' he smiled. 'I *have* decided I shouldn't like to be a farmer.'

Mary narrowed her eyes in question, but he merely shrugged.

'Well, you have time. You're still young.'

'You may ask,' he said, sensing her hesitation.

'How old are you?'

'Two and twenty.' Mary nodded, sighing as she gazed up at the beam-covered eaves above them. 'tis not that much younger than you.'

Though, come to think of it, he wasn't *exactly* sure how old she was.

'Nearly a decade, Luca.'

'As I said,' he smiled, and she looked at him, a grin growing on her lips even as she shook her head. 'But we were speaking of life's pleasures. What of yours, Lady Mary?'

'I have none, Luca,' she said sadly. 'I'm thoroughly accomplished. I can draw well enough—my watercolours have livened many a drawing room, as have my musical talents. I sing, play the pianoforte and the harp with ease, I've embroidered countless cushions, and other things. I speak four languages, read Latin, and can play any acceptable game—be it cards or croquet. I have a good knowledge of plants, flowers, and can arrange a bouquet like the best of them. But these are things I learnt because I was supposed to learn them. I find some pleasure in them, but I would never say I pour my soul into them as you do.' Luca nodded, her sadness permeating his own heart. 'I've found though I have no talent for it, I quite enjoy baking,' she said with a surprisingly eager smile.

'Truly?'

'Yes. My sister-in-law, Genevieve, she's a good cook—even gave my brother lessons once. She started working on improving her baking with…the housekeeper of Yew Park House,' she said quickly, as though…correcting herself. 'I'm quite competitive, and last Twelfth Night, I helped Mena and a girl who works with her, Susie, to bake King's Cakes, and I admit, it began as a way to measure up to Genevieve, but in the end, I've kept at it occasionally, for I quite enjoy it.'

'Cooking can be art. Someday, you'll have to let me taste one of your creations.'

'Perhaps…'

They gazed at each other, until Mary cleared her throat,

and pushed away from the table, wandering across the room to examine a stack of charcoal sketches.

'I recognise this view…' she said softly.

'From Frances's house,' he said, nodding, and going to her.

'Will you paint it?'

'No… I could never capture the vibrancy I saw. And so, I don't attempt to. I only sought to immortalise the peace, and the richness of the light.'

Another wall came tumbling down before him, her eyes softening, and he worked hard to keep breathing.

After a moment, she turned back to the sketches, unveiling a few *études* of Deirdre, in the general pose of Ingres's *Odalisque.* Luca wondered if Deirdre would mind, but then he recalled she'd given him permission to show *anything* at Clarissa's *salon*, and so he didn't think she would.

She was as proud of these as he was.

'They're beautiful, Luca,' Mary breathed, her fingers dancing over the lines, never touching them. '*She's* beautiful.'

'Yes, she is.'

'You love her.'

'Very much. She's my dearest friend, and I admire her greatly. Once, I think we were *in* some fashion of love, but now, it's different,' he said, unwilling to lie, hoping Mary understood.

'She seems so different,' Mary said quietly, fascinated by the pages laid out before her. 'And yet, more…*herself*.'

'The highest compliment you could ever pay an artist.' Mary glanced up, and he smiled gently. 'To imply they managed to capture a truth others couldn't see without the artist's guiding hand.'

Slowly, Mary nodded, studying him, though he felt it was herself she was examining.

It really was the queerest—

'How would you capture me? Charcoal? Pencil? Paint? Sculpture? Something else?'

'Sculpture,' he answered unhesitatingly. He hoped… her questions were leading where he thought. Long had he dreamt of being given the chance to use her as his muse—he'd never wished to do it without her consent, not even in mindless sketches. 'Terracotta.'

It was perhaps his favourite work, making figures such as the oldest civilisations had.

Gods, idols, mementos, spirits…

'Would you? I know you don't do commissions,' she added quickly. 'I just think… I should like to see myself through your eyes.'

Unable to speak—too full of pride, exhilaration, and joy at being trusted to do this—Luca nodded, swallowing hard.

Non rovinare tutto. Do not make a mess of this chance.

Chapter Fifteen

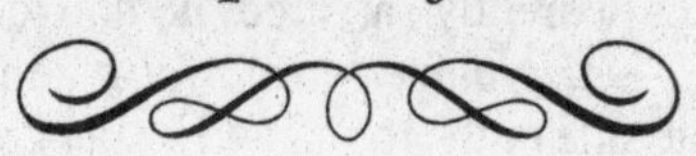

Luca was adorable. A thousand times more charming in his anxious, fluttering state than when he was…being charming. Mary found his own nerves, and harried, determined dash to make her comfortable and get everything ready, actually calmed her. Odd, but welcome. For nerves such as she'd felt when she'd asked him to do this…well, she hadn't felt those for a very long time.

Fluttering, adorable butterflies that swooped and soared in her belly—nerves she'd last felt as a young woman first encountering handsome young men, giggling, and flirting…when she was carefree, and hopeful; before her interest in men turned primal, and functional. Less…sentimental. It felt good to feel that again, only it was disquieting. She'd thought that part of her long dead, but Luca… he'd revived it, like dying embers.

She wasn't sure what possessed her to ask him to capture her—but then she wasn't sure what possessed her whenever she was with Luca. Basic, natural, and unconquerable impulses which pushed her to say, and do, what she wasn't even *aware* she wanted to say or do, but which felt…truer than anything. And today…

Today I won't think so hard.

And yes, his own eager nerves settled her. Enough to

be…sure of what she would do whilst he pottered about, first fetching coffee and biscuits—which he set on one of the few available surfaces—then clearing and setting up a spot by one of the windows away from his primary workstations, with pillows, and a chaise-longue, and, thinking better of where he'd set the refreshment tray, he cleared a small table, and set it by what she surmised was to be her *posing area.* Apparently satisfied, he nodded to himself, smiled at her—*make yourself comfortable*—then went back to the opposite side of the room, and began getting his materials ready.

So invested was he that he didn't notice her undress, carefully setting her clothes on a chair whilst he went to and fro, carrying clay, water, a table, a stool, tools, and other assorted things she would discover the use of eventually.

Now naked, hair unbound, sitting on the chaise-longue, and sampling the delectable butter biscuits, and admittedly delicious coffee, she watched him, a smile playing on her lips. It felt…

Queerly natural, sitting there, nude. Not only because this was an artistic exercise—because undoubtedly there was more to this—but because…she felt comfortable as she never had with anyone, in Luca's mere presence. Unabashedly, her barest self—and not just in the physical sense.

Not an entirely *new* revelation, but she did realise—

'*Mio Dio,*' Luca exclaimed, frozen, the tools in his hands held like the King's sceptre and globe.

'Took you long enough,' Mary laughed, and he blushed, blinking himself from his gawking appreciation which unquestionably made her… *Very warm.* 'How would you like me, Signor Guaro?' she asked, setting down the cup, gesturing about her.

He blinked again, trying very hard to keep his eyes on her face.

Endearing.

Yes, she was teasing, only it wasn't malicious or her usual *toying*. This was…gentle, intimate fun, and was…

Glorious.

'Um, I… I think… That is…'

'Luca, I didn't mean to make you uncomfortable,' she said, realising perhaps she had…*imposed*, in pursuit of her own desires. Which she would never do. 'If you'd rather I put my clothes back on… I will.'

'I'm not uncomfortable. I was surprised.'

'All right. How would you like me?' she repeated seriously.

Taking a breath, he settled.

'If you are comfortable, could you stand?' he said, gesturing towards the area before the chaise-longue. 'We can take breaks—just tell me—and if you are cold…'

'I'll tell you,' she nodded, rising, and standing where he'd indicated. 'Should I…pose?'

'No, just as you are.'

Nodding, she took a deep breath, and prepared for… what came next.

Standing there, letting him, see…all of her. For however long it took. She'd always felt he could see more of her than any other, yet she'd never felt able to accept it. *Withstand it*. Today, she felt ready.

It was…terrifying.

Standing there, forcing herself to just *be*, without planning, reserve, schooling her features, or hiding away her thoughts. She watched Luca set himself up, and begin his work, bending over a little table, still in his shirtsleeves, barefoot, hair tumbling into his eyes as he went from wetting a mound of clay, to her, back and forth.

It helped to watch him, to feel him *there*, entirely present—involved in his work, but not…*removed*. Closer than they'd ever been. Just…breathing together. It helped, not to clear her mind—*full, as always*—but to steady it away from thinking about her posture, or how silly she looked, or how this was inappropriate and scandalous. Instead, it focused on what was important—which right now, was her grand, yet glaringly simple realisation from earlier.

Which was, that she trusted Luca.

Mary trusted *no one*. Not completely, ineffably, and naturally. The part of her that *could* trust was damaged long ago, then beaten down, until she'd thought it quashed out of existence entirely. Yes, there were people she trusted *to a degree*, but she couldn't even say she trusted her mother completely. Once, yes. Her mother had been the last vestige of total trust. Then two years ago, the family secrets Spencer had unwittingly unearthed...shattered that.

Those revelations had sent Mary further down her path of bitterness, anger, fear, and...aloneness. Further cemented the beliefs she'd held most of her life—that no one could be trusted, that people were hypocrites, that one could only ever rely on oneself—as if the door to a pathway of hope, and trust, had been closed off inside of her; sealed up, never to be opened again.

And Luca... He'd found that walled-up door, and brick by brick, set to reopening it. Yes, she was terrified of what happened when the door reopened, and she was able to tread down that hidden path again. Afraid of what she would find, or how she might stumble, and be hurt, yet... she was also curious. Curious what version of herself she might find there, and if, perhaps, that version would be altogether better fitting than the monstrosity she'd become and now seemed to fit so ill.

But to what end?

Changing herself, becoming vulnerable... What purpose would it serve, beyond weakening her? Making her ill-suited for the world she lived in. Her power would disappear as surely as if some ancient god robbed her of it, and...she would have nothing. She would be changed, transformed, certes, but *why*? Luca may be unintentionally opening the door to that path, but deciding to walk it because of him, it would be…counterproductive.

Firstly, because nothing had changed about who they were, and what they could have. Not that she was saying she *wanted* something…other. And secondly—most importantly—changing *for* another person, it wasn't right. One had to change for oneself, to be…truer to oneself. Still, the unknown possibilities down that path whispered to her, like some siren song.

Shaking her head, she shook those thoughts away, to be…examined later.

Right now, she just wanted to…bask in this moment. To enjoy this newfound trust, which had seemingly opened her chest so that Luca could see her thumping heart. The sun streamed through the window, warming her almost as thoroughly as the slow, gentle caress of Luca's gaze—which she felt as surely as she might've his touch. Standing there, basking in the light, and lightness, it felt…like she was becoming one with the sunlight. She felt freer than ever before, so open, as though her body couldn't contain her. Not like her skin was too tight, as before, but like she might explode into a thousand shards of sunlight.

Luca would put me back together. Gather me up; reshape me.

Smiling, she let her own gaze rake over him, not looking at the form rising between his fingers. She didn't want to until it was finished, lest she analyse it. No… She wanted to see herself through Luca's eyes. In the meantime, she could…*enjoy the view*. Which certainly wasn't a hardship. And not merely because he was pretty.

Fine, *beautiful*. No denying that now.

But it wasn't merely his beauty that was mesmerising. It was…his soul. For he didn't hide it; it shone through, and for so long, Mary had tried to convince herself it was…a trick of the light, or merely a trick. That no one could be *that* true, open, and earnest, except Luca *was*. From the very first, when she'd met him at that ball, she'd sensed his...gentleness. Kindness. Warmth. And she'd dismissed it, chalked it up to his facade as a charmer, a *fancy man*, but now she knew it was *him*. He was a kind, gentle, warm, and passionate soul, who saw the world for all its wonder, and had hope. *That* made him mesmerising.

And when he was thus—fully invested in his work, damp clay slipping and sliding through delicate fingers with grace and ease, as he moulded, and defined it, every so often glancing at her with those unguarded dark eyes... It was watching a master at work.

Breathtaking.

Admittedly, also very...suggestive. Erotic.

Mary felt her body responding, flushing, slickening, tightening; her mind wondering what those fingers might feel like against her skin if given free rein. She wondered what that drip of sweat beading at the base of his neck might taste like, and she'd be lying if she said she hadn't thought about what those silky, impertinent strands of hair would feel like against her skin. She let the sensuous sensations take hold, and noted that though she was more...*excited* than ever before—not like this, alive, afire, awash in a slow, decadent desire that awakened the forgotten corners of herself—her heartbeat, her breathing, remained steadfast, and steady.

Luca's, however, she noted, quickened as every minute ticked by. He licked his lips more frequently, flicking hair from his eyes more often.

I'm not the only one affected...

It wasn't...what she'd *expected* of this—nudity meant nothing; Luca was professional, and she trusted him—but if this was the turn it was to take... After all, she'd come here to seize…*something*, so if this was how the day *evolved*, well, so be it.

Anticipation grew, for them both, as they remained thus—he sculpting, she standing there, open to him—for how long, she couldn't say. Nor care. It was too…sumptuous.

Eventually, he did finish. Washed his hands, stood up, and examined the figure she refused to peek at from every angle, until finally he nodded, then met her gaze, apprehension flashing in his.

Briefly, she considered slipping on her chemise, but instead, gathering her courage, she walked over to him.

'If you hate it, you can smite it,' he shrugged, raking his fingers through his hair.

Nodding, she turned, and glanced down at the figure, which was about ten inches high. It looked like an ancient idol, and was a gorgeous study in stationary movement—so alive…captivating, and…

Heartbreaking.

Sliding onto the stool Luca had vacated, Mary felt tears gather but did nothing to stop them, too stunned by the work. She recognised her own form, knew the dips and valleys were hers, but the face…

There was no face.

A tiny hand was lifted, drawing on an eye, but the rest was blank. Below the figure's feet, shattered shards of a mask. It was…

True.

And it hurt. It burned, and tore at her, because although she'd known she was a painted doll with a mask held up to the world—she'd never been *confronted* by that truth. She'd never hated it as she did now. She'd wanted…

For Luca to see something more. The truth beneath.

But then, perhaps he had.

For the figure wasn't still, doomed to being faceless, a

void beneath the disguise; it was…shaping itself. Making itself anew. Casting away the veil of falsity, and slowly revealing itself—starting with the eyes.

Mary wanted that.

Not for anyone but herself. She wanted to be that figure. Fully, when it had finished revealing itself.

Hot tears fell on her cheeks, and she swiped them away.

Luca came to, kneeling beside her, frantically searching her face, uncertain of what to do.

'I'm sorry, Mary,' he said hurriedly, pain in his own voice that only made the tears fall freer. 'I didn't mean to upset you, I—'

'Stop, Luca,' she breathed, shaking her head, and sucking in a breath. He stilled, and she smiled a wobbly smile, swiping at her eyes with the back of her hand. 'It didn't upset me.' He frowned, unconvinced. *Fair, considering the tears.* 'I was moved. There's truth in this piece… Hope in it I hadn't expected, nor wished to be confronted with.'

Luca softened, understanding; though he couldn't understand the intricacy of it, he understood enough.

'Perhaps not,' he whispered. 'Yet it is there, in you. I saw it. The hope. And so much more. Thank you, for showing yourself to me, Mary. It was a privilege.'

She didn't like the use of *was*.

As if he knew he was doomed—the experience never to be repeated again. Which…was likely, except that Mary resolved she would always show herself to him. For as long as they might have—even if only today. She would have him know all of it.

All of me.

But first things first.

I need...him.

Chapter Sixteen

Luca watched as Mary came to some decision, then leaned forward and captured his lips. He'd have been lying if he said he hadn't been…*affected* by that session, but he didn't want to presume anything would happen. Particularly since Mary was raw—he felt it, saw it—and he would never take advantage, however, since she was making her desire clear, well. He wouldn't refuse what was given.

The kiss was…perfection. It thrilled him in a way none of her other kisses had—not that there had been many. In the library, he'd been excited, eager, yet also felt her…reluctance. Her need for *impersonal*, and whatever the opposite of *intimate* was, and because that was what she'd needed, he'd shuttered the part of himself that wanted *personal* and *intimate* away. At Fenton Hill, her kiss had been sweet, as this one was, but today…

Today, she kissed him like she *cared* for him. With the tenderness, and intention, he'd longed to show her, but been unable to. Her kiss was as unguarded as she'd been, standing there with all she was. And he didn't mean *naked*—though he'd had a shock when he'd witnessed her in all her spellbinding, mouth-watering glory. He hadn't expected that; even if he had, nothing would've prepared him for the sight of her, unbound and unashamed. Luminous, and magnetic. As timeless, and blinding as the sun.

But no, it wasn't merely her body she'd entrusted him with. It was herself. He'd *seen* it, and nearly cried. Watching the emotions, doubts, hope, joy, and pleasure flit across her unguarded eyes. It was perhaps the most beautiful thing he'd ever witnessed. He'd wanted to tell her…so much. *Thank you*, he'd managed. That it was a privilege, that too. But there was so much more.

It was an honour.

I won't betray your trust—I would rather die.

I'm so proud of you, your bravery, in shedding what you did so that I might glimpse your soul.

Don't be afraid.

Seize whatever it is you wish for—I can see you wish for so much more.

Only he hadn't got that far, and he didn't want to sound… patronising? Idiotic?

But I can tell her now.

Yes, he could. He could tell her with every touch, every kiss, every sigh, every look. He could show her everything he felt; adore, cherish, and…

Love her.

Yes, he loved her. Had, for some time, though he still didn't fully *know* her—if such a feat was even possible—but he did know her well enough to know he loved her. Someone might argue it was merely the first flitting of young love, but Luca knew, in his heart, his soul, his bones, that this love inside of him, which had bloomed from the first into a thing of…immeasurable power, grace, and light, was something more. A love which completed, reshaped, and remained infused in your being until your dying day. Perhaps longer.

It was a love that breathed life into him, made him ready to conquer the world, yet soothed, and calmed, as if reassuring him that he'd found…his place in the universe. He didn't…expect Mary to love him back. This gift, of loving her, was enough. And he would show her all he felt; give her…some of the light in him now. Share his gift.

Mary's hands slid up his chest, over his shoulders, leaving warmth in their wake, until her hands tangled in the hair at the base of his neck, and she moaned contentedly. Shuffling closer, he slid one arm beneath her knees, and the other around her waist, rising to his feet with only a little difficulty—from being careful not to injure the precious woman in his arms. Mary squeaked in surprise as they rose, breaking the kiss but not full contact between their mouths, her eyes flying open as her body came to nestle against him, the feel of her distracting him.

Then, realising his intention, she relaxed, tightening her own hold around his neck, and smiling as she resumed kissing him…thoroughly. It wasn't a trial, keeping his eyes open whilst they delved deep into each other's mouths, tongues curling and searching, lips caressing, and mapping. Not when watching her…strange as it was—not merely falling into sensation, but watching as it was provoked—was even more fulfilling. Erotic. Raw.

He watched the fluttering of her lashes, the quirks of her brows as she drank from him, and he from her, her scent—*salt, sweat, nutmeg, orange blossoms in the sun*—rising between them, and making him…more light-headed than he already was. Without stumbling or mishaps, he brought her over to the chaise-longue, laying her down as he dropped to his knees, and only then did he slow, and break the kiss. He gazed down at her, flushed, thoroughly kissed, eyes bright and afire with desire, and gently smoothed her silken gold strands away from her face.

There was no reticence, no doubt, still…

'You must tell me… If I should stop. If anything…isn't to your liking.'

'As must you, Luca,' she breathed, a relaxed smile on her lips, fingertips dancing down his torso.

'I will fetch a… French letter.'

Mary grabbed his shirt, preventing him from rising.

'I've always used one,' she told him. 'I am…healthy, and…my time has just passed. If you…wished to do without.'

'I've always employed one,' he assured her. 'And am also healthy. If you're sure…'

Mary nodded, and he took a breath, steadying his heart so he could focus on his task.

He breathed her in too, studying every line and detail he felt he already knew so well, and yet…new ones appeared with every passing second. Leaning down, he caressed her face, from temple to jaw, peppering every inch with kisses. Her brows, her nose, her eyelids, her lips… Pouring every ounce of love he had into…her.

One of her hands snaked around his waist, holding him close, whilst the other found his hand where he braced himself on the chaise, and he shifted so she could take it. She did, tangling their fingers, and bringing them to lie against her heart.

Slowly, intricately, Luca finished his journey around her face, then continued lower, to neck, shoulders, collarbone… Mary shifted to grant him better access, her breathy inhales and the flush appearing on her pale skin, reassuring him that…she was enjoying his ministrations. As he descended further, Mary moved their joined hands so they rested near her head, leaving him to explore what had lain beneath them.

Explore he did.

Studying her to sculpt her, he hadn't…focused on the intricate details. The constellations of freckles across her chest. The bumps and tiny hairs around her…delectable, and glorious nipples, where he and his tongue lost themselves for a very long time, laving, sucking, and…loving. Listening to every breath, every pant, feeling every rise of her against him, pillowy flesh encircling him. It was…like coming home. As he imagined sailors or explorers felt, after long journeys traversing oceans and lands.

Mary's hand slid from waist to shoulder, pulling at his shirt restlessly, and he disengaged enough to strip it, catching her gaze as he did. The blue oceans of fire burned with appreciation and hunger, and before he resumed his exploration, he leaned up, kissing her deeply and passionately, but swiftly.

Despite her squeak of protest when he pulled away to return to where he'd left off—*the rise of flesh just beneath her breasts*—he did return, holding fast to his directive of loving every inch. From her soft belly via the tips of her fingers which, when they could, trailed against his own skin, sparking life as they did, to the tips of her toes—adorable things, the second longer than the largest. From the dent beneath her solar plexus, to the underside of her knees.

All the while, Mary…took. Let it seep into herself as much as he did her touch—though whether she felt the love, was a mystery. Laughing sometimes, if he found a ticklish spot—*the dip of her hips*—or guiding him away from others—*inside thigh, just above the knee.*

Then, and only then, when he'd mapped her best he could, he pulled her down on the chaise gently, guided her legs open, the tips of his fingers nearly coalescing into the impossible softness of her thighs, then, after one last look in her eyes—*yes*—he leaned against the bottom of the chaise, and began his exploration of her innermost self. With all the tools he possessed—eyes, hands, mouth, tongue. She was…

Delectable. Sweet. Tangy. Satiating. Thirst-inducing. Everything.

He licked, caressed, mapped, traversed, lapped, laved, teased, and watched ripen and open. Until Mary was sucking in gasps of air, writhing in his hands, singing the oldest melody of humans. He loved her thus until she clenched beneath and around him, curling and seizing, a picture of ecstasy no artist could reproduce. He watched her rise and fall, stayed with her until she had, then when her eyes fluttered open, searching for him, he rose, divested himself of what clothes were left, and slid against her, into her beckoning arms.

Her hands caressed his face then, eyes mapping his features, awe and satisfaction lighting the silver specks like beacons. Her leg rubbed against his own, before curling around it, as if to prevent him from falling backwards. But the only thing he was in danger of falling into was *her.*

Perhaps she sensed that, for she closed her eyes, kissing him then, their scents, their tastes mingling into what he found was ambrosia. Together, they adjusted their bodies so he could cradle, then slide into her, and when he did…

Dio Mio.

Her teeth scraped against his tongue, and they moaned in unison.

This was…beyond pleasure. He knew she felt the connection—the one she'd refused in the library—and he understood why someone would want to shy away from it. It was…so much. Too much. Blinding, and heart-stopping.

Lazily, but intent on loving her, he rocked in and out of her, her own hips and core helping him find the pace. All she was, held tightly against him, holding him, burrowing into him. Melting, melding, meshing; their slick bodies joining. He understood that word in a way he never had—having never *loved* someone, not like this.

He took his time—*they* took their time—time slowing, the world pausing. His grip tightened as his release neared, their breathing shallow pants when they broke from the kisses they'd tumbled into. Spine tingling, he watched

Mary's face, white teeth peeking out to bite her lip. Closer he held her, cradled, wishing…

Her eyes opened as his thrusts—no matter his will—quickened inside her, and that connection between them, it was alive then. A thread, an energy, as visible as the infinite twilight blue pools of her eyes.

Ti amo. I love you, he told her silently. In the splinter of a second before he came inside her, before the specks of silver in her eyes expanded into bursts of colour and light, he thought he saw an acknowledgement, a relinquishment in her gaze. She took all he had, clasping him tight, holding him to her, grounding him, their gazes never breaking, until she too, joined him in soul-shattering pleasure.

Floating down from that unique, fulfilling pleasure, a feather on the wind, Luca knew…life would never be the same. He would never be the same. And for a brief moment, he let himself dream… That he could keep her. And she him.

Ti amo. I love you.

Chapter Seventeen

Dust motes danced in the rapidly lessening sunlight which heralded the approaching disappearance of the afternoon. Mary wished she could live here, in this attic, with its walls of solid wood, dancing dust, and warm sun. Luca curled behind her, holding her tight.

That had been…*extraordinary.*

And the otherworldliness hadn't frightened her. Perhaps she hadn't had anything left—no strength or energy to *be* scared. No, it was *him.* Coaxing her, inviting her to connect in a way she'd never been tempted to. In a way she'd never trusted herself to with anyone. Connecting her to *herself* in a way she never had. When they'd been together, it had felt…

As if he was trying to tell her so much. He, his body, the way he moved with her, within her…*that* was the siren's song. Dragging her down into unknown, glorious depths, where she could be free, and live.

It felt like—

'Why did you never marry?' Luca asked softly, toying with her hair with one hand, his other caressing the bottom of her ribs.

Instinctually, she stiffened, her heartbeat quickening. Prepared to leap, *run*, dismiss him, but then she focused on his thumb against her skin, and the rise and fall of his chest against her, and she fought the impulses, reaching for the calm he poured into her.

She should've known there would be *talking*; it was what lovers did, wasn't it? Not that she knew from experience. Still, she should've known Luca would wish to…*talk*, and hadn't she resolved to have him know her?

Why not begin with one of my greatest secrets?

He couldn't know what the answer to his question involved, and it was *so much*, so quickly…

'You don't have to answer,' he said, sensing her reluctance. 'I thought… Well, that night, on the road to Sussex, you mentioned asking Walton to marry you once. Though marriage would've been expected of you, I thought you'd merely exercised a desire for freedom, then reconsidered, and asked him. That there was some simple explanation—that you'd perhaps never found anyone you liked enough—but now… This is neither a simple, nor pleasant explanation, is it?'

She nodded, no longer surprised at his ability to see…

Everything.

'No, Luca. It isn't. I've never told another soul in my life what I would tell you now. But if you still wish to know… I will tell you. I want to,' she breathed.

Well, she didn't *want* to, but she did…

Want to.

'I would hear whatever you wished to share, Mary,' he whispered in her ear, kissing it lightly. 'I'm grateful you would trust me with something you've never told another.'

Turning in his arms, awkwardly at first then more smoothly when he helped, readjusting their position so she could look him in the eye, Mary grasped her courage, to say what she needed to before beginning her tale.

It was vital he knew this.

'I trust you more than I've ever trusted another,' she admitted, and something uncoiled within. 'I can't explain it, nor do I wish to.'

'I will never take that gift lightly. I never have, and never will, lie to you.'

'I know,' she smiled, inhaling deeply of *him* to give her strength.

How, and where, to begin?

I need to move.

Mary untangled herself. Reluctant as she was to leave his warmth…she needed to move. Rising as Luca sat up, she fetched her chemise, slipping it on whilst Luca grabbed a pillow from the floor, placing it on his lap; his small gesture of modesty for this serious conversation, sweet, in a way only he could be.

Genuinely.

Striding to the window, Mary gazed out at the city, letting its business, its seemingly infinite scope half distract, half centre her, as she slid her fingertips along the rough edges of the sill.

'You were right; I was always expected to marry. My whole life, I was told the sooner I was settled, with a husband and heirs, the better,' she said, knowing he knew as much, but it was a solid, safe place to begin. 'With my looks, my name, my dowry, if I applied myself, it wouldn't be difficult to secure a good match as early as my first Season. My father had been dead some time, and my brother… Didn't need to be concerned about me. He had better things to concern himself with. So… I launched myself with determined enthusiasm into the Marriage Mart,' she laughed bitterly, recalling her youthful naivete, and…*hope*. 'And I met George. George Claeyton. At a garden party, as it happens. He was handsome, witty, thoughtful, and though not heir to some great dukedom, a good prospect.'

Against her will, memories of the wretch as he'd been… *before*, assailed her, but she held fast to Luca—his presence, his breathing, all that he was—determined not to let the other man take anything else from her.

Including her own story.

'Altogether, a good match, and everyone was sure to tell me so, including my mother, and in a rare show of opinion, Spencer. They also said he was a good man, and I believed that, but then, perhaps I was merely…enthused. I'd never… That is a lie,' she chuckled softly. 'I'd received attention from men—*boys*—before. Looks, comments of appreciation. I'd flirted—even been instructed on the whole business.'

'But George was different,' Luca offered gently.

'Yes. He seemed kind, and warm, and after a lifetime in a cold house, I welcomed that warmth.'

Having experienced Luca's true warmth, she wondered how she'd been so fool so as not to see the lie of George's, but then, growing up in Clairborne House had made her desperate to feel anything *but* cold.

And…

'He made me laugh, took care of me, and it felt…*real*. I trusted him. That was the last time I trusted anyone.'

Well, she'd still trusted her mother then, but in time, that trust too had been shattered.

A story for another day. Or perhaps never.

She was so lost in thought she didn't hear Luca throw on his shirt, or come stand beside her.

Not until he laced his own fingers through hers on the rough-edged sill did she notice him, jumping at the contact.

'I didn't mean to startle you, I'm sorry,' he said, moving to take his hand away, but she held on tightly, unable to look him in the eye.

Though she did glance down at their hands, preparing for what came next.

He won't judge. He won't reject. He'll be here.

'It was a house party,' she told him, cold certainty invading her veins.

Strangely, this part of the story, it…

The memories, though vivid and clear didn't touch her. They felt…*other.*

Detached from her own experience.

'It was to be a chance for many of us to get away. All very proper. Encouraged, to cement links, and relationships. Mother came, and so many others too. There were games, and dancing, and then George and I went for a turn about the garden. I'd never been kissed before, and I thought…*this is it*. It was all very romantic—shadowy mazes of hedges and trees, lanterns in the branches, roses and jasmine in the air. He gave me punch. It tasted…bitter, but I didn't think much of it, as we walked through the gardens, and I felt… safe. Little idiot that I was.'

'Don't,' Luca ordered, his hold firmer now. 'None of whatever occurred is your fault, an error in *your* judgement.'

Mary appreciated his words, and tried to believe…

Only, it wasn't so easy. Not after years of convincing herself of the opposite—of hearing others say such when speaking of people falling prey to predators.

Even my own friends' mothers when they learned...

'By the time we returned to the house,' she said, determined to be done. 'I couldn't see straight. I was dizzy… yet, pleasantly warm, and sleepy… I didn't even notice we came in…surreptitiously. I didn't notice we weren't going back to everyone else.'

Her voice rose slightly as she fought panic, not remembered, but from watching her younger self walk the path she had.

If she could just scream loudly enough, the young woman might wake up, and turn back.

But it is not so simple...

'I followed George blindly. Through the house, up the stairs, to a room far away from the party. I remember…the smell of hot wax. Too many candles. And…the sour smell of sick. After that, it's mostly a blur. Of faces, laughter, sweat, brandy, and moans, and crying. I remember…my clothes being taken off. Not torn, but taken off, lovingly, almost. I remember far too many hands on parts of myself I'd barely ever touched. And I sadly remember my first kiss, though it feels wrong to call it that.'

Shaking her head, Mary sucked in a deep breath, and pushed the memories away.

It felt…easier, now that she'd brought them to life. No longer like fighting some mighty hydra, trying to stuff it back into a chest too small to contain it, but as though the hydra was now merely a drawing. Or many drawings. Which she could steadily put back in a box, and tuck away.

And here I thought the beast would devour me should I speak of it…

'They called themselves The Second Sons. They'd perfected their…technique since their first time, perhaps a decade prior. Only, that night they miscalculated. First, they didn't count on my mother. On her noticing my prolonged absence, knowing something was amiss—rather than believing I was *solidifying ties*—and finding us. Them. Secondly, one of them had…been too ambitious. One of the other girls—there were five of us that night—was a duke's only daughter. It gave Mama the leverage needed to end their reign of terror. If not for that… I doubt she would've been able to accomplish all she did.'

'What did she do?'

'She gathered all the parents, The Second Sons' and the girls'. A deal was struck. No word would be spoken of what had happened. We…girls, would retire from Society under the guise of illness until we recovered from…*the ordeal*, and until it was certain there wouldn't be…*consequences*.'

'Were there?'

'Yes.'

She recalled the day the letter had come—she and Mama had been in the Sussex house nearly a month by then. Mary had gone down to breakfast and seen a darker shade of sadness in her mother's gaze, and then she'd seen the letter beside the plate of untouched food…

Her mother had passed it to her, and she'd read the disgusting lies that said absolutely nothing of how Catherine truly fared. Merely that *the physician confirmed that Lady Catherine had contracted a contagious infection and would therefore remain in the country, recuperating for some months.*

The truth—obfuscated as always, lest someone read it and tell the world.

Lady Catherine was viciously assaulted and will bear a child by the man who raped her.

Lady Catherine is...angry, sad, tired...

Whatever Catherine had been. Mary never knew. Oh, Mary had written—they'd been good enough friends *before*—but she'd been instructed to keep it…*simple.* As Catherine undoubtedly had. No clues could ever reveal the shame which wasn't theirs to the world. Something else which made Mary…*hate* the world.

Luca's thumb slid against the knuckle of her little finger, bringing her back to the room.

'Two of us weren't…*spoiled,*' she told him, employing words not hers for lack of better ones, trying to rid herself of the bitterness—more infectious than anger towards the actual perpetrators just now. 'Myself, and another. Mama arrived just…before, though… I have regretted that often. It feels as if… I didn't deserve to be *one of the lucky ones*',' she admitted, voicing one of the most twisted, incomprehensible remnants from that experience. 'I feel guilty for not suffering as much as the others. But in answer to your question, yes, one of us became with child. She was forced to give it away, naturally.'

And then the Duke's daughter married a duke as she was always meant to.

'And The Second Sons?' Luca asked, tension now in his voice.

Oddly, it soothed her—to think that, perhaps, he was…

Ready to plan their demise if they weren't dealt with properly.

Only they had been. Her mother, the great sorceress, had seen to it. It was what she'd wielded the full force of her power for—hers, and that of the other parents, gathering it all to…*smite*. It was all this—how her mother had… *changed the status quo*—that had made Mary crave to wield the same power.

And so I do.

'They were sent far away, with nothing in their pockets.'

Mary finally looked over at Luca.

He was…harder now, warm, and gentle, yet there was a sharpness to his edges that reminded her of…some animal that could be the sweetest, gentlest being—until something it cared for was in peril. And when those dark eyes met hers…she saw no pity. No change in how he looked at her beyond…

More of that light I cannot name.

'If any aid was given them, or they hurt anyone else, my mother and the others—including the Duke—would know, and their lives…would be forfeit. One was sent to America, one to Canada. One to Africa, one to the Navy to serve in South America, and George was sent to India.'

'The terms were respected?'

'As far as I know. One of the women…received a letter begging forgiveness perhaps five years after it all happened. The man who went to America found God. Presumably saw the error of his ways, though who truly knows beyond

God himself. Never heard much of the others. George died two years after his exile. I was…glad, yet regretful that…'

Searching for the right words, Mary glanced down at their hands, still wound together.

Wondering how much of her…*ugliness*, of her darkness, she could show Luca before he baulked.

All of it…though there is only one way to know.

'You'd not received a letter?' he offered. 'A request for penance?'

'That I hadn't done it myself.'

'You don't mean that.'

'Don't you dare, Luca,' she warned, her heart beating a tattoo suddenly, at the idea that really, he didn't understand…

'You're right,' he said, stepping a little closer. 'I'm sorry. I cannot understand what you went through, or what it might've…brought forth. I merely meant… I don't believe you would've wanted him dead. To suffer, a long, desperate life perhaps, but to kill him…end his torment quickly… No, I don't see that in you.'

'Perhaps you're right,' she smiled wanly, thinking that he did, after all, understand her. *And still he doesn't baulk.* 'Though we'll never know.'

'You did know your brother would kill him, didn't you?' he asked suddenly, his eyes narrowing. 'You never told anyone, and I suspect it wasn't only distance which made you keep it from him.'

'You're right,' she murmured, impressed. 'Mama and I knew… *I* knew, that even despite the distance between us… Spencer would've killed George without hesitation. Be it for honour, duty…love. It would've ruined him; his… *goodness*. Ruined his life, and Mama's and mine.'

They looked out of the window, falling silent, and Mary's mind was…

Blissfully quiet—if only for a moment.

'Frances…she was one of the women?'

'Yes.' It wasn't her secret to share in some respects, yet Luca knew already, and she wouldn't lie. She would tell Frances that Luca knew, and beg forgiveness, but she wouldn't lie to Luca. 'The day we went to her… It had been fourteen years to the day.'

She felt Luca nod, and paused before…

Saying things I've only ever thought, yet here, I feel I could eviscerate my soul, and still Luca would look on it with...

Wonder and reassurance.

'I always…looked down on Frances,' she confessed, her voice barely audible. 'She's accused me of it, often, and it's true. I thought her weaker, for not…*moving on*. Living normally, putting it all behind her. Yet I envy her. For not forgetting, and pretending it was nothing at all because so many have experienced such horror. I envy her for raging, without end. For voicing what we've always kept silent.' Luca raised her hand, and kissed it gently. 'She hates me, for not having suffered as she did.'

'I'm sure that isn't true,' Luca frowned.

'It is, and I don't…begrudge her. Had our roles been reversed, I would hate her with everything I am.'

'You didn't suffer any less, Mary,' he said, as if his words were so obviously true, it was baffling she couldn't see. But she couldn't—she shook her head—of course she had suffered less. 'Mary. You suffered *differently*, but there isn't some…gauge measuring suffering.'

He must've seen her rejection of that, for he took a breath, glancing out of the window before turning back to her, a seriousness, and authoritativeness in his gaze she had no choice but to heed.

Reaching around to grasp her other hand, he forced her to face him fully, and Mary waited with bated breath, knowing whatever he said next might just…

Be another thing to change my life. As so many things with Luca do.

'Were I to cut us both now, take the same knife, make the same mark on each of our fingers, still, we would feel the cut differently. One of us might cry, or shout. One might feel a sting, another a prick. One might bear a scar for years, whilst the other will have no mark. The same cut does not produce the same wound. I'm not saying what Frances might feel is wrong, but *you* shouldn't diminish your pain because you believe it less than another's. That is not how pain works. And I think, in her heart, Frances knows that. As do any others who might harbour such feelings. You have a right to feel the wounds inflicted upon you, Mary.'

I was right; something to change my life.

Unable to truly understand the repercussions of his words, let alone express them, Mary simply released Luca's hands, stepping into him, sliding her hands around his waist and laying her head on his chest, letting herself just feel *him*.

And so they remained a long while, merely holding each other tightly.

Though *merely* was far from the truth of it.

Chapter Eighteen

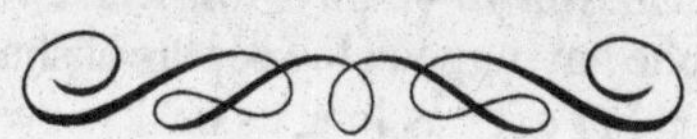

It was very queer, feeling at once angry, sorrowful, to hurt for another, and also…*honoured*. Glad. Luca had never felt anything like it, and at first, the…*positive* feelings brought forth guilt. Who, when told such a tale as Mary's, felt… *glad*, in *any* measure? Who, faced with such a disgusting, heart-wrenching tale, felt anything remotely *positive*?

Quickly he realised that he felt *honoured*, glad, because of what Mary gave him. Truth. Trust. A window to her soul, her life; *her*. Yes, he hurt for her. In a way…he'd never experienced. But then, that was love. He felt her pain, in his own heart. Felt it surer still, for the deepness of the wound, which even she had trouble seeing. The way she spoke of it…*removed*, and nearly emotionless… It spoke of wounds on the soul. The kind which hurt so profoundly they *didn't* hurt any more.

Yes, he was angry. Angry at all those who'd hurt her, and others. Sad for her, for all she'd not only endured *that* night, but every night, every day since. He was sad for the woman she'd forced herself to become; that she'd been forced to become by circumstance.

Yes, some animal part of him had visions of tearing those who'd hurt her—those men, and anyone else who had done such, anyone who had ever looked away from such things—limb from limb. Even as he knew the best, and only thing, he could do, was be *here*. Listen. Love. Hold.

So he did, holding her silently. She needed time to grapple with it all—emotions he was certain she'd never quite faced before, living in silence, with a hurtful perspective of her own experience. If he was honest, he needed time too.

When he'd asked her about marriage… Well, he'd never expected the answer to be anything close to what she'd shared—despite having seen the depths of shadows, anger, and sadness in her eyes as long as he'd known her. When he'd asked, he'd…been trying to find a reason. A reason from *her*, which would…stop him dreaming. Getting carried away with his love.

Years of believing he couldn't share anything but a few words, a jest, had made everything else which happened with her…a dream. First, her—albeit reluctant—friendship. Her softening. Her kiss. That interlude in the library. Every step, he told himself *more* was impossible, and he accepted that; yet, in time, they took another step, and he…hoped some more. Loving her, having her in his arms, to touch, to kiss, to watch—even if for a moment—had turned that hope into a raging inferno, which he knew, left unchecked, would consume him. Make him…*believe*. That perhaps he *could* keep her. That they could have more than stolen moments, an *affair*. Perhaps, they could have *a life*. Even as he knew it was impossible.

So yes, he'd asked her about not marrying…selfishly. Not only to know her, but to *remind* himself that a life, more together, wasn't for them. If reminding himself of the worldly reasons why—Society, his own lack of… *everything*—didn't work, then hearing a reason of her own would. He'd thought, as he'd said, she'd say something of wanting her freedom, her fortune, to be her own. That she'd never wanted a husband; that her family had been agreeable. That…*anything*. Anything but the truth. Anything but *a* truth which didn't deter him from believing they could have something…*lasting*. Magnificent. In fact, her show of trust, of *giving*, only made him hope, and dream, more.

Il mio più bel sogno. My most beautiful dream.

A dream most unlike one, when he held her thus, her soft hair beneath his fingers, her heartbeat thumping a gentle rhythm against his chest. No… It felt like a reality within his grasp.

One which I will savour for as long as it is.

The slowly sinking sun reminded him that today at least, he might not have much longer—life, and obligations beckoning—however his time hadn't run out yet. And there was still much to be said.

Not least of which...

'Thank you, Mary,' he whispered, kissing the top of her head. 'Again. For sharing… *Showing*…all you have. Letting me understand you; telling me what has had a hand in making you who you are.'

'It would be so easy, wouldn't it?' Mary sighed, slowly pulling away, and Luca frowned, as the chill swept over him, and as he tried to make sense of what he'd said wrong. Mary went over to her clothes and began slowly redressing, sitting on the chaise to slide her stockings on. 'To put it down to *one thing* making me what I am. One single ugly thing, transforming me into an ugly creature. But life, people, are not so simple,' she said, shaking her head, as if he were the dullest man alive, and he understood. 'That experience shaped me, Luca, yes, but it alone isn't responsible for what I've become.' He found a clean basin and took it, along with clean linens, and what remained of the water in the pitcher, over to the table before her. 'What I made myself.'

'I know, Mary,' he said gently, settling beside her, and she stilled, those luminous blue depths meeting his. He smiled, and nodded slightly. 'I never meant to imply it did.

As for you being an ugly creature…we will for ever disagree on that count.'

Nodding half-heartedly, she noticed the water and cloths, and quickly but efficiently made use of them.

Luca longed to offer her a shared bath, so they might… do many things, *and* clean themselves, but Mary wished to dress now—put her armour back on—and so he would ease her way in any way he could.

No matter how small.

As he watched her, not avidly, not lustfully, merely… observationally, her words swirled around his mind. She was convinced of her…*ugliness*, as she put it—this wasn't the first time she'd said something similar—and though Luca wished to convince her otherwise, he knew it wouldn't be easy, accomplished in one conversation. It wasn't something she needed to *be convinced of.* She needed to *realise it herself.* Perhaps he could have a hand in it—either way, some day, he prayed she would see the truth.

There is good and bad within us all.

'Please don't take this as it isn't meant,' he said slowly. She neither spoke nor looked back at him, busy tying her stocking ribbons. 'I think perhaps you should speak to… someone. Any of the other women from that night. Speaking to someone who can…understand better than I, might help. Perhaps, in time, give you…courage to share with your family, your friends. Secrets are poison, Mary.'

'I won't disagree with you there,' she muttered bitterly.

There are still so many secrets within you, Mary; I see that too.

Not that he would push her to reveal more—he hoped, in time, she would trust him with everything.

'May I ask what happened to the others?'

'Two married, as befitted their stations. Another…well, I'm not entirely sure how it happened—it was all kept very quiet—but from what I understand, she rebelled against her parents, and was engaged as a companion to an ageing widow, who took her to the Continent. There she met a woman, and they've been travelling together ever since.' A small smile graced Mary's lips, a whisper of happiness crossing her eyes, but it was gone in an instant as she rose to continue dressing. 'They've all made good lives for themselves. Likely what made Mama believe I could… It took her a while to understand… She gave me some time, but after a few years, started encouraging me to move on, and settle again. Spencer joined the charge, and I played along for a while, but then finally, I told her it wouldn't happen. So she turned her attention on Spencer instead.' Mary grinned wryly.

'And what of the others?' he asked casually, not ignoring the rest—what it meant, how he felt about it—but focusing instead on the point he was gently trying to make.

Mary stilled, frowning at him as if questioning, though she knew very well what he meant.

'I just told you,' she said dismissively, busying herself with her dress buttons.

'You told me of the women with you *that night*,' he agreed, rising to help, though he knew she could button her own dress. Likely why it had been made thus—buttons on the side—when a lady such as herself would typically have gowns requiring another to fasten them. She didn't fight him, merely moved her arm and looked away while he slowly did the work for her. 'You didn't, however, tell me of the others before you who suffered the Second Sons.'

There was challenge in his voice—only she didn't take it up.

I know what sort of woman you truly are, Mary. Though you refuse to see it, I know you cannot blatantly lie to me either.

'Married, mothers. Working as governesses, companions, even tradeswomen,' she sighed, capitulating. 'Some retired from public life, one unfortunately… Ended her life entirely.' Luca nodded, placing a kiss on her shoulder as he slid his fingers to her waist, gently holding her. 'It was years before I thought to seek them out. And it took years to find as many as I did, and still there are more I'm sure. Those men…didn't merely prey on Society women; alone, each of them had…a sordid history. In any case,' she continued, clearing her throat as she stepped away, running her fingers through her hair, preparing to put it back into something respectable. 'I, and the solicitor I engaged to… handle my enquiries… We had nothing to go on but rumours of whispers. Why I even sought them out… It isn't as if I wrote them, nor spoke with them of what had happened to us all. I just…wanted to check on them. See if I could ease their way, any of them. Any who hadn't had such a mother as mine. Now, don't even think to try and paint me a saint, Luca,' she warned, whirling back, a pin in her hand pointing at him menacingly. 'A saint would've reached out, and spoken the truth, and *fought*.'

'As you fought for the women abused by Viscount Mellors?' he countered, raising a brow of his own.

Mary couldn't hide her shock at his mention of the man who had terrorised Rebecca Reid, Countess of Thornhallow for years—then subsequently been transported not only thanks to the Earl of Thornhallow's efforts, but also those of the Spencer family.

Thanks, in great part, to Mary's quiet, *fervent* fight for justice—an open secret.

'That was the Reids' fight,' Mary retorted, fixing her hair. 'And my brother's. Had I not helped, Spencer would've seen us doomed to scandal by his involvement. Rebecca—Lady Thornhallow—she's the one who sought out the others whom Mellors had harmed. I merely assisted.'

'Of course. That reluctant *charity* of yours,' he nodded.

'Like that which you show at Nichols House. And to all of your friends.'

'What are you about, Luca?' she demanded, frustrated, mostly herself again—a *lady*—though somewhat...*softer*. Unguarded. *Ruffled*. 'This conversation has taken a turn, and I...need to go. As do you. You haven't even washed or dressed, and Lady Granville will be waiting.'

Grabbing her coat, she made to just *leave*, and Luca smiled to himself, stopping her by putting out his arm—not touching her nor *preventing* her leaving, merely *asking* her not to...*thus*.

'I'm sorry,' he whispered, and though still stiff and defensive, Mary softened. 'I...' *Love you and wish you could see yourself truthfully.* 'Merely sought to deepen my understanding. I suppose I got carried away, and pushed. Only, it's drugging, getting to know you, Mary Spencer.'

Beseeching eyes met his, as a quiet sigh escaped her lips, taking with it the tension within her.

Begging him silently not to...give her too much care.

That is all I would ever give you, amore mio.

'You make it very difficult to be angry with you,' she breathed, and he grinned, leaning down to capture her lips swiftly, eyes never leaving hers. 'Very difficult to leave, too.'

'Though I know you must,' he agreed, lifting his head so he wouldn't be tempted to encourage them both to eschew their responsibilities. *Dream, meet reality.* 'As must I. Tell me you won't try to end this, however. I feel we're only just beginning.'

'The rational part of myself knows I should,' she grinned, shaking her head. 'Yet somehow another part has taken hold, and so I won't. I want more time with you, Luca.'

'Then you shall have it.'

A nod, and she raised herself to kiss him—swiftly, but deeply.

Not that even the slightest touch of hers didn't reach into his heart and soul.

'I would offer to see you home; however, I know you'll refuse lest you be seen in my company.' Her eyes dropped to the floor in assent, and his heart twinged—reality quashing the dream some more. 'Send a note, and we shall find a time to meet again.'

'Good evening, Signor Guaro,' she smiled, running her fingers down his chest.

'*Buonasera*, Lady Mary.'

And with that, she was gone; though thankfully, not from his life.

Yet.

Never, his heart demanded, as he tidied the studio, collected his things, and basked in her lingering scent.

Never, he begged the little goddess he'd created.

Never, amore mio.

Chapter Nineteen

If Mary had known how…delicious, liberating, and…calming a long-lived affair could be, she might've indulged earlier. Well, her affair with Luca couldn't be considered *long-lived*—it had only been a couple weeks of…*indulgence*. A handful of mornings, afternoons, or very late evenings in his home—whatever time they could spare, though something within begged her to spend *all* her time with him.

It was *long-lived* only in that it was comparatively longer than any of her…*romantic relationships*—unless one counted George's courtship, which she categorically refused to mark as a *romantic relationship*. Her previous dalliances had always been short. Scratches of itches. The only closeness, the only carnality she would ever have; part of the vow she'd made after the night George had taken what he had. Oh, she'd pondered reneging, loneliness creeping at the doors of her heart—hence proposing to Freddie all those years ago—but then more secrets had been exposed, and she'd known she was right to make the vow she had as a girl.

Never trust anyone with your life.

Never trust anyone.

Hence, *dalliances*, and scratching itches. The rational

part of her told her to think of…this affair with Luca as nothing more, either. It scratched *another* itch. One for closer companionship. Didn't change that there would be nothing more than…a longer-lived affair in the end. Though that rational part struggled to explain certain facts.

Like why, when she said if she'd known the…*benefits* of indulging in a long-lived affair she might've done so earlier, why her heart screamed that *it wouldn't have been the same without Luca.* Just as it screamed she would never experience what she had with him again.

And? You'll have pleasant memories. Experienced... loveliness for a time.

Then, someday, it'll be gone. That is life.

'So it is,' she muttered, ending her…*staring out the study window like some dawdling schoolmiss.*

Honestly, it was becoming…a nuisance, all this thinking. *Pondering.*

Pleasantness, loveliness, *goodness* invading her life… was a surprisingly welcome change from what *had been*, except she could do without the haze of…*lust.* Yes. Lust. That's all it was. Luca was…very attentive. Very talented at…*sexual congress.*

Precisely.

Regardless, she could do without the haze. It was distracting—why only this morning she'd congratulated Lady Fellows-Johnson on the birth of her latest granddaughter when she'd welcomed a grandson. This haze…delicious though it may be, was leading to mistakes. Mistakes led to losing power.

That won't do.

'Concentrate,' she ordered herself, forcing her gaze to the letter-strewn desk she was sitting at.

Right.

That's what she was meant to be doing. Writing letters.

She'd done the easy ones, responding to invitations and

friendly notes full of drivel, filling up her calendar nearly to the brim—*must leave time for Luca*—and now she was left with those that shouldn't be difficult but were.

Letters from Yew Park House. There was *another* letter from Genevieve—why her sister-in-law insisted on writing so…*frequently* with no real news to share, was beyond her. Actually, it wasn't.

She's trying to be a friend. To help.

It annoyed her.

Flicking through the pages with a sigh, Mary tried to decide which would be the least painful to reply to.

And reply I must...

Mena's, perhaps.

> *Freddie and I are doing our best to distract your brother, and mother, however being here is aggravating their nerves... The McKennas—*

No. Not that one.

Freddie's?

> *You should be here, Mary. You've been...different these past years...*

Not that one either.

Perhaps Genevieve's?

> *I know how difficult being here for your birthday would be, Mary, still I pray you will be here to meet our child. Wounds take time—*

'Absolutely not.'

Spencer's then, novelty that it was.

> *I know I haven't written... Mama shared all the*

news from your last letter... I appreciate all you do to be present in Society, for us all. Never forget, however; Society is not the world. There is so much more... I wish you were here... That we could speak... Please—

Not that one. That one…last.
Mama's.
The only one remaining...

Do pass on my congratulations, condolences, and apologies to those who require. You will remind Lady Sailsham of her promise to forward the name of that architect—I should like to engage him to review Clairborne House's gardens... Mary, you have been mentioned in a few letters I received, and I wonder what this business is with Viscountess Porens. Are you quite well... Reports of queer behaviour...

'Damn it,' Mary exclaimed, slapping the paper onto the others.

Peace.

Liberty.

That's all she wanted, and she'd thought she'd have it with them off in bloody Scotland, but *no.*

'I shall simply focus on the unimportant sections of Mama's letter,' she decreed. 'Ignore…the rest.'

Brilliant.

Thus decided, she dipped her pen into the ink, prepared a sheet of paper, and—

'Yes?' she sighed, inviting in whoever was scratching at the door.

Brooks, aged and respectable, strode in, a note on a silver platter.

'This just came, Lady Mary,' he said, offering out the

thing. 'The gentleman was most insistent you receive it immediately,' he added as she examined the note, bearing her name in Luca's handwriting.

Brooks's voice held no judgement—not that he wasn't better trained than that.

Though Mary wondered if the servants knew, or suspected. Doubtful—she was secretive and prone to disappearing enough as it was *before* Luca—though she did need to be careful. The servants in this house were loyal, well-paid, *trusted*—only she didn't trust anyone.

She nodded thoughtfully, though just as Brooks reached the door, she stopped him.

'Signor Guaro delivered this?'

'Yes, my lady.'

'Thank you, Brooks.'

A bow, and he was gone.

Mary frowned as she opened the missive, wondering why Luca would veer from their agreement and deliver a note himself. Why he would do so when they were meant to meet that night—after the engagement ball she was to attend, and the dinner he and Lady Granville were. Though the reason became clear when she read the dashed note.

Lady Mary,

My sincerest and deepest apologies, however I will be unable to return that book you were so kind to lend me as agreed.

He would not make their next meeting—book-lending being the agreed upon subterfuge for their notes, should anyone become...*interested* in their correspondence. A twinge of annoyance at having to use subterfuge twisted Mary's heart briefly, but she pushed it away.

A last-minute request has been made for my pres-

ence, so I will be departing from London for a day or two. I will return that book duly when I return.

Until then,
I remain yours,
L. Guaro

Disappointment flooded her; ridiculous, considering they weren't...*promised* to each other or anything so trite—and without realising, she crumpled the paper in her hand. Such...unpredictable happenings were bound to upset plans. It was natural. She appreciated him sending a note. Very thoughtful.

Very thoughtful indeed.

Tossing the note into the wastebasket, she turned back to the other letters, however her mind veered into unfamiliar, and disturbing territory.

I wonder what this last-minute request was.

He would undoubtedly tell her when he returned.

I wonder from whom the request was.

He'll tell me when he returns. Though it was surely Lady Granville.

But why didn't he say?

Because we don't write such things in our notes. Obviously.

Still, he might've said it was Lady Granville.

Unless it wasn't.

Who else would he leave London for? With?

No one.

That she was aware of.

That doesn't mean there's someone else. It could be a friend...anyone.

Even if she didn't know of Luca having friends, beyond Lady Granville.

An acquaintance, then. One he would drop everything to help.

If help was what he was about.

That's Luca. A kind, and thoughtful man.

'Yes,' she breathed, shaking off her…silliness.

Her idiotic mind rambling into directions it had no business going.

They owed each other nothing. His life was not her business, and vice-versa. She ignored the hurt of that.

We don't even owe each other fidelity, her mind whispered perniciously.

True. They hadn't said outright they wouldn't…engage in certain activities with other people, only she'd felt it was understood. Implied by what they'd shared, and he'd promised to never lie to her, so he wouldn't…

Go find another woman willing to pay for his life? Perhaps Lady Granville seeks to withdraw her support. Perhaps he's had another offer.

A better offer than you.

'He wouldn't do that,' she told herself. 'He would tell me.'

In a note you warned him against saying anything of import in?

Yes.

No.

I don't know.

Mary struggled to draw breath properly, as, without her consent, doubts, and the gnawing of jealousy assailed her.

You'll know the truth when he returns.

Unless he lied to her. Unless…he'd been lying all along. Playing her the fool. Pretending to be caring, thoughtful, and…worthy of trust, when really, he was just following his…*baser instincts* about town, and she should know the truth of it. She deserved to know the truth.

I thought you trusted him, the evil little voice mocked.

I do. I did. I will.

When I...see the truth with my own eyes.

Reason completely abandoned, Mary left the study, and went to change into riding clothes. She told the staff she would be visiting a friend outside of London—let them think it was Frances. Wouldn't be the first time she'd left thus.

Then she took her horse, Hera, and herself over to Luca's house as quickly as discretion allowed. More doubts rose—*he would've already left, he's gone to Lady Granville's, this is absolute nonsense*—but she pushed them away, intent on her purpose now. She just…*had* to know. To make sure. If Luca was already gone…it would be a sign. That she would have to wait, trust, be patient, and—

Luca.

There he was, on his own mount, a small bag behind him, just at the end of the square ahead.

You shouldn't do this. How will you pursue him on empty roads should he take some?

A problem for later.

Right now, her problem was…pursuing him on busy streets without being noticed. Right now, her problem was trust—*unsurprising.* However, for the first time, as she followed Luca northeast, she didn't feel…righteous, vindicated, or safer, for her lack of trust. Instead, she felt… guilty. And…*dirty.*

Well, we'll see how I feel once I know the truth.

Something told her it would be much the same.

Chapter Twenty

The further Luca travelled from London, the tighter the invisible string in his gut pulled, urging him back; the harder he had to force himself and York onwards. It wasn't that he didn't *want* to go; *need* to go. He would never *not want* to see Mamma and Sofia—it had been too long since he'd last visited—and according to Sofia's letter… That lapse had consequences.

There were bills to be paid. Despite Sofia's tight control of the purse strings, money had run out. Partly because Mamma had…managed to order extravagances, but mainly because it had been too long since Luca visited, and brought funds. He'd meant to, but then everything had happened with Mary, and it wasn't that he'd *forgotten* his family—how could he when they were the reason he did all he did?—but he had… Got involved, and thought they were fine, and could wait a little longer. Until…

Well, until *what*, he wasn't sure.

These past weeks—these past couple especially—he'd been granted a gift he'd never thought to dream. Time with Mary. So yes, he'd been selfish, and snatched, *succumbed*, to every moment he was given, no matter how small. He needed to shore them all up, collect them for when…

She…leaves me. Dismisses me. Ends things.

Whatever it is she'll do.

Before any of that, he needed to…fulfil his love. Fill his soul with as many memories as he could, so that he wouldn't…suffer so much. Though he knew his heart would break, and that he would never love again as he loved Mary. Some might argue again that was *first youthful love*, but Luca knew differently. Spending the time he had with her these past weeks, learning her, *knowing her*, soul, mind, and body—heart, to a degree, as she still…held back—he felt his love only deepen. Strengthen, and…sharpen, as he'd predicted that day in the studio. Cementing his conviction that his love for Mary was something…extraordinary. Different to any other, for he believed each love was tailored to each person, and he didn't like to think of love in terms of *amounts*—loving one *more* than another—however, he could still say without doubt that he would never be…the man he was with Mary with another. He would never be able to give as much of his heart, soul, and being to another, for some pieces would always be *hers*.

Luca didn't believe in Fate, but he did believe in…*soul mates*. Pieces of a whole coming together, and complementing each other.

And Mary is mine. I feel it, though I still don't know the entirety of her.

But even a lifetime wouldn't be enough for that.

The point was… What was his point?

Ah yes. That he'd been distracted recently, selfish, and not taken care of what he needed to, so today he must. Wanted to. Would.

Though none of that knowledge diminished the pull tugging him back to the city as he traversed brilliant and bustling countryside. It wasn't tugging him back to Mary—he felt *that* pull in his heart, more of a…*connection*, than a pull, tethering him to her—no, this was a *tug in his gut.*

As one felt when one left a candle burning or forgot some important appointment.

It was the note he'd left her; he knew. It...*rankled* him. Though in fairness, all their notes did. More so with each new one he wrote or read. They bothered him because... They were untruthful.

Some might enjoy the subterfuge, the *sneaking*, the innocuous notes hiding *desire* and *intent*. Luca did not. Not one bit.

This morning, all he'd wanted was to knock on Mary's door. Tell her *everything*. Even...invite her to meet his family. He'd known that was...impossible, and *too much*. Impossible, for what *leaving London together again* would signal to Society, and *too much*, for inviting her to meet his family would...imply... That he wanted what they couldn't have. That they were something they could never be. And by doing that, he might...scare her.

So he'd settled for an innocuous note even though he'd longed to just *tell* her he had to visit family, and that he'd miss her, and...

Many things I couldn't lest someone discover...us.

It wasn't the notes rankling him. It was all of it. The untruthfulness of their situation—which he understood the necessity of but which directly conflicted with his love. He *knew* he couldn't be selfish, and demand what Mary wasn't willing to give; demand Society give a blessing they never could. Still, his love wanted to be shouted from rooftops, and live in the light. Not the shadows. It demanded to be *expressed*, not stifled, and...

Can't change a damned thing.

Così è la vita. That is life.

Determined not to dwell on the unpleasantness, to instead do as he'd told himself...his entire life, actually—*enjoy the good*—he pushed on, forcing himself to enjoy the birdsong, sunshine, and pastoral vistas. In no time, he arrived at the cottage just outside the tiny village of Downsham.

Nestled beside a lane, among fields and farms, much like Frances's house, it was small—too small according to Mamma—but large enough for both Sofia and her to live comfortably, with two respectable gardens, for herbs, flowers, and vegetables. They had a small gig, a horse, and whatever Downsham couldn't provide the larger surrounding towns could. He'd chosen this place as it wasn't far from London, yet…far enough from temptation. From extravagant shops, any manner of society, and anyone Mamma might try to…force Sofia into becoming interested in.

In the long term, he wasn't entirely sure what he planned—it largely depended on what Sofia wished to do, which, as he would *very* soon, she would have to decide. She was only nineteen—but a girl no longer. She was a woman, and one already rushing out the door to greet him as he opened the gate, walked York through and tied him up beside the cottage—he would properly settle him later—and he smiled as he opened his arms.

In the short glimpse he got before he enveloped her into a tight embrace, he found she looked well, if a bit tired—circles beneath her eyes, and wisps of hair escaping her tightly braided locks.

He held her tighter, and longer, than usual.

'*Ciao, bella*,' he murmured into her hair, before kissing her cheek. '*Come stai?* How are you?'

'*Va bene*, Luca, I'm well,' she said, smiling as she released him. 'How are you? You look…different,' she frowned, quirking her head enquiringly, and Luca blushed. Sofia grinned wider. 'Luca…'

'Later,' he promised, shaking his head. 'For now, let's inside.'

'You should go, say hello to Mamma. I will take care of

that gorgeous gentleman,' she said, nodding towards York. 'You are staying the night.'

'I thought it best,' he nodded, making to do as he was told.

'Mamma will be pleased.' Luca smiled, heading for the door. Only Sofia's voice stopped him. 'Luca,' she said, her voice strangely...*serious.* 'Do you know that woman? She seems...upset.'

Frowning, he turned, then followed Sofia's gaze to the lane—back in the direction he'd come from.

Mary. How...?

'Mary!' he called, his feet already carrying him towards her.

It couldn't be, yet it was.

Sofia was right; she looked *upset*—sad, angry—and she stood so still, just *staring* as he vaulted over the gate into the lane. His heart beat fast and he was grateful she wasn't fleeing—whatever shock *she* had keeping her unmoving—though he was also...confused and angry, yes, but happy, all at once.

He didn't understand how or why she was here, or perhaps he did know instinctively *why*, and that's what made him angry—*she doesn't trust me*—but also...*she's here.*

'Mary!'

Amore, you're here.

Why couldn't you trust me?

Chapter Twenty-One

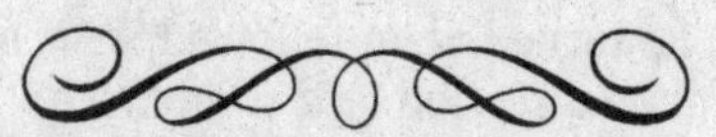

She's beautiful. That was Mary's first thought. That the *other woman* she'd known she would find—even though she'd tried hard to convince herself she was being silly and distrustful—was stunning, young, and…everything *right* for him. Tall, with a lovely form, sharp features, a blinding smile, gorgeous dark hair, and a complexion which suggested a heritage similar to Luca's…she was perfect.

It… Well, it didn't break her heart—impossible, considering though she *liked* Luca she wasn't so foolish as to be in love with him—but it did hurt.

To a nearly unbearable degree.

More than it should've—because she'd *known*—and it hurt because she'd allowed herself to trust him, and been betrayed. In a very queer sense, it hurt more than it should've because…it hurt more than it should've. Because until she'd seen them embrace, she hadn't realised just how *much* she liked Luca. How much…she'd grown attached. Even though she knew they didn't belong to each other—*never could, never would*—well, she'd…wanted him for her own.

She'd never been…*jealous* before, and she didn't like it. It made her long to do darker things than she ever had—destroy this unknown woman though she'd done nothing to deserve it beyond love the man Mary liked. She wanted to rage, scream, strike them both, or humiliate them, make them feel her pain, and she felt out of control…

And sad. So very sad.

Hera snorted and pawed behind her, either sensing her emotions or objecting to Mary's tight clutching of the reins, and Mary forced herself to loosen her white-knuckled grip, so the mare could wander a few paces and calm down.

Would that I could do either...

It was the unfamiliar jealousy, and surprise at the depth of the wound Luca inflicted on her unknowingly, which kept her feet firmly rooted on the lane long past the time she should've left. Gone before they'd noticed her—suspicions confirmed—Luca to be dealt with later. It kept her rooted there even as they noticed her, and Luca came running, and she didn't want to do this now, she didn't want him to see how much he'd hurt her, because it was her own fault, and she just had to *move*, only she couldn't, even as he skidded to a halt before her, out of breath. She only had enough strength to keep the tears threatening at bay, especially when she looked into his eyes, and saw confusion, mingling with…

Anger and excitement?

'Mary,' he breathed, his hand rising to touch her, then, realising that was *not* a good idea, lowering again as he set his jaw. *Preparing for the unpleasantness.* 'We'll speak of this properly later. For now…come meet my family.'

What?

'What?' she managed, feeling as though her head had been knocked about, her mind and heart struggling to return from the dark path they'd been on.

'That's my sister, Sofia,' Luca told her seriously, disappointment in his voice which made those feelings of *dirty*, and *ashamed*, brew hot, until her face was flaming.

Yet there was also understanding in his gaze; he knew

precisely what she'd been thinking, and it made *his* heart break, but still he didn't fault her, because he knew *her.*

That realisation made her even sadder, and tears dripped onto her cheeks.

'Oh, Mary,' he sighed, wiping the offending things away, and pulling her into his arms. She dropped Hera's reins—not that she could worry about the mare absconding while her mind and heart wrapped themselves around the truth—and Luca held her tighter. 'Mary, Mary, Mary…'

His voice soothed her, a knight in and of itself, slaying the demons inside, swiftly and surely.

He didn't betray me. I betrayed him. I didn't trust him.

He cannot be yours and yet in this moment he is, and ever has been.

'I'm so sorry, Luca,' she mumbled into his waistcoat. 'I…'

'It's all right, Mary,' he said gently, untangling them. 'We'll speak later. For now, as I said, come meet my family.'

He shot her a soothing smile, which did its work, and well.

With a nod, he offered his hand, and without thinking, Mary took it. They collected Hera, and Luca marched them to the cottage she'd thought would be the focus of nightmares for years to come, and which suddenly seemed less grim. Less terrifying and more…

Cosy. Sweet. Welcoming.

Luca's sister had disappeared, as had his horse, but Luca led her along the side of the cottage into a larger garden, surrounded by grand oaks, complete with a small lawn, patches of vegetables, a henhouse tucked away at the back hedges where they abutted surrounding fields, and a tiny barn with surrounding space for barely one horse—though Luca's was there too, munching on some hay with an older mare. His sister was there, leaning on the thick fence keeping the horses from the garden, and when she heard them, she turned, smiling at them both.

Mary smiled back. She *was* happy to meet the young woman—a large part of her heart which shouldn't be was *very* excited to meet his family—but she still felt foolish, and guilty…and so the smile ended up being sheepish. Luca squeezed her hand, and her smile relaxed.

Don't think too hard. You can untangle this mess later. Enjoy the gift this day has given you.

'Lady Mary,' Luca said, as formally as if he were introducing them in a drawing room. 'May I introduce my sister, Sofia Guaro. Sofia, Lady Mary Spencer.'

'A pleasure, my lady,' Sofia said, dropping into a curtsey.

'Please, Mary is fine. I'm very sorry to have…come unannounced,' she said diplomatically, and Sofia nodded knowingly. *These Guaros and their ability to…understand others.* 'It's a pleasure to meet you.'

'Luca, you should introduce our guest to Mamma, who I'm sure is already anxiously awaiting you,' Sofia said pointedly. 'I will take care of this lovely lady,' she added, taking Hera's reins and letting the horse sniff her hand. 'Your bag is already inside, and I'll finish making tea when I come in.'

'*Grazie.*'

Luca turned them around and led Mary towards the cottage, but rather than head for the rear door—likely leading into the kitchen—he led her around the front.

'Mamma will have a fit if I bring a lady through the tradesmen's entrance,' he explained quietly. 'Not that it is…'

'I understand, Luca,' she reassured him, squeezing his hand this time. 'And I—'

'No more apologies, Mary. You're here now.' Throwing her a smile as they reached the door, he opened it and ushered her inside. 'Welcome.'

It was all just as simple and cosy inside as out.

A tight little corridor, likely ending in the kitchen, stairs to the upper floor just past the line of coats, hats, and shoes nestling on the wall behind the door. Two doors ahead on their left, a few pictures on the simply furnished walls, a vase of fresh wallflowers on a tiny table between the doors. Worn, but good wooden floors.

Luca held out his hands and she hesitated, but those dark eyes ensnared and reassured her, so she gave him her hat and gloves, which he put away, before divesting himself of his own hat, overcoat, and gloves.

Taking her hand again—his warmth flooding her better now, quashing the nerves she felt at meeting his mother—he led her to the first door, and knocked once.

'*Si*,' a voice called.

Luca opened the door, and led Mary inside the delicate drawing room, simply, but as stylishly furnished as could be.

Two chairs, a sofa, and a variety of tables, rugs, pictures—some, Mary was certain, Luca's—flowers, and decorative figurines were packed into the rather small, square space.

A woman rose from the chair closest to the window, and Mary instantly recognised the familial link between her, Luca, and Sofia. She was as stunning as both her children, with thick, dark hair peppered with grey pulled into an intricate coiffure, the same dark eyes—though hers seemed slightly colder—and the same sharp features. Tall, slightly more endowed than Sofia—*motherhood*, Mary suspected—she was clothed in a rich forest-green silk gown more suited to a Society dinner than one's own drawing room; as was the emerald set decorating her ears and neck.

No surprise on the woman's face—but then, considering the whole…episode outside, it was likely she knew very well a *guest* was coming. In fact, the woman seemed… proud, and *pleased*.

Though it warmed Mary, she also felt…it wasn't just a mother's pleasure in meeting one of her son's *friends.*

'Lady Mary, may I present my mother, Signora Isabella Guaro. Mamma, Lady Mary Spencer.'

'A pleasure, Lady Mary,' Signora Guaro curtseyed, her voice slightly more accented than her children's. 'Welcome to our humble home, though I must apologise for our lack of…welcome.'

'Not at all, *signora*. I'm the one who has imposed on you with my surprise visit. I'm most grateful for your welcome, it's a pleasure to make your acquaintance.'

Signora Guaro gestured to the sofa before her, and Luca led Mary over, settling beside her, still not releasing her hand—not that his mother seemed to mind *that* lack of etiquette.

'How was your journey?' Signora Guaro asked. 'I didn't see a carriage. Did you ride, then?'

'I did, *signora*. Such a glorious day should not be spent locked in a carriage,' she smiled, again, diplomatically side-stepping her egregious behaviour—riding after Luca like some…secret agent. 'It was a most pleasant journey.'

Might've been, had I the heart to enjoy it.

Luca ran his thumb along her knuckles, and she relaxed, expelling tension she wasn't aware she was holding.

'And what, may I ask, brings you to Downsham?'

'I…'

'I mentioned what a lovely place it was,' Luca said before Mary had to think of any lies. 'Lady Mary is a friend, and needed an escape from the city for the day.'

'Yes, well, it's a lovely enough place, for England,' Signora Guaro acceded. 'Dreadfully small, though. Nothing to do here, but—'

'Tea,' Sofia said brightly, not *barging*, but *spiritedly* entering, a tea tray in her hands.

'Perfect timing,' Luca smiled, and Sofia threw them

both a wink, before dutifully arranging the tray, handing out cups, then plates of delicious-looking biscuits and cake, as they fell into a…not awkward, but somewhat *strained* silence.

'That one is orange cake,' Sofia told her, pointing at the mouth-watering slice Mary was about to taste.

'Everything looks absolutely scrumptious, Sofia, thank you. Did you make it all yourself?'

'I did,' Luca's sister said proudly, settling in the chair beside her mother. 'Luca has his art, I have mine.'

'Mary has an interest in baking, Sofia. Perhaps you could share some recipes.'

Sofia's eyes widened, and Signora Guaro frowned slightly.

'I would appreciate it if you would,' Mary said, soothing both their concerns and surprise. 'If you have the time, that is. I think I would require…added notes and instructions.'

'Of course,' Sofia smiled, recovering. 'After tea, perhaps you could show Lady—that is, *Mary*—around. I can prepare some for you.'

'Thank you.'

'How did you meet my son, then?' Signora Guaro asked in the ensuing, more comfortable silence, pointedly looking at their still joined hands. Mary made to disengage—she hadn't realised she'd linked with him again after being served, and then proceeded to eat and drink onehandedly—but Luca held fast. 'Your family perhaps?'

Luca sighed, making his opinion of his mother's *very* leading question—*who are your people*—known, but Mary smiled graciously, and answered.

To the best of her abilities.

'I met Luca at a ball, shortly after he arrived in London,' she said. 'We've been acquaintances ever since, though I'm sorry to say my family hasn't yet had the opportunity to meet him. My brother, the Marquess of Clairborne, has been…busy. Luca has met friends of mine, and been of great assistance.'

'Good, good,' Signora Guaro nodded; the answer which wasn't truly one satisfying enough.

At least, enough for what she needed to know.

The conversation continued until all had their fill of tea or sweets, though it returned to the polite, insignificant conversation of drawing rooms the world over; everyone's health, parish news, and the unseasonably warm spring.

Though a sense of strangeness never quite left her—nor the awkwardness of having put herself in this situation—Mary felt also…at home. Relaxed, calm. But then, she always felt thus with Luca beside her.

Especially at home.

Not that it means anything.

'Mary,' Sofia said. 'If you wouldn't mind accompanying me to the kitchen, you could tell me which recipes you're particularly interested in, and I can show you where to refresh yourself before your walk.'

'That would be lovely, thank you, Sofia.'

She wasn't entirely sure if Sofia was attempting to leave Luca and their mother alone, or if she was hoping to speak to Mary in private; either way, it didn't matter.

Perhaps both.

Everyone rose, Luca giving her another squeeze before releasing her hand, and his mother curtseyed.

'A pleasure to meet you, *signora*,' Mary said with a nod. Though she would like to dream—*not the word you should be using*—that after her walk with Luca, she would return, and get to know his family better…she knew that wasn't to be. She would return to London, where she belonged. 'Thank you for your most gracious and warm welcome.'

'It was delightful to make your acquaintance, Lady Mary,' the woman smiled.

Mary responded in kind, then followed Sofia out of the

door Luca had opened for them, which he then shut with one last look that made her want to…

Stay in there, with him, for him.

Instead, she followed Sofia down the corridor into the brightly lit, and clean, but packed kitchen—full of ingredients, herbs, and cooking implements. Traces of their tea lingered on the worn wooden table at the centre, as did a variety of delectable smells. Kitchens were somewhere a *lady* should never dwell, yet Mary had always felt them to be…places she should like to live in.

Inanity, considering she had no concept of what it took to properly *run* a kitchen, even one in the home—

'Were there any specific recipes you were interested in?' Sofia asked as she began clearing the tray.

Mary might've offered to assist, but she knew Sofia wouldn't accept, and so instead she lingered at the door.

Something in the young woman's tone, however, told her something.

'I would be appreciative of anything you'd be happy to share. The easier to execute, the better.' Sofia nodded, and Mary took a breath before continuing. 'I don't think you asked me here to speak of recipes, however.'

'No, I didn't,' Sofia agreed seriously, seeming much older than Mary supposed she was. She gave Mary a searching look reminiscent of Luca's piercing yet soothing gaze, then continued her work. 'You'll forgive me my impertinence, and candour, Mary, but I wouldn't forgive myself if I said nothing. I don't know what lies between you and my brother—I can venture a guess—but I do know it's nothing like…his *habitual* relationships. My brother's life is his own, as yours is. However…my brother is a *good* man, Mary,' she said, stopping to look her directly in the eye, and Mary fought the urge to squirm. *He is a good man, and I'm not a good woman, and she sees that.* 'He…

he's a kind, gentle soul, who…loves with all he is. Please, don't hurt him.'

Speechless, a riot of emotions twisting, and wrenching her heart, Mary could only stare at Sofia; every second worsening the tumult because of the heartfelt plea in those eyes so like Luca's.

I don't want to hurt him. I already have. I undoubtedly will.

You should warn him from me. I've tried to walk away but have no strength to do so.

He doesn't love me. He does love me. That's what I've felt.

I wish—

'No one can promise that,' Mary breathed finally, swallowing the lump of emotion. It tasted…bitter; like shards of glass mingled with honey. 'I wish I could,' she said, hoping Sofia could see how dearly she did. She must, for she nodded solemnly. 'I do know what kind of man Luca is. Just as I know…what kind of woman I am. So all I can promise, is to never forget that. Promise I'll never…intentionally do anything to damage Luca's beautiful soul.'

If I haven't already.

'Thank you,' Sofia whispered.

After a moment, she continued her work, before remembering to show Mary where to refresh herself.

Mary did just that, not that it made her feel better.

Whilst she was alone, she prayed to whoever might be listening, that those promises she'd made were ones she wouldn't ever break, for they were…perhaps the most important she would ever vow. Yet a terrible voice whispered as she emerged, and Luca gave her her things, took her hand, and led her outside, that she was doomed to shatter them.

Them, and him.

Chapter Twenty-Two

'*Showing Mary around*' likely meant around the tiny gardens, however Luca needed to expend energy, and he didn't wish to have the conversation they must within earshot of the house. So he led her into the lane, past the cottage, until they met a footpath which led through miles of open fields he knew the landowners and farmers didn't mind casual visitors upon, having taken it often with Sofia.

Mary was quiet beside him, and he was grateful for that, and the continued presence of her hand in his. They had much to speak of, but he needed to get his thoughts… *somewhat* ordered. It wasn't just Mary's sudden appearance, nor the pleasant shock of her meeting his family, it was also the short talk he'd had with Mamma when Sofia and Mary had left. His sister had known he needed to have a word before Mamma…*got ahead of herself.* The rest—her extravagances, funds, etc., that could wait until Mary was gone. Not that he wanted her to leave, but they both knew she couldn't…stay.

But yes, he'd known—as Sofia had—that Mary's *surprise* visit, and their relationship, needed addressing before Mamma…*excited* herself. Unfortunately, even as quickly as he'd acted, it had been too late. His mother was already planning his wedding, moving to London, planning Sofia's

Season, deciding where to summer, and *wouldn't it be nice to have a marquess in the family, oh the advantages, and...*

He loved Mamma, dearly. All he did was for her and Sofia. Sometimes, however, living with someone who patently refused to see reality, who lived in a world of lost dreams, and long-lost futures…was *trying*. Luca had tried to bring Mamma back to reality gently, only she hadn't been in a *proper* mood to hear it, and so he'd left to deal with it later.

And now you're here, walking in this beautiful countryside with the woman you love.

Indeed, he was. The artist in him wished he could capture this image, Mary…more herself than ever, gloriously beautiful and unguarded, amongst the lush green, yellow, and cerulean backdrop. The romantic realist in him knew he could never capture it, so he would need be satisfied with keeping it in his heart instead.

He was just coming to a place where he felt able to talk—centred by Mary's presence—when she spoke first.

'What does your mother think of your occupation?' she asked, looking down at the well-worn path. 'Or doesn't she know?'

Briefly, he considered arguing this wasn't what they should be speaking of, yet he knew…

She was trying to bridge a gulf. To know *him* better; to know the people she'd just met better. To understand him.

So he answered.

'We've never really talked about it,' he admitted, and she nodded, her head raising to look ahead, leaving him space to continue. 'I think it's easier for both of us *not* to confront it, though I think she knows very well.'

'Families have a tendency to do that,' Mary shrugged, her fingers trailing along a hedge of grasses that started beside her. He appreciated her not asking if his mother thought *her* to be one of his…*protectors*, because he would tell her what Mamma really thought, and saying the word *marriage*... Well, he knew it might scare her. Give her an excuse to leave him again. 'Avoid speaking of anything of import,' she clarified, with a wry, but wan smile.

Luca returned himself to the conversation, which was...

Families, not confronting things.

'Is your family thus?'

'They were. We were raised to believe that emotion, *the self*...wasn't for us. You know all the grand ideals of nobility, and our family—at least, my parents... They taught us to *be* those ideals. To wash away the sins of our forefathers, or because they truly believed we should be thus... I don't know.'

'You said *were*,' he pointed out, and Mary grimaced, annoyed, he thought, at her own slip of the tongue.

Stopping, she glanced out over the fields, and pondered whether to respond.

No matter all they'd shared, no matter how much she'd trusted him—today notwithstanding—he knew she still found it difficult to bare herself. He understood. It made it all the more meaningful when she made the difficult choice to speak the truth, rather than platitudes.

If I were granted a lifetime with her, perhaps it wouldn't be so difficult, eventually, for her to always be thus.

A silly thought; a silly, impossible dream.

'When I went after Spencer two years ago,' Mary said finally, staring down at a stalk of grass she'd plucked, as though it held the words she searched for. 'When he decided to bring Genevieve and Elizabeth into our family, we were forced to confront...many things.'

She looked up at him, and he saw more secrets, more truths, hidden in the blue depths, but also a warning.

That she wasn't ready to speak of them today.

And so you don't have to, my love.

'Something shifted,' she continued, clearing her throat,

walking again. 'Mama, Spencer… They tried to change. To become…*different*.'

'Not you.'

'Change isn't so easily, nor quickly achieved, Luca,' she admonished gently, with an indulgent smile as she raised a brow. He inclined his head, and she became…*serious*. No other way to describe it. 'And change requires sacrifice. It's complicated.'

He longed to press her, if only to offer to carry whatever burden she still did, but he didn't.

In time, perhaps, she will let me see everything.

'How many were there before Deirdre?'

'Two,' he told her. 'Henriette and Constance. Lovely women. Very…kind. I travelled across Italy with Henriette a while—she was my first—then she left for Switzerland, and I remained. I met Constance in Venice, and we shared some months, before we both returned to our respective homes, where I then met Deirdre. I knew I couldn't survive thus, so I… Was honest with Deirdre, about what I wanted. As she was.'

'What prompted you to seek out your first…*maîtresse* to begin with? Or did you simply…fall into this line of work?'

'Mother was…becoming desperate,' he grimaced, unable to find a better word, yet feeling guilty employing one so…ugly. 'Our circumstances *were* desperate. Creditors knocking at doors whilst we climbed out of windows to new horizons. She began talking about finding Sofia a husband… My sister was barely fifteen. Even so, even then, I knew it wasn't what Sofia wanted. So I did what I had to.'

Mary nodded, understanding, and admiration in her gaze that made him feel…

Good.

'I met Henriette at the gaming tables one evening, and thought it would be…something for a night. Something to pay for a meal or two. Only, in the morning, she spoke of a *proper arrangement,* and I went along with it because that was…much better. We were together nearly nine months, and in that time, I paid off the creditors, and made sure Mamma and Sofia had all they required to live in comfort. Henriette also made sure I knew… Well, I wasn't her first *fancy man*, as you English say. She taught me my profession, in a way.'

'You're a good brother, Luca,' Mary said, halting, and putting her hand on his arm. 'And I don't mean because of what you chose to do, but because you did it to give your sister a choice.'

'What of your brother, then? I know… You aren't close, but still, you said he's tried to improve things. Complicated it may be… I believe that shows a measure of love, at least.'

'He's a good brother, in his own way,' Mary smiled wanly. 'I never doubted…that Spencer would do what he thought best for me. And I've learned…been *trying* to learn, as he has, what it means to love when one has barely ever felt such a thing. So yes, complicated.' Mary cleared her throat, and threw him another smile before changing the subject. 'What of Italy? Do you miss it?'

'Not really. I thought I would. It's a beautiful place, and felt like home as long as we lived there. Only, once I left… I suppose I saw it for all it was, and *wasn't*. It's a wondrous place. Yet it's also…in transition. Volatile, somewhat. And we didn't…*flee*, however admittedly, I would be wary to return. But there is good and bad anywhere, and I saw that everywhere I travelled, just as I see all the good, and all the ill here. I must admit however, strange… I feel I've found a place here. A home. The grey skies, the rolling hills, the mists… Days like this too. I never would've expected it to suit my temperament, yet it does, and I feel…connected to this land as I didn't even my homeland. What of you? Have you ever desired to travel?'

'Desired, yes,' she chuckled gently. 'When I was a girl,

at Clairborne House… It was very cold, and very lonely. I dreamt many times of a life of adventure on the high seas like some pirate of old, with nothing but ocean, sand, and freedom. And then I grew up.'

She shrugged, looking away, but not before he glimpsed the sheen of tears.

Luca pulled her to a stop, and faced her.

'Your life isn't over, Mary,' he said seriously, and though he knew she wished to look away, to not have him say such, she fought her instincts and held fast, and his heart grew even more as his love for her grew then.

It wouldn't be so hard to memorise this moment precisely.

The way the sun flickered in her golden strands, or how those specks of silver in her eyes glistened like waves in moonlight. The steadying warmth of her hand. The pulse at the base of her neck, even the ladybird on her shoulder.

May it bring you luck, and dreams, amore.

'I know… I cannot convince you of what you wouldn't be convinced of,' he began, taking a breath, trying to find his words. Letting his love take hold so they would just *come* to him. 'Whether it be that you have a choice, the freedom to live whatever life you wish to; or whether it be that you can trust me. I know… Though you wish to believe me, some part of you seeks to preserve you from harm in preventing you from doing so. I won't lie and say knowing that makes me any less angry that you didn't trust me today. That you followed me, and thought what you did… It hurt, despite my understanding. The thing is…'

He frowned, looking at their hands for a moment, trying to find…*courage*?

Trying to determine whether or not what he needed to say most would…do more harm than good. Pressure her, or scare her, or…anything *but* what he wished to do. But when he met her gaze again, he knew…

This is the time.

'I love you, Mary,' he told her, and there was no surprise in her eyes.

She clenched her jaw, steeling herself against…the words, the emotion, herself…he didn't know.

All he knew was that she held his gaze, and his hand.

'I'm *in* love with you. I know…love is a complex thing on the best of days, and that it's entangled in so much more for you. I do. I don't say these words to… I ask nothing of you; not even for you to reciprocate. I don't say them because I think they will magically make you trust me. I say them because they are *my* truth, and I promised you that. Someday, in time, you might see that love, and trust, are possible.'

Luca watched as a world of questions, objections, fears, and hope—*yes, hope too, and that is all she needs*—swirled in the crystalline blue depths of Mary's gaze.

Until finally, she…surrendered. Not to his words, but to the hope kindling inside her. And then, much like that first time in the library—though today couldn't be any more different—she pulled him close, and raised herself up to capture his lips.

If Luca hadn't known better, he might've said there was love in her kiss—so different from any they'd shared, or ever would again. Though he knew kisses to be like falling snow—ephemeral, ever-changing, infinite—he also knew it *meant* something different. The tenderness, the *give*, Mary demonstrated in the middle of those fields, were proof of her sharing her soul. Of her sharing that newfound—no—*newly rekindled* hope, for he didn't think she'd ever truly lost it, with him. Helping her, even in some small way, to find that hope again, would for ever be one of the greatest achievements of his life. If that was to be the only purpose of his love… What an exceptional purpose that would be.

They remained there, entwined, a long while. Then they

walked some more, in quiet contemplation, still—*always*—hand in hand. Before long, it was time to return.

Sofia reappeared as he and Mary prepared her for the journey back, and Sofia slipped her hand in his as they watched Mary disappear down the lane.

Luca had no idea what lay ahead, and by rights he should've felt…*lost*.

Except Mary had given him a sliver of her hope, and so he felt whatever the future held, it would be rather exceptional.

Chapter Twenty-Three

A week since Mary had…*met Luca's family.* Followed him out of inexplicable—well, not *inexplicable*—dizzying jealousy. A week since…he'd said all he had. Since he'd told her he loved her. A week of grappling with the emotions not only his confession elicited, but also all she'd learned of him; and herself.

The week had been unsurprisingly busy—she'd only managed to see Luca privately once, both of them occupied with Society frippery. It had been…*succinct* that meeting between her and Luca. Everything had still been tangled, and he'd sensed that—or perhaps it had been tangled for him too—so they'd both just satisfied their need for the comfort each other's body could give. Mary couldn't say her emotions any less tangled now, however she could say… the path forward was clear.

This past week, since that walk in the fields, she'd fought her instincts. Abandoned reason, and done what she'd scoffed at others purporting to do. She'd listened to her *heart*. She'd let *it*…*guide* her. Perhaps she'd willingly scoffed at others' ability or desire to do so because she'd never felt her heart had worthwhile things to say. Her mind, logic, instincts, yes, but not her heart. However, since Luca had uttered the words which were no true surprise—for hadn't she felt it; seen it in his eyes? Ever since he'd offered his love, his heart—freely, with no price nor demands attached—she'd felt…clarity of spirit. A shining, guiding light, illuminating her world, unveiling a truth she'd never have been able to divine otherwise.

Breathtaking and extraordinary that light may be, it hadn't made the road she had to travel—emotionally, spiritually—any easier. It had been jarring, unsettling, and more than once during this conversation about horses, or that about fashion plates, she'd felt entirely of another world. Removed, from what she'd fought long and hard to not only be *part of*, but *central to*. All the words friends, family—even strangers—had uttered to her, finally made sense; resonated with unquestionable truth.

Society isn't the World.

There are things more vital than power.

Love is...liberating.

There is hope.

You are capable of great love. Worthy of it.

Mary had come to two very important conclusions. Well, three. Two, wholly more significant; another *part of* the others.

Mary loved Luca. Mary was *in love* with Luca. Desperately. Undeniably. Irrevocably.

She wasn't entirely sure *when* her heart had, against her will and better judgement, made the leap. She suspected it was much earlier than she realised, even perhaps…

Glitter and frost sparkling in moonlight. Silence but for the horses being prepared so they could continue on quicker; so they could make it in time to save Freddie.

Tea had been offered, and refused. The three of them stood silently, separately, waiting with bated breath.

Mary told herself not to look—she had since they'd started up the drive.

Told herself not to look at the house she'd not been to in fourteen years. Where she'd recovered, with Mama.

But she did look. It was beautiful tonight—of the realm of the Fae. And like the realm of the Fae, it was...hidden from this world for a reason. For all the darkness and sorrow it contained.

Mary shivered; not from the cold. Tonight was all too much—

Luca was beside her. She felt him edge closer, his heat, his presence...soothing.

She hated, and welcomed it.

He said nothing. They stood there...a while, their breaths little clouds in the night, until they were called. Everything was ready.

She glanced at him before turning back to the stables. He had this look...

As if he felt her pain. Knew...there was something about this house.

And a look which said simply: I am here.

Later, she would refute it. But in that instant, her heart... beat steadier.

Not that it mattered *when* exactly she'd fallen for him.

What did matter was… Her second conclusion. Mary wanted a lifetime with Luca. A lifetime not in shadows, and secrecy, but in full view of the world. In the light. If he would have her, she would do as her friends, and brother had. She would tell Society to go hang itself—meet whatever consequences, whatever ruin came—and marry him. Damn everyone's objections—*too young for you, we don't marry fancy men*…whatever else they'd dream up.

Those two conclusions might've seemed…rash, impulsive, *quick*, and in fact, her decisions *were* all that. Yet Mary's heart told her, that didn't make them any less *right*.

She had two paths before her. One, she could take by following her heart; the path past that door marked *hope*

Luca had slowly cracked open. It led to an unknown future, full of beauty, trials, love, and adventure. The other, she could take by continuing on the same path she'd been; leading to a life of relative safety, comfort, and perhaps, in some measure, contentment. A life too, of regret, bitterness, at the end of which she would look in the mirror, and find herself transformed into that monster inside—with no hope of ever turning back.

Before she could, however, ask Luca to marry her, share a life, she had to be…brave. Show what she still kept hidden. Bare all her secrets, and wounds. Finish painting the picture of exactly who Luca would be sharing his life with. Which was why she was here. In his kitchen. Doing something even more improbable than following her heart: cooking. And baking.

All on her own.

It was…not going well.

She'd thought she could do this. Often enough in the past couple years—more often than a lady should—she'd been in kitchens, seen what was done, and how. She'd received recipes from Sofia with *very* clear instructions—and chosen the orange cake, which appeared simple enough. She'd called on Susie for a fish pie recipe which, again, couldn't be *that* hard.

Somehow, still, smoke billowed from the range, and out of the door and windows she'd had open since she'd boiled the fish and *it* had leaked everywhere, and she was flapping about like an angry hen—more food on her than in the damned pots—and…

'How do you burn mash?' she cried, feeling stupid and useless as she stared down at the fish pie in her hands, before setting it on the table, disgusted. 'I don't understand…'

Tears filled her eyes, and she swiped them away.

Tonight was meant to be perfect, and she'd ruined it. She

should've...brought cheese and bread, wine, and fruit, and not believed she could do this.

You've managed to muck up Sofia's fool-proof recipe too, she thought grimly, setting the...*thing*, which had overflowed and resembled dried muck, with slices of taunting orange popping up.

'Mary?' came Luca's voice, just as she plopped herself despondently into a chair. She didn't have it in her to move, or respond. *Such a mess...* 'Mary...? Oh.'

Glancing up, she found him frozen at the door, surveying the chaos below amidst which she ruled supreme.

Even the beautifully laid table, with romantic candles, flowers, and shiny crystal was a mess. Originally she'd wished to have dinner in the garden, but thought better of it because *they could be seen*—particularly since they were meeting at a not-so-late hour today, *for this special occasion*—so she'd thought the kitchen would be informal, *homely*, and now that idea had been proven to be as much a mistake as the rest.

Where is all your perfection now?

'I'm sorry, Luca,' she mumbled, as he slowly made his way over, her gaze returning to her hands—*burnt, cut, mangled*—as they sat in her lap. 'I ruined everything. I thought I could do it, but it turns out, I cannot. I hope you aren't hungry, for there's nothing to eat.'

'Nonsense,' Luca declared assuredly. *Tenderly.* He knelt before her, brushing back some of the many loose curls which had escaped the scarf she'd used to hold them back, and bade her silently to look at him. 'There's plenty to eat,' he smiled, mischief, and that love she'd come to know so well, so quickly, despite its alien nature, burning brightly in his eyes. 'And it smells delectable.'

'Don't be nice, Luca,' she shrugged, trying to remove herself from his touch, but he didn't let her.

'I'm not being *nice*. I promised never to lie to you.' Eyes wide, she stared at him, convinced this might be the time to find a lie. Only…*he speaks the truth.* 'So you've burnt… everything,' he chuckled gently. 'It won't be the first time I've eaten a meal which has suffered too much time in the fire. We can easily scrape off the top of the…fish pie?' he asked, and she nodded. 'As for Sofia's cake… I'm sure despite its presentation, it'll taste just as sweet.'

He kissed her cheek, smiling reassuringly.

'I wanted it to be perfect,' she argued, trying…to make him understand. 'Instead I… Made a mess of everything.'

'It can be cleaned up easily enough,' he told her, meaning it for so much more than supper, and the kitchen. And she felt it, reverberating through her, touching the place in her soul which forced her remorselessly to never…*make a mess.* 'And wasn't it even a *little* bit fun, making it?' he teased, taking her hands in his. 'Oh, Mary, your hands.'

'It's fine.'

'Let me put some salve on at least.'

Without waiting for her to object or agree, he rose, heading for a shelf by the corridor leading to the pantries and upper servants' quarters, and grabbed a small chest.

Sliding her cake to the side, he set the chest on the table, dragged a chair around, then sat, and began tending to her minor wounds. With so much care, and affection, it made Mary speechless.

With so much love I know I'm not wrong in what I still must do.

'You shouldn't have gone to so much trouble,' he chided gently, applying salve with a featherlight touch. 'When you said you wished to cook dinner, I thought… Well, I thought it was for your own pleasure. Instead, I fear you've tortured yourself trying to do something for me, and I appreciate it, I do—it's perhaps the sweetest thing someone has done for me in a long time, but… You could've asked for help. We might've made a mess together,' he smiled.

'I wanted… To prove I could do it. To myself, and…'

'To me,' Luca finished seriously, studying her carefully. 'Why? Why would you ever believe you needed…prove something to me? Especially that you could cook? If this is about my declaration—'

'It isn't,' she reassured him. He watched her carefully, to ensure she spoke the truth, then nodded, and carried on with his work. 'Or perhaps it is.'

He said nothing until he'd finished tending her hands, then put everything away and sat back down, waiting for *her* to finish.

Sighing, Mary screwed her courage tight, trying to find the words to…

Express it all when I never thought to do such a thing.

She'd had this grand plan to make it all perfect, and ease them into this conversation…

Life does not go according to plans.

A lesson she'd learned long ago, yet refused to accept.

'Luca, I…' Grounding herself by meeting his comforting gaze, she drew another deep breath, and let her heart speak. *I'm trusting you, heart, don't let me down.* 'I wanted to prove, to you, and myself, that I had something, *anything*, to offer you.'

Luca frowned, quirking his head, but remained silent, ever patient.

'I wanted to show you… For it to be perfect, romantic, and sweet, so that I could say the words, a little more easily. I love you,' she breathed, and Luca softened, or *lit up inside as though the sun shone from his heart*; but still, he neither moved nor spoke, knowing that wasn't the end. 'I never thought I would, *could*, but I do. I'm…in love with you, and I… You are an incredible man, Luca Guaro,' she smiled. 'Generous, with your heart, and soul. Kind, thoughtful… you give all of yourself. Have given all of yourself to me. Strength, when I needed it. Comfort. Love. Understanding. Advice. I may not know much about love, but I do know…one person cannot give everything. It's a give and take, and I… In a roundabout way, I wished to show you I had something—even the simplest thing—to give you before I asked… Whether you might be willing to share a life, and marry me.'

It was her turn to make *him* speechless.

He gazed at her, stunned, but like she'd just gifted him the entire Universe. The hope, love, excitement in him… gave *her* hope, warmed, and made her giddy—but she tempered it, because…

I'm not done.

Before she could continue, her courage faltered, because a shadow of regret passed over Luca's face, and she knew he would refuse her, which…broke her heart, shattered her hope—the worst of it being because he hadn't even heard it all, and already meant to refuse…

A declaration of love does not equal a desire for a lifetime commitment...

'Mary, I'm honoured, my heart is crying with joy, hearing your feelings, and the thought of what you're asking… But you speak of give and take, and you must know, I have nothing to give you. No fortune, no title, no honourable name, no prospects but scandal.'

Her heart relaxed, making her dizzy as hope ignited once again.

He refuses not because of my lacks.

'Didn't you hear me?' she asked, recovering her wits and strength. 'You've already given me so much. All of what I never dreamt could be mine. I don't need a fortune, a title, nor anything so…material. I'm not afraid of ruin any more. I will brave it, for you. For us. I see now…what truly matters, and what doesn't. However… Luca, there's more I must tell you before you say anything else.' *Before you say yes, and I know you would in an instant.* 'More you must know, before you consider what I ask. Have asked. Lord, I'm making a mess of this too.'

'Tell me then,' he said, placing his hand on hers, and it worked, quietening her doubts and nerves.

'I wanted to prove I could give you *something*, because the truth is, I cannot even give you what you think I am. Like all the rest of me, it's a lie. A mask—though not one I created. You see, Luca, I'm not a lady. I am not my mother's daughter.'

'I don't understand…'

Neither did I, for so long...

'I'm a bastard, Luca. As is Spencer.'

'Tell me, Mary. Tell me everything.'

Chapter Twenty-Four

When they'd been very young, his and Sofia's favourite pastime was to find a spot full of tall, luscious grass, grasp each other's wrists, and twirl, twirl, twirl. As children the world over did, turning and spinning until ground and sky blended; until they were dizzy and breathless. Then they let each other go, and fell into the grass, laughing as the world upended itself.

In this moment, sitting in his kitchen with Mary, he felt…not dissimilar. Minus the laughing—though the joy remained. But then, joy filled his life since Mary became even the smallest part of it.

The past week had been good, apart from not seeing Mary…*every day.* Confessing his love, everything they'd shared in Downsham…it lessened the sting of secrecy. Put it all into perspective. Freed him. Showed him that what they could or couldn't have didn't matter—all that did, was being given the gift of loving her. Constraints, rules… were of no import when he'd been gifted a chance to love her, in any way.

It had been a busy week, full of engagements, but he'd embraced it with an alacrity he'd never known. Yes, he'd wondered how Mary fared, longed to speak with her, longed to…hold her, but he'd also known she needed time. Since the garden party, he felt…she was discovering herself as she allowed him to see ever more. And he understood such a…journey was not made lightly, or easily. That time in the studio, when she'd shown herself, he'd focused on simply being. On enjoying the gift he'd been given, and throwing himself into giving her what she needed—which had merely been…*him*. His love. And that had been enough. It would always be enough.

When she'd told him of her plan for this evening—her cooking supper—he'd been touched, certes, but he'd also known it signalled a shift. The change in their…*modus operandi* heralded a change in their relationship, and though, yes, he'd hoped it was for the better—a deepening, a strengthening—he'd never thought… The night was to be anything like this.

And it's only just begun.

Never, in a million dreams—or perhaps in one in a million—would he have imagined Mary would not only declare her love for him, but ask him to marry her, say she wasn't enough, then tell him she was a *natural* child.

So yes, his head was spinning as it had those times as a child with Sofia because it again felt like the world had been upended. Blurred, until he no longer recognised it. Oh, his heart cried with joy, at the hope bursting from it—*she loves me; perhaps we do have the chance of a lifetime together in the sun*—whilst he also felt honoured, terrified, and unworthy—because no, he *didn't* have anything to offer of what Mary deserved or expected—but he also felt confused. Shocked.

He hadn't meant to be short with his *'tell me everything'* only he'd had all *that* coursing through him, and he'd known her revelation, this secret, was what she'd been keeping within her—that last great, weighing shadow of darkness, the one he'd sensed, which knowing now, explained so much—and the gift of *that*—her trust—made him…

Lost for words.

Now he tried to make up for it, smiling gently, holding her hand tightly, willing her to see that no matter what she said, he wouldn't abandon her, love or want her any less—for he saw now that's what she feared.

And he appreciated her honesty—her unmasking before she asked *him* to share a life.

'I found out two years ago when I went after Spencer,' she said softly, and he recalled how…different she'd been when she'd returned to town that autumn. 'That's where we were born, at Yew Park House. Where we were conceived, and where my…parents met the woman who gave birth to us. Spencer…he started remembering things, remembering *her*, and by the time Mama and I arrived, he'd uncovered the truth.'

Mary took a breath, and Luca took the opportunity to slide his chair closer, so their knees were touching, and he rubbed his fingers against her hands, careful not to hit the injuries on which he'd just put salve.

'Apparently, our mother couldn't conceive. She and Papa tried, but no child came. She offered to leave him, but he loved her too much, so instead they devised a plan to have another carry his child. They went to Yew Park House, and that's where they met Muire McKenna, the daughter of the housekeeper and butler. It all worked out just fine, obviously,' Mary said bitterly, her gaze turning to the open door from whence the cool evening air crept in, shaking her head. 'Spencer arrived, and by Mama's account, they were all very happy for a time. Then I was conceived, and…it all ended. Muire died…the night I was brought into the world.'

Tears glittered in Mary's eyes, sadness brimming up from where she'd kept it so long, and Luca was about to reach up, and…touch her, in every, *any* way, but she sniffed, and shook her head again, looking him straight in the eye.

Her features harshened in the flickering candlelight as she guarded herself from him, the memories, all of it.

'So there you are,' she said flatly. 'The truth. Of me, my family. I'm not a lady. My family…isn't some great titled, irreproachable thing. Everything we are, everything I am, is a lie. Should it ever be discovered…it would mean total ruin. You deserved to know that.'

Luca nodded, her words tangling, knotting in his mind, until he slowly, but carefully, pulled on the threads, one by one, determining all which his heart told him he needed to say.

Tutto quello che ha bisogno di sapere. All she needs to know.

'You thought this would change how I felt? Thought it would change how I would answer if you asked me to marry you?' Though slightly thrown by his opening salvo, she quickly nodded, her expression saying: *it should.* 'It doesn't,' he reassured her, because yes, that was the most important thing. 'Mary… I know it's hard for you to see it, understand it, but everything I've said since I've known you… I meant it. Hard as you've tried to keep yourself hidden, I *see* you. The truth of you.' Her jaw clenched, and he willed her to see herself through his eyes. To believe him. Hear him. 'You said all the ineffable, intangible things I've given you are all that matter, and so it is for me. You may not realise it, but you too have given me so much. Love, strength, courage, knowledge, challenge… You could be a pauper, a travelling actress, I would care for you no less. I would want you no less. I'm grateful you told me,' he smiled, brushing his fingers against her cheek. 'For your trust, your honesty. I'm grateful you gave me this new piece of yourself, of what you've lived, and lived with. That's all I'll ever ask, or need of you. *You.* So tell me…everything. For I can see there is still so much you keep for yourself, but if you do intend to ask me to share a life, begin with sharing the burdens you carry now.'

Mary's breathing had quickened, shallowed, and without thinking, Luca gathered her up and took her onto his lap.

She squealed in surprise, but quickly nestled against him—either too tired, or determined to no longer fight his comfort, and more importantly, her need of it.

'I trusted her,' she murmured against his chest. 'Mama… she was the last person I trusted, and then… I found out she'd lied to Spencer and me all those years. I understood why, but that didn't make it any easier. We'd been… through so much together. Spencer I understood, but not telling *me*... It shattered everything.' Luca stroked her hair, gently encouraging her to out with it. All the poison; all the hurt. 'And then…they moved on. Spencer married, forgave Mama, and we talked sometimes, and met with the McKennas, visited Muire's grave together, only…it was as if everything was *fine* once the truth came out. As if we should all be happy, and close, and *transformed*. As if it made everything better.'

'Rather than worse, which is what it did to you.'

'Yes… Spencer, he… Sensed something wasn't right, tried to reach out, as did Genevieve, Freddie, Mena, and the rest of them. Only I couldn't trust them, and I couldn't just…*move on*. Not again. And Spencer…he remembered the love, from before I was born. Before Clairborne House became cold, and our parents… He had memories of Muire, happy ones. He knew her, and I…had nothing. I asked questions, to get to know her, that part of myself, but it hurt Mama, and Mrs McKenna so much, and I only wanted to understand *myself*, and who I was when the last piece I thought certain turned out to be mere illusion… All they could do was move on, be happy, and not look to the past.'

'I'm sorry, Mary.'

'McKenna…my *grandfather*…' Mary sucked in a breath,

and Luca knew whatever came next… He held her tighter. 'McKenna was the only one with the courage to tell me the truth. To speak of Muire, and tell me what no one else would. The truth of the night I was born. How he had to tear me from his own daughter's womb. Cut open her lifeless body, and take me from her… Spencer has his happy memories of Muire. All I have are her eyes, and the haunted look in my grandfather's when he told me of what he'd done.'

Gazing down at her, Luca found her cheeks soaked—tears streaming endlessly as she clutched him tightly.

And though it hurt his heart to see her in pain, he knew she would be better for crying tears she'd no doubt kept inside for such a long time. He knew they were not only tears for her losses, her wounds, relating to her origins, but also…from all the rest. So he held her, and let her cry, grieve, and release.

The candles had nearly burnt to their end by the time she finished, and he would've sworn to anyone asking that she felt lighter in his arms. Slowly, she pulled herself away, and he fished out a handkerchief, which she made very good use of. Smiling, he noticed the shadows had finally released their hold—they still lived with her, but didn't control her—even though the dim light might've made anyone else think the contrary. Red-eyed and blotchy, still she was…freer.

Più luminosa. Brighter.

'Well now, are you hungry, my love?' he asked, and she stared. He grinned. There was…so much more to be said, spoken of, healed. For now, however, all which needed to be, had been. The rest…they had time. 'Cold though it may be, I'm still looking forward to this feast.'

Mary laughed, the sound lifting his heart.

This, this is my purpose. To make Mary Spencer happy.

'Luca, wait,' she said, as he made to grab the fish pie—plates, servings, and proper table manners be damned. He stopped, waiting, gazing back at her. 'I know this is…seemingly sudden, but I for one am certain. I… I don't know what our life would look like. I'm not entirely certain what I wish it to look like, beyond us being together. I suspect my family, and friends, will support us, and I think yours will too, but we might… Even if Society doesn't shun us, I think I should like to spend time away from it. One day, I would like to travel. And I… I've never wished for children. I don't see that changing. Bearing all that in mind, Signor Luca Guaro, will you marry me?'

'Yes, Mary, I will,' he said simply, though his heart screamed in jubilance and elation.

Some might argue it was *his* duty to ask, or that it shouldn't be done thus—her family, *his* family should be aware—but he knew…this was right.

Just as it should be.

The smile—the beaming, heart-stopping smile—Mary gave him cemented that belief. As did the kiss they shared. Full of…*love*. Unconditional, blinding, searing, hopeful love.

Some time later, they came up for air, to the sound of candles spluttering. Luca settled Mary back in her chair, closed the door so the chill wouldn't be too profound, then lit new candles, revived the fire in the range, and served them healthy portions of cold fish pie—after scraping off the burnt top.

It was the most delectable meal he'd ever eaten, and as they ate, they spoke of all their plans—small, and great—with an ease and settled quality that was both achingly strange and utterly natural. After they'd finished, they cleaned up together, then he carried Mary upstairs, and loved her until dawn.

As I will love her until the end of time.

Chapter Twenty-Five

'My, my, aren't you early this morning?' Deirdre said, removing her spectacles as Luca entered her study. Well, the study she'd made her own after her husband's passing, transforming it from the severe, ostentatious thing it was into an elegant, soft haven. He knew, for he'd witnessed it when they'd returned from Italy together—even assisted in choosing the wall hangings; finely striped yellow and blue with sprigs of wildflowers.

Deirdre's marriage, like many in Society, had been a cold, formal thing, during which she'd lived heavily pressed beneath her husband's authoritative, unyielding thumb. To boot, he'd been a liar; a wastrel in more ways than one. Her sons had suffered in their own way, not that they could admit it. They'd built the lives they were meant to—full of power, riches, good marriages, and heirs—and hadn't appreciated Deirdre's quest for happiness following Lord Granville's death, separating themselves from her eccentric refusal to maintain the prescribed status quo. One day, he hoped, they might find a way to each other again; estranged though they may be, Deirdre loved them.

He wasn't sure why he was thinking of this just now; but then again…

Because I'm about to abandon her too.

He knew he shouldn't see it thus, still he felt a pang of…a smidgen of regret.

Striding over to her, he kissed her cheek, and ignored the fluttering nerves in his belly—amplified by his lack of sleep—as Deirdre scrutinised him carefully.

'I hope I'm not disturbing you,' he said, glancing at the pile of correspondence she was working on. 'I wished to speak before we left for our morning calls.'

'I welcome any reprieve from this tedium,' Deirdre grinned, waving at the desk. 'Here, take that chair, and let us talk.'

Luca did as bid, fetching a chair set by the window and placing it before Deirdre's as she turned so they could face each other.

Taking a breath, and her hands in his, he readied himself to speak words he'd never imagined he would. In the short time since Mary had left him this morning, he'd tried to think of the best way to say what he had to Deirdre—to ask all he must—in the end realising he should merely…

Tell the plain and simple truth.

'I'm to be married, Deirdre.' Her eyebrows shot up and she stared at him, her emotions veiled for once, which was…*unsettling.* 'Say something, please.'

'I… I'm surprised, Luca,' she stuttered, still studying him. 'Lady Mary?'

'You're the first to know,' he nodded, smiling, his joy unwilling to be contained, and he understood this was a shock, but he hoped Deirdre would share his joy. 'She asked last night. There's much to be done, but I wanted you to know. I…' Drawing another breath, he tried to find the words to express…everything. 'I'll always be grateful, for everything you've done for me, Deirdre. Being with you these past years… It's been wonderful. I hope… I know it's rather irregular, and sudden, but I… I don't want to lose you, because I make this choice.'

Deirdre softened, smiling a small smile, and Luca felt some of his tension subside.

'Luca, my darling, you won't lose me. I'm happy for you. And Lady Mary. I admit, I never thought… Well, that doesn't matter,' she said, shaking her head, and though Luca understood what she meant to say, why, and that he shouldn't be concerned about how it felt…*prophetic*, well, he did feel…something ominous. 'You surprised me, that's all. Now, tell me everything. When are you leaving for Scotland? Or will you be waiting for her family to return here? And what of your mother, and Sofia?'

'We… Mary and I thought it best to be married…quickly, and quietly,' he said, repeating what had been agreed the previous evening, and which then, made sense. But which now, with how Deirdre regarded him, almost…worried… It didn't bear thinking on. He and Mary had made the decision together. It was the right one. 'Society will no doubt have their say on our union, so we thought presenting it as *fait accompli* would diminish the…theatrics. Mary is today obtaining a licence so that we may marry at St Gregory's, a week from today. She didn't wish to upheave her family,' he explained, not that he needed to. *Ovviamente no—of course not*. 'Not with Lady Clairborne expecting in a couple of months. I'll advise Mamma and Sofia, and have them here for it, and then we'll all discuss plans for…after. That's part of what I wished to speak to you today of, actually. Well, that is, I don't wish to abandon you, as I said. I'm happy to finish the Season with you, and I would never wish to bring mockery, or ridicule upon you—'

'Luca, you could never,' Deirdre reassured him, patting his hand. 'You'll be beginning a new life, and I'll be just fine on my own, though I'll look forward to meeting you in Society with your wife, should you decide to remain after you're married.'

Luca expelled a long breath—unaware he'd been holding it so long.

He wasn't afraid Deirdre would…deny him happiness, but he did feel guilty since he was essentially abandoning her, his duty to her, for…himself.

'Thank you, Deirdre. I'll set the house to rights as soon as possible, and find myself other accommodation until Mary and I have wed—'

'Don't be ridiculous. The house is yours. I've no other use for it, remain there as long as you need. As for setting it to rights, I quite like what you've done upstairs, and I think, when you leave, I'll consider getting tenants who will enjoy the studio.'

Deirdre winked, and he let loose a nervous chuckle, grateful yet again to have such an incredible person in his life—and even more anxious.

For what he still had to ask her.

'Deirdre…' Clasping her hands tightly, and looking her in the eye, he steeled himself. 'Would you…stand with me at the wedding? Mary will be asking two friends to bear witness, but I should like you there with me, if you'd do me the honour.'

'The honour would be mine, Luca.'

'Thank you.'

Deirdre nodded and they fell silent, though Luca sensed she had more to say.

'Luca…' she began carefully, her tone setting him on edge. 'Please don't take what I'm about to say as a contradiction of what *has* been said. Only… I wouldn't forgive myself if I remained silent.' Luca swallowed hard, preparing; he had a feeling he wouldn't like what was coming. 'I'm happy for you, that you've found this woman you love, so dearly. I can see that. I have seen it for some time. I'm happy you've found your way to each other, and that she has…acted in a way I never imagined she could. Accepting this love, shirking off the expectations of Society to grasp it. And I understand in principle why such hasty arrangements would be made—you wouldn't be the first eager lovers to wed hurriedly, and quietly. I'll gladly stand beside you, and see you begin a new life. However,' she said meaningfully. 'I also must caution you. Not against Mary, but against… *Lady* Mary. I worry, knowing what I do, seeing what I have, that she might not have the courage to face what will come of this marriage, when the time comes for her to. I worry that in the end, her love for you won't be enough for her, as yours is for you. Everything you do, you do unreservedly, and passionately. Not everyone does, and I just don't want to see you hurt, Luca.'

'What are you asking me to do?' he breathed, his heart…

Drowning, in worry, and fear, for the truth was, her words *didn't* injure him, or even strike him as unbelievable.

The truth was, Deirdre voiced thoughts which plagued him since he and Mary had made these harried plans over their cold dinner last night.

'I'm not asking you to do anything, Luca,' Deirdre smiled gently. 'Well, perhaps I'm asking you to…consider everything carefully. I may not have first-hand experience, but I do know that love can…sweep us away. Sometimes we miss those things right before us, and then, end up… dashed on the rocks.'

'I understand, Deirdre.'

And he did; more than he wished to.

But all will be well. Mary trusts me, and I her.

'Good. If there is anything I can do—be it organise a wedding breakfast, or help choose your *accoutrement*—please, tell me. In the meantime, you may go see the carriage is ready, for I believe it's time we were off.'

Luca nodded, relieved, grateful, and…*excited.*

He grinned widely as he rose, and kissed Deirdre's cheek again, before doing as he was told. Though somewhere, in a shadowy recess of his heart, he couldn't stop the slow burrowing of doubts and fears.

Non è niente. It's nothing.

Chapter Twenty-Six

People often spoke of the absolute madness that was organising nuptials. So many arrangements! So little time! Mary, however, was finding it…straightforward, and easy. It helped that her own wedding—*something I hadn't thought would be mine for a long time*—was to be quiet, simple, and small, so there were only few arrangements to be made.

Essentially, it was one step above elopement—not that she minded. In fact, the choices they made were mainly due to her own desires—Luca's only wish being that his family and Lady Granville be present, hence no *actual* elopement. Lady Granville who, according to Luca, had been most pleased for them, something which warmed and reassured Mary more than she'd thought it would.

It wasn't that she didn't wish for her family to be present—despite her feelings, and resentments, which she did hope now to resolve someday, perhaps with Luca's support and guidance—merely that she wished to be married. To Luca. Without delay.

They may be shocked, but deep down she knew they would be happy for her, and with Spencer's child on the way…this was easier. She would write them once the deed was done, then she and Luca would go to Scotland after a week or two in London. She wasn't *avoiding* telling them—a letter posted now would be lucky to arrive before the wedding—she wanted…to keep this…*all* to herself. It felt something which needed…

Protecting.

The lack of grandeur or fuss to the wedding also felt…more suited to her relationship with Luca. Small, just for them. Far from the eyes and reproach of Society—though she knew someday soon she'd need face both.

Unless they cut me.

Doubtful. Far more interesting to keep me about—and though I'm marrying a fancy man, I will be married.

Besides, I haven't yet lost all my power.

No, she hadn't—which helped when expediting a licence so they could wed without banns. She might've obtained a *special* licence, only they had no need, and badgering the Archbishop wasn't keeping things…quiet. She would see well enough how Society behaved after news spread she was married, and she and Luca faced them before leaving. Running away *directly* to Scotland had been discussed, but Mary knew better than to flee without feeding the wolves their pound of flesh.

Beyond that—obtaining the necessary papers, making arrangements at the church—Mary hadn't had much to do. There was the celebratory part—a wedding breakfast, to be held at the townhouse; *nothing to get servants' or merchants' tongues wagging*—travel arrangements, and that was it. She would wear an old gown of silver and blue silk, and Luca was arranging the rings—another of his choices. She'd written to Susie and Frances, asking them to be present at St Gregory's in Bloomsbury at the chosen date and hour—without explaining the *whys* or *wherefores* of the sudden marriage, but promising she would explain it all at the breakfast. When the subject of *guests* had come up, she'd instinctively known she wanted both women present.

Mary was slightly concerned as to how Frances might take the news, but in the end, they'd been friends for over sixteen years. It didn't matter how close they were, or difficult their relationship was sometimes. Frances was a big part of Mary's life—and not solely because of...*that night*—though it wasn't until she'd had to think on who she *wanted* to witness her wedding, that she fully realised it. *Accepted* it. That she had *actual* friends—even such as Susie, who she had a sort of...natural kinship with. She had friends who were *people*, not merely those terrors that lived in her heart, and were slowly being cast into shadow.

By Luca's love, and mine for him.

Accepting his love, realising her own, making the decision to reveal *everything*, and agreeing, together, to share a life... It transformed her. So much, in what seemed days—though she knew it was longer. She knew she wasn't a new person *overnight*, but she was...on that new path love had illuminated. It was terrifying and exciting.

Just as these past days had been, inching closer and closer to the hour of her...wedding. Every time she'd needed to make a public appearance—one didn't shirk off one's entire social calendar lest one *truly* wished to set tongues wagging—she'd felt both terror at anyone discovering what she was planning, and also raucous joy urging her to shout her news from the rooftops.

She visited Luca every night, reckless though it was, traipsing across town like a thief in the night, and their lovemaking transformed into...something fun. Giddy, and clumsy...as she imagined the love of youth was. Holding him in her arms, being with him...it made her excited to soon be wed. She'd never thought she would want that—though loneliness had prompted her to consider Freddie once—but to be wed to Luca... It wasn't about the institution, the holiness of the blessing; it was about the pledge they made to one another. Having the language to describe it to the world, so the world could understand their bond, was…reassuring.

Though my love—the love of my life, the surprise I never expected—I suppose works too.

And happy as she was to *marry* Luca…if she could have a lifetime with him, in the sun, the rest didn't really matter.

A scratch on the door tore her from her musings, and she glanced down to find her fingers stained with ink, having left them on the list of things she needed to pack.

'Come in!'

'Apologies, my lady,' Brooks said, looking uncharacteristically…*harried.* Mary frowned as he bowed, and crossed the room. 'There is… A lady demanding to speak with you. We've refused her many times…'

The way he said it…made her wary.

'Who?'

Brooks held out the platter, and when Mary glimpsed the name on the card, her hand curled into the back of the chair until wood scraped deep below her nails.

How dare she?

Rage, and a twinge of fear bubbled up, and she forced in a breath before rising.

'I'll take care of it.'

Bowing, Brooks stepped aside, and let her lead the way to the entrance hall.

Of all the…

I don't need this today. Ever.

What can the damned wretch want?

It eluded Mary, and that worried her more than anything, though the casual manner in which the *damned wretch* stood in the midst of the hall as though she had *any* right was also extremely concerning.

George's mother—Viscountess Claeyton—hadn't changed in the past fourteen years, not that Mary didn't already know, considering whether or not she wished to be confronted with the sight of the woman, on many a social occasion, she hadn't had a choice. Even if Lady Claeyton had been…*encouraged* by Mary's mother to avoid certain gatherings, and on the whole, Viscount Claeyton, before he died, hadn't been part of the *upper echelons*.

No, the woman hadn't truly changed. She was still beautiful—short, petite, with shrewd, cat-like features, and light brown eyes which had darkened as her lines had deepened after losing her son; bitterness replacing what Mary had once thought *clever kindness*. Though one thing *was* different today, Mary noted, forcing her stomach *not* to rebel, and her heart to steady.

The woman seemed…*happy*.

'Though I'm sure it was made clear years ago, you aren't welcome in this house, Lady Claeyton,' Mary said without preamble, stopping before the Viscountess, with as much cutting ice as she could, hoping the frost in her voice would invade her veins, and keep her calm. 'Brooks will see you out, be sure never to darken the doorstep of any Clairborne home again.'

Mary turned, ready to march away, determined not to wonder *what* had brought the woman here, except she didn't get very far.

And a chill finally did invade her veins, only not because of the Viscountess's words—innocuous enough—but rather the woman's tone…

'You will want to hear what I've to say, Lady Mary.'

It was chilling, and Mary clenched her jaw to stop from shivering.

Still, gooseflesh appeared on her arms as she turned back, and she knew then, when she glimpsed the Viscountess's face—full of glee and twisted satisfaction—that whatever came next would be…

Terrible.

Though I'll face it, with grace, and fortitude, for I won't give her any more of that disgusting satisfaction.

'Very well,' she said, inclining her head, more to Brooks and the assisting footmen—for he looked ready to throw the woman bodily from the house. Loyalty which might've made her heart joyful, had it not been full to the brim with dread. 'We don't require refreshments, Her Ladyship won't be staying long,' she told Brooks, before leading the Viscountess to the closest room—the library.

Shutting the door, Mary followed the Viscountess to where she'd planted herself beside the empty hearth; the woman had the decency not to presume to sit.

'What do you want?'

Yes, she'd been taught to mind her manners, *especially* when dealing with enemies, however, right now she didn't quite have it within herself.

All she could do, was stand strong and face whatever oncoming storm this was.

The worst I shall ever face again, I think.

The Viscountess chuckled, nodding, and Mary wanted to scream her question again, but the woman answered.

'I'm here to return the favour you once paid me,' Lady Claeyton smiled viciously. 'I'm here to break your heart, girl.'

Mary stared at her, uncomprehending.

Though the dread and terror didn't dissipate, she found herself…*laughing*. As if the Viscountess had told some great jest. A hysterical laugh that left her shaking and breathless when she finally managed to stop.

Pulling herself back together, she shook her head.

'Are you done, girl?'

'*Are you done*, Lady Claeyton? I have little time for your nonsense.'

'Yes, I imagine that Italian boy keeps you busy,' the woman retorted, and though Mary was unsurprised she knew of Luca, it did quell what little relief she'd felt from the laughter. She waited, letting her adversary make the first move. 'Or at least, *has been* keeping you busy. Soon, your time will no longer be taken up by him, nor wedding planning.'

How the hell does she know?

A servant, an eager clergyman, no doubt. She'd been careful, but apparently not careful enough.

And really, it didn't matter *how*.

'I'm not entirely sure what you're about, Lady Claeyton,' Mary sighed, uneasy at the Viscountess's *suggestions*, yet… less afraid. Or so she told herself; it wasn't as if Lady Claeyton could force her and Luca apart. *We are strong. Stronger than anything.* 'I have half a mind to call you a doctor.'

'I'm not mad, you little viper,' Lady Claeyton hissed, and Mary froze as the woman's black heart and soul made an appearance. 'Though you might've driven me thus by taking my son from me.'

'Your son took himself from you, abusing others.'

'And now I'll take your precious Luca from you,' the Viscountess smiled. 'Or rather, you will take him from yourself. You will break it off with him *today*, or the world will know the truth of what happened the night you ruined my son's life.'

'I don't care,' Mary breathed unhesitatingly, utterly… *free*.

Dizzy with the knowledge that with Luca by her side, she didn't care who knew her tale.

With him, I can face anything.

Smiling herself now, relief replacing ice in her veins, easing her breathing, and slowing her heartbeat, she felt…

A great, mighty warrior queen. What power love can give…

'Publish the tale of your son's wretchedness in the papers, shout it from the steps of St Paul's if you will,' she told Lady Claeyton. 'I *don't care.*' Shrugging, she chuckled. 'Your grand plan is foiled; you may go now. Disappear for ever under whatever rock you crawled from.'

It was the Viscountess's turn to laugh and, *damn it*, but it was a potently eerie thing.

'Fourteen years I've waited. *Fourteen years* of watching, planning, listening, ferreting out every secret, and you think *that* was my grand plan?' Lady Claeyton laughed again, and Mary shivered this time. *No. No... You didn't acquire all your power to be bested by...her.* 'I'm...thrilled you would so easily have your secret exposed. It reassures me I wasn't mistaken in believing your heart belongs to that poor boy.'

Mary was speechless; her teeth surely ground to dust considering how she ground them together.

Desperately she searched her mind for something, *anything*, to use in defence, only her mind wouldn't work. Nothing of her body would.

Of all the times to do this to me...

No matter the pleas to herself, all she could do was stand there, a terrified rabbit before a wolf, unable to even scream that Luca was more of a man than George Claeyton could ever have hoped to be.

I won't lose Luca because of her, I can't...

'Anything less than heartbreak wouldn't have done,' Lady Claeyton continued, growing in power and malice, as her words had the intended effect. 'I thought long and hard about your punishment, and that of your mother, and I realised it should be as the good book tells us. *An eye for an eye.* Your heartbreak for mine. Then, in turn, a mother's heartbreak for the great Dowager Marchioness of Clairborne. Though I must be honest,' she sighed dramatically. 'I did begin to despair. Always alone, and such a vicious creature you can be. I began to wonder if you had a heart to break, and considered just having you killed—however boring, and unsatisfying—but then one after the other, the pieces fell into place.'

Something worse than dread, something resembling *relinquishment*, seeped into Mary's body, making her tired, and apathetic.

I haven't lost; I cannot...lose...him.

'You may be willing to risk your own reputation for this great love, Lady Mary,' the woman said sweetly, approaching until they were nearly toe to toe. 'You may be willing to see your life go up in flames, however, will you risk the lives of others? What would the Duke of Barden say, I wonder, were he to discover his beloved wife Catherine was defiled? If he were to learn of the child she bore before his? What would Society say…? Or your dear friend, Eliza… I doubt the Marquess of Winternell would appreciate learning of his wife's past. And one must wonder what shame would be brought upon her parents, the ambassadors… Then, of course, there's Simone, travelling the Continent with her *friend.* The daughter of an earl, cavorting thus… And there are so many more secrets,' Lady Claeyton sighed, stepping away, pacing the space before the hearth, not that Mary breathed any easier. 'For years, I've amassed them. Not only those of your friends, but of every other woman who was clever enough to keep silent once my son and his friends had taken their due. One secret alone, you might be able to contend with. You might be able to turn the tide, as you did with that unfortunate viscount all those years ago. As you did with Lady Clairborne—the once *Great Whore of Hadley Hall.* You are good, girl,' the Viscountess conceded with an admiring smile which made Mary want to slap her—not that the impulse was new, and not that she could move. 'You and your mother...are masters at this game we play, no denying that. Only, you're not *that* good. You…*got* attached. An unfortunate, novice mistake. You believed yourself akin to

Choderlos de Laclos's heroine, when you're no better than the idiotic young Cecile. So here we are, at the end now. Keep your precious Italian, or preserve the lives of others. Your choice. You have until the end of the day. Oh, and I nearly forgot. It goes without saying that neither the boy, nor anyone else, will ever know of this. And once you have ended things with him,' she finished casually, as though discussing the weather, slowly making her way towards the door. 'There will be no hiding from the world. You'll live as you always have, in full view of Society. Any hint of your heartbreak, and the deal is off. No need to send a note. I'll know what choice you've made.'

'You will know it now,' Mary said flatly, managing to find her voice at last.

Her heart *would* break.

She *would* feel the rage, impotence, sadness, injustice… in time. She would weep, and rack her brain for another way out, and bemoan ever allowing herself to love anyone.

For this is what comes of it.

Not now, however. Now, a drugging numbness had a hold over her, and she welcomed it. A warrior's last moment of defiance; laying down arms before a conqueror, refusing to yield grace.

Mary turned to face the woman, who raised a brow expectantly.

'I will end things with Luca. And I will live with a smile on my face in Society until the end of my days. I recognise when I've been bested. However, you bitter, twisted old hag,' she said, ever so sweetly, ever *so* politely. 'I'm still young. You've taught me well today, and I thank you. I see now that I still have much to learn, and so *fear*, you demented viper. For I *shall* learn. And destroy *you* before you meet your maker.'

'I look forward to you trying,' Lady Claeyton sneered,

though Mary was pleased to notice a flash of fear traverse the woman's eyes.

'See yourself out. I'm sure you can find the door. Brooks will no doubt assist you if you cannot.'

Lady Claeyton inclined her head, as if unaffected by Mary's threats, though she still scurried away.

Scurry, scurry, demon of Hell.

Unbidden—perhaps to give her courage to face what lay ahead, though all it did was twist the knife deeper into her heart—a memory, her first of Luca, flooded her mind.

A hush, followed by tittering tongues swept through the crush of the steaming, cloying, glittering ballroom.

Lady Granville had returned from her travels with a young Italian. They'd all known, heard as soon as she'd stepped onto English soil, but there had been no public appearances yet.

Mary wasn't curious. Mary didn't care. Neither did Mama nor Spencer.

Mary laughed at them all silently, ruffled fans and ruffled egos for miles, and shared a complicit glance with her family. The most complicity they seemed to have.

Then she saw them. Lady Granville and the pretty boy on her arm.

And she was struck...dumb. Her heart stirring in a way...

Lady Granville was...changed. Happy. Glowing. Free.

Mary envied her. Ruthlessly.

The worst...

Lady Granville was hesitant, outwardly challenging, but inwardly wary of her own re-entry into this world, Mary could see it.

Just as she could see the way the boy at her side soothed her. Touched her, gently, shielded her with his own daring presence. The softness about him, the warmth.

Mary wanted...

Warmth. Soothing. Happiness. Freedom.

Mary envied Lady Granville. Though Mary knew it was foolish.

It didn't prevent her feeling that envy gnawing ruthlessly when they were finally introduced to the boy.

Luca.

A man of...

Gentle warmth she could never have.

'Lady Mary,' Brooks said tentatively, scratching at the open door, carefully venturing in. 'May I be of assistance?'

'Please send a note to Signor Guaro,' she said hollowly. *For I haven't the strength to put ink to paper—not with what lies ahead.* 'Ask him to come, today, as soon as he's able.'

'Of course. My lady—'

'That will be all, Brooks.'

The butler dutifully bowed, and shut the door.

That was the last thing Mary saw.

The world faded into a blur as she stood there, staring at nothing, her mind, heart, and very soul reeling, though she knew the worst was yet to come.

That storm I just faced was nothing compared to that on the horizon. That which will surely drown me. Or...

Not me.

The me I might've been with love in my life; Luca by my side.

The me I shall never be.

Chapter Twenty-Seven

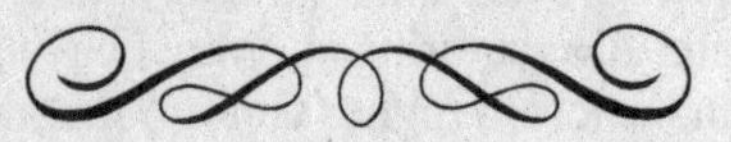

Luca tried in vain, for the short time it took him to get to Mary's—Nigel had caught him as he returned from a morning engagement with Deirdre—to convince himself nothing was amiss. That something terrible *wasn't* about to happen. There had to be some *good* reason why Mary would send for him, immediately, and not write it in her own hand. Wasn't there?

Everything had been going so well. Arrangements were being made. She'd obtained the licence. He'd bought the rings—simple gold ones, though hers bore an engraving which read *ti amo*. He'd begun tidying up the house in preparation for his departure, and was planning on visiting and fetching Mamma and Sofia in two days. He'd spent every night with Mary, and it had been…glorious. Free, relaxed… In the moments when they hadn't been alone, but chanced to meet in Society, even those moments had been good. Full of stolen glances, touches, and…

Perhaps there's some problem with...the wedding breakfast.

Even to him that sounded absurd.

Something is wrong.

Still, he dismissed his fear, blaming it on his difficulty believing such a gift as a shared love and life with Mary could be his. On his former conviction that…it would be tantamount to reaching for a star, and being able to pluck it from the heavens.

We're fine. We're strong.

Right. *Were* there to be a problem, they could fix it, together.

Certamente. Certainly.

Repeating those positive words, Luca managed to push away the dread for a time. Long enough to give York's reins to…someone at Mary's door—he couldn't have said whether it was a footman or a circus performer, so eager was he to see her, and reassure himself all was *certainly well*—and go inside, and follow…another someone to the library, and there she was, *amore*—

Something is wrong.

She was…herself. The woman he'd known *before*; Society's creature. There was no…warmth. No light. No… *love*. The mask she'd worn so long was back on, and it terrified him more than if he'd found her…pale, crying, or *anything but this.*

No, no, no...

'Mary,' he breathed, searching her eyes for any clues as to what made her thus, ready to go to her, hold her, and see if he could bring the true Mary back, but her words stopped him.

'Good morning, Luca. Thank you for coming so quickly.'

So formal. Emotionless...

Frozen, he scrambled to make sense of her; still denying what his heart screamed was coming, no matter his churning stomach, and twisted chest, which prevented him from breathing properly, while Deirdre's words taunted him.

'Love can...sweep us away....and then, we end up... dashed on the rocks.'

'Mary?' he asked; begged, pleaded.

'I suppose there's truly no easy way to do this, is there?'

she said casually, dismissively, with a little laugh—as though about to inform him green was simply *not his colour*, and not…what he knew she would. 'I'm afraid I must end our engagement. I cannot marry you, Luca.'

The words…

Though he knew they were coming, hurt more than he expected. Still, he fought the disappointment, *heartbreak*, fear of losing…*her*, and steeled himself. He wouldn't just… stand here, and let *this* be the end. He would fight, discover what had prompted this sudden change, because he just…

Couldn't understand.

'Why? What prompted this…change of heart?' he demanded, louder, and harsher than he meant to.

'It's complicated, Luca.'

'I'm sure you've explained more complex things,' he bit back. Taking a breath, he forced his anger down, refusing to believe…she was as Deirdre had warned. 'If marriage, a wedding is what scares you, we don't have to do that,' he offered gently, grasping at straws. *I'll do anything to keep her; keep our love alive.* 'We can live, as we have. We can find a way to be together.'

'I'm not scared, Luca,' she said, warning in her voice as he made to step closer. Something…flickered in her gaze, but it was gone before he could think to name it. 'Pleasant though our time together has been, we cannot continue thus. We cannot continue together at all.'

'Pleasant? That's what you call it?'

'Yes. That is what it was, and now it's over. Such is life, Luca.'

So…callous, careless, and cruel.

Deirdre wasn't right. I know Mary; this isn't her.

'Mary… I know you. The *real* you,' he pleaded, stepping forth, still not touching her, no matter how he wished to. He didn't think it would help—to remind her of how it felt to be together—instead, he sensed it would push her further away. 'I don't know…why you're doing this, why you've become this…*old self* of yours, but whatever has prompted this, we can fix it, we can find a way to be together—'

'If I wanted to, perhaps. Only I don't, Luca.'

I don't believe you.

'Mary… Why are you doing this? What happened?'

'Nothing *happened*, Luca,' she said, with that dismissive laugh again. 'Beyond me coming to my senses. I got carried away, as we women are wont to, and that is regrettable. I am sorry to have hurt you, but surely you must've known it was all naught but a foolish dream?'

'No. I don't believe you.' He didn't. He couldn't. Not after…*everything*. 'You love me, and I love you,' he said, desperation clawing at his voice, his heart, everything within him, begging him to fight.

And perhaps she saw that, for with her next words, Mary ensured he had no fight left.

With her next words, she ensured his heart was well and truly broken.

'That is not in question,' Mary stated flatly, thankfully stopping Luca in his tracks yet again. If he touched her… Well, the lies which up till now had so easily tumbled from her lips might not any more. It wasn't lost on her how easily, *convincingly*, she'd spoken such affronts to *truth* and *honesty*—all she'd promised him, and he'd given her; just as it wasn't lost on her just how much was at stake should she fail this task.

A skill not easily forgotten, thank God.

Though the one skill she would need to finish it, was one never practised. One she'd never even thought to learn, but which now, the lives of countless others depended on her acquiring, in an instant.

How to break someone's heart.

She'd tried to divine *how* in the small amount of time

she'd had to prepare herself for this harrowing task. In the end, all she'd come up with was…telling the truth. As her old self, the woman who took the *other* path. The path of fear, not that illuminated by love.

It was easier than expected to slip that old mantle back on; just like the lies. Unfortunately, she hadn't counted on Luca…fighting so hard. She should've; he wouldn't be the man she loved if he didn't challenge her, and see… What she didn't wish him to. Only…she had to finish this. Before she lost what little strength she had.

God...gods, someone, forgive me what I do.

'I do love you, Luca,' she said, trying not to lose herself in those pleading eyes, so full of love. She had to act fast, before he started fighting again. *Speak some version of the truth, or he'll know.* 'I love you more than I ever imagined I could anyone. But you're a boy, and cannot understand. I love the power I wield more.'

He shook his head, and she forged on, knowing her words were having the intended effect.

'You've been good to me, but the power has kept me safe, all these years. I thought… For a moment, I thought I could risk losing it. For you. Only…the sad, hard, and harsh truth is, I can't. I won't. What Spencer did… First standing by the Earl of Thornhallow, then marrying Genevieve… He nearly destroyed our family name. Our standing, our credibility. It took *everything* Mother and I had to survive those scandals. We wouldn't survive another. And I won't live as I would be required to should that happen. You always knew who I was. Better than anyone, I think. Though we may have believed otherwise for a glorious moment, in the end, this was inevitable. I'm sorry, Luca. But you're young, you have your life ahead of you. In time, as I said before, you'll recover, and set your sights elsewhere.'

'As I said before, you're wrong, Mary,' he breathed, his fight gone now. *Good.* He cleared his throat, and straightened. 'I may recover, a sliver of my heart and soul, someday. Perhaps I will love again. But I will never love anyone as I love you. Will always love you.'

A perfunctory bow, and he turned to leave, making it as far as the door—making her believe for a split second that the worst was over.

'I'm not a boy, Mary,' he added, turning to face her. 'I'm a man, and you know that very well. And this man pities you for the life you'll lead. I *do* know you. The woman you are, underneath. The one you long to be—who isn't filled with bitterness, but hope. The one who doesn't see the world so cynically, and tries to make it better. So I pity the woman you'll become. I never saw your cruelty, your weakness, until today. Still, my love forces me to wish you well. To wish that you may find as much happiness as you can ever hope to with your choice. Goodbye, Mary.'

With that, he was gone.

Mary had always thought *heartbreak* to be profoundly exaggerative. Hyperbole. Despite all the pain she'd suffered, all the supposed heartbreak, betrayal…she'd never felt the actual cracking, tearing, shredding of her heart before.

It was…fascinating, strangely. The pain so vivid, so encompassing, so brutal, all she could do, was stand there and let it consume her. How long…she didn't know. The sun had set by the time she regained any senses, only then realising her cheeks were coated with dried salt—from tears she couldn't recall shedding.

The greatest pain, the greatest curse of all, was realising then it wasn't her own heartbreak which tore her apart. It was the knowledge she'd inflicted such wounds on Luca. That she'd done as she'd promised Sofia never to. She'd broken his soul, and doomed him to be harder, and less… *Luca.*

I would ask your forgiveness, Sofia, but none can for such a sin.

Worst of all, we both knew I could never keep my promises.

Chapter Twenty-Eight

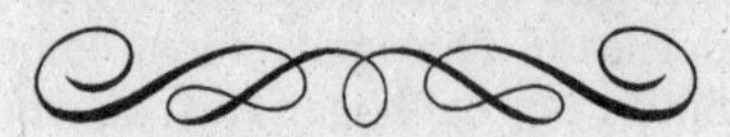

The last thing Luca wished to do was...*anything.* All he wanted to do was find a hole to curl up in, sleep, forget his sorrow, and forget the pain splitting him in half. The pain, which was his own doing, because he'd not listened to others' warnings, but most of all his own.

Lady Mary isn't for you.

Luca had let himself fall prey to hope, love, and a belief they could...be something he'd always known was impossible. He didn't blame her—oh, he was angry, disappointed, more heartbroken because he loved her, saw who she could be but refused to. He'd stared at the statuette he'd made of her a long time before he managed to dress tonight—romantic ninny that he was, he'd put it on the mantel in his room—fighting the urge to launch it at a wall, and see it shatter as his hopes had.

Instead, he'd left it untouched—a reminder of...unfulfilled destiny and dreams. Still, as he'd told her, he wished her as well as she could ever be, because his love demanded it, and he would pray to the goddess of her every night for Mary to find some measure of happiness.

He was angry most of all at Society; the world. Even her family in some measure, for moulding her into this...creature who would suffer a lifetime of torment—anyone who denied their true self did—because of them. He wanted to rage at them all, to parade Mary before them, forcing them to *look, look at what they'd done to her.* Instead, he would parade himself, pretend nothing was amiss, for that was how it was done.

And he may not have much—but he still had a duty. To one of the only people who had never abandoned or disappointed *him*. So here he was, outwardly all he needed be—dressed, and ready for dinner—while inside, he felt… *excavated.*

He smiled, striding across the hall as Deirdre descended the stairs, and offered out his arm, thinking he was hiding his turmoil convincingly.

Apparently he wasn't, he knew, as soon as he felt Deirdre's eyes roving over him, though he pretended not to, walking her across the hall to get her things.

'I just need a moment,' she told Henrikson, her butler. 'In fact, I think I need refreshment before we go, Luca,' she added with a smile, guiding him over to the study. 'Luca will take care of me, Henrikson, thank you. We won't be long.'

No hiding anything from Deirdre...

Luca knew he'd have to tell her what had happened at some point. Only, he hoped perhaps…for *one* evening. The first evening to just…*pretend*, get his bearings, and a hold on his pain, before he had to say the words. Make them real.

Unfortunately, he wouldn't get that. Deirdre walked them into the study, closing the door and releasing him before heading for the drinks cabinet in which she kept a single bottle of the very best cognac. A glance back, a silent question, and he nodded. He joined her as she finished pouring them each a glass, and they stood in silence, warming the liquor for a moment; Deirdre allowing him time.

Staring down at the richly coloured liquid, he tried to find the words which were so simple, yet difficult to speak.

'The news of my engagement was rather premature,' he said flatly. 'As was the invitation to my wedding. I would've told you, Deirdre, I just…wished for an evening to forget, and you don't deserve to be burdened by my…personal complications.'

'Luca…'

'Please, don't, Deirdre,' he begged, finally meeting her gaze.

In some way, yes, he'd also come here for comfort, for friendship, but saying the words aloud, revealing his foolish dreams had been *just that*, he felt…

That he couldn't bear much more.

And not that she would, but hearing any hint of *I warned you*, or *I told you*, would only break him more.

'I'm so sorry, Luca,' she said gently. 'Please, sit with me awhile. We won't speak of anything you don't wish to.'

He hesitated, then did as bid, and they both settled on the small leather sofa.

Setting down her untouched cognac, she took one of his hands and cradled it in her lap.

'I shouldn't have come…burdened you with this, Deirdre, I apologise,' he said suddenly, her care…wrenching against the part of him which just wanted to hurt. 'I thought I could manage this evening; my personal affairs shouldn't affect my duty to you. After all, we've only a few days before our arrangement ends—don't worry, I won't beg you to take me back now that I'm…forsaken.'

'Don't be foolish, Luca,' she sighed, tightening her hold, preventing him from leaving—which truthfully wasn't hard, because he didn't truly wish to go. 'We're friends, aren't we?'

'Of course,' he breathed, setting down his own glass. 'You are…the best friend I've ever had,' he admitted, more vehemence in his tone, for he'd never forgive himself if she didn't know that much.

'And you are the best I've ever had,' Deirdre smiled. 'I love you, Luca.'

'As I do you—'

'I know,' she said gently, patting his hand. 'Which is why I hope in time, you'll feel able to share what has occurred. And which is why, I think, you should come with me to Norfolk after all.'

'But—'

'Luca,' she said, teasingly, warningly almost, and he quietened. 'Our arrangement has been…very different from what it began as, for a long time. We are friends. And friends, help each other through life's most difficult moments. I know…you're still finding your way. That this… disappointment will likely shift your path even more. Which is why, some time in the country, to think, would be beneficial. I was already considering leaving earlier, and I would very much enjoy your company.'

'I don't think I'll be great company,' he muttered.

'Then bring your mother, and Sofia,' she said casually, and he stared at her wide-eyed. 'As I said. Our arrangement changed from what it was, why shouldn't it again? You kept them…locked away from your life, and I understand. Why you chose to do so, and why it was in a very sad sense, necessary. However, now, we are past that. Bring them along. It will be good to have the house full again.'

'Are you sure, Deirdre? You've already done so much…'

'People have always looked down on me, Luca. Pitied me. First, for such an unlucky match. For what I endured. Then, for choosing to…embrace a new life, a new side of myself I might've never imagined had I not met you. They pity me for…*buying* what they see as untrue affection. But then…we all exchange something, for something else. Love for love, or coin for food. Whatever it is, is an exchange, and there's nothing inherently wrong with that. I always knew…with you, however, that what you gave me—joy, love, and kindness—I didn't *buy* it. I may have helped in the only manner I could—with money—to ease your life, but what you gave me… No one could ever buy *that*.'

'I don't deserve you,' he breathed, tears falling down his cheeks.

Tears he hadn't cried when Mary broke his heart—and to some extent, these were those he'd held inside—but they were also tears of gratitude, and love, for the beauty of Deirdre's soul, and heart; and the great good fortune he had to have her in his life.

'If kindness, and friendship, *can* be deserved,' she said gently, holding his hand tighter. 'Which I don't believe, then I can think of no one more deserving.'

They sat together there some time, while Luca expunged what he could, then quietly cleaned himself up.

Thank goodness I hadn't yet gone to speak with Mamma and Sofia.

At least I don't have their pity and disappointment to contend with, though I'll have to tell them eventually.

'So,' Deirdre said, sipping her cognac as he did so too. 'Wretched and distasteful a place it may be, how are we feeling about honouring our engagements in Society? I wasn't lying when I said I hoped to leave earlier for Norfolk—I'd planned on perhaps quitting town after the Duchess of Fanshawe's spring ball—however, if you wish to go now, we can.'

'No,' Luca said, knowing that no matter how dearly he wished to, quitting town now would only…inflame matters.

The arrangements Mary had made were designed to be discreet, however they'd been made under the assumption there would be a wedding within a week.

There was no telling whether the secret would be maintained longer—though Mary would do her best to keep their short-lived engagement a secret—and if it did out, it would be best to face it, by Deirdre's side.

'The ball is in three weeks. We can survive Society that long,' he smiled wanly. 'It'll give us time to make the necessary arrangements. Deirdre, you should know, there's a chance the truth of what nearly happened will come out—'

'I know. Don't fret, Luca. We'll face it if it does.' He nodded, grateful yet again for this incredible woman. 'Perhaps you can help me find tenants for the Bloomsbury house before we leave for the summer. It would be good to have your help.'

'Of course.'

'Now, drink up,' Deirdre ordered before rising, downing her own cognac as she did. 'I have a feeling we'll both be needing that liquid courage this evening.'

Smiling, Luca did as he was told, before returning the glasses to the cabinet.

'Thank you, Deirdre,' he said seriously, as he went to her.

'Thank me by…having some fun with me this evening. I know your heart likely wants nothing more than to grieve, and there will be time for that. But no matter how it feels, your life isn't over, and you should remember that tonight.'

He nodded, unconvinced—though it wouldn't stop him from trying to have some measure of *fun*, if only to make Deirdre happy.

Opening the door, he offered out his arm, and once kitted out with their gloves, hats, and coats, they were off.

And though Luca still felt excavated, heartbroken, he did feel…slightly better, for having a friend by his side.

Chapter Twenty-Nine

'Are we ever going to talk about it, or simply carry on for the next thirty years pretending you weren't supposed to be wed today?' Susie asked as they knelt together, sorting crates of donated clothes for Nichols House.

And we'd been doing so well, Mary thought grimly; the silence in which they'd worked for hours convincing her she might escape discussion of the...*disappointment*, as she'd taken to calling it.

It helped...not minimise the pain—Mary doubted anything could, even time—but lessen...the importance of what she'd suffered. If she thought of it as a disaster, a ruination of her entire life, soul, and heart, then she wouldn't...

Move on. And move on I must, for I've no choice.

It's what she'd *been* doing, moving on. Doing as ordered. Resuming her old life—and cleaning up the mess she'd nearly made of it, before someone found out what she'd dared to dream. That last part...what she'd done beyond writing to Frances and Susie advising them of the *cancellation*, and rescinding all breakfast and travel arrangements—i.e. bribing people—she'd done it not only for herself, but also for Luca, and Lady Granville. He'd been hurt enough, and she...deserved better than to be ridiculed because Mary had thought herself...

Smart. Untouchable. Powerful. Hopeful.

She'd paid the price for that hubris, and there was nothing to be done but forge…if not onwards, then somewhere. She'd done as the bargain with Lady Claeyton required, she'd not shirked a single engagement, and attended every tedious, mind-numbing event with a brilliant smile. All she'd wanted was to be left alone to her misery, perhaps shatter the townhouse's collections of crystal, crockery, art, and ceramic. However, good, perfect, contained and controlled girl that she was, she hadn't. Merely wrapped herself in silk, linen, cotton, diamonds, and jewels, pasted that trusty smile on, laughed, mingled, danced, and…

Now she was here.

Her calendar for today had already been cleared, because as Susie so *kindly* pointed out, today was meant to be her wedding day. There were hundreds of other places she could've gone, but she wanted to be…

Somewhere I wouldn't be alone. Somewhere I could be...what little of myself I can. Somewhere I can be useful. Keep busy.

Somewhere with...a friend.

Only, now, she regretted that choice because friends wanted to *speak*, and she…had nothing to say.

There's nothing I can say. Or the bargain will be broken.

Mary had to admit, Lady Claeyton knew…well how to strike.

'Mary?' Susie prompted, tearing her from her reverie as it veered into something altogether more…vengeful.

'There's nothing to say,' she answered simply, running her fingers along the hem of a girl's dress. *Light mending needed but nothing more.* 'I'm not the first to cry off days before a wedding.'

'But *why* did you cry off?' Susie insisted, her tone… annoyingly gentle and kind. *You wanted friendship, this is what you get.* 'Your note merely said: *the wedding is off.*

And that was after your other letter which read: *I am getting married on Saturday, I would appreciate your presence as a witness, breakfast and explanations to follow.* I don't even know for certain *who* you intended to marry; I can only imagine it was that Luca fellow Mena mentioned—'

'What does it matter?' Mary retorted harshly, picking up some trousers. *Seams need resewing, buttons missing.* 'My moment of folly is over.'

'Mary…'

'Fine,' she hissed, glaring over at Susie, whose eyes were so full of…*sympathy. Which I don't deserve.* 'If you must know, yes, I was going to marry Luca. I was swept away in a moment of…madness and lust, but I came to my senses, realised we weren't suited, now it's over, and I should like to get on with my life if that's all right with you.'

Susie watched her, and Mary glared back, raising a brow in challenge.

'I won't force you to speak of it if you don't wish, Mary,' Susie said softly, relenting after a time, and they both returned to the work at hand. 'Only… It was all so sudden, and unlike you… I was worried.'

'There's nothing to worry over, I'm perfectly fine.'

Unbidden, Luca's voice echoed in her mind.

'I don't believe you.'

She shoved it away, as she had the rest of him.

She couldn't keep any of him, not even the good memories, for with them she could never…be who she had to again.

'Well, if you ever do wish to speak of it, as I've said, you're welcome to speak of anything with me.'

'Thank you, Susie,' Mary managed to say, convincingly enough.

'Most of this is usable,' Susie noted. 'Some isn't, but most is, and what needs mending and repairing will be good work for those learning the skills.'

'Indeed.'

On they went, sifting and sorting through the crates, before distributing it to the necessary places—laundry, rubbish…though not much went there, as even scraps were used for cleaning.

All the while, Susie chattered on about the local news, the weather, international news, Nichols House, and so on. In the end, as Mary returned home that evening exhausted and worn, she also felt…grateful. For all Susie had done to keep her mind and hands busy, so that she could fall into bed, and perhaps, for a few blessed hours, forget she was meant to be beginning a new life today.

But that was never to be.

Chapter Thirty

Ten days later

There was noise. So. Much. Noise. *Why?* Blinking rapidly to wake her mind and senses from the deep, but fretful slumber plaguing her every night now—and likely would until the end of days—Mary dragged herself to sitting, rubbing a hand over her face and glancing to the window.

Dawn hasn't even broken, why in the hell is there so much bloody noise?

'Jacqueline,' she called, her voice hoarse with sleep, and annoyance. 'Jacqueline!'

No sign of her maid—only silence.

Well, silence in her quarters, from below it sounded like Napoleon descending with his army.

Where the hell is she?

Ripping back the covers, Mary tore from bed angrily, sliding on her slippers and fumbling in the half-darkness of the last embers until she found her dressing gown. Tying it tightly, she threw open the door, the cacophony from whatever was occurring downstairs assailing, and fully waking her.

Had she heard any shouts of alarm, she might've been concerned—about a fire, burglars, or another Norman invasion—but there were none, so she felt only frustration and annoyance. She had enough trouble sleeping as it was; not that it was restful, but there was no possible way she could face another day and night in Society without *some* measure of rest.

Bright light—unusual for this hour—poured up the staircase, and Mary stomped towards it, making her way halfway down before she stopped in her tracks, grabbing the banister for balance as she recognised some of the voices.

It cannot be...

Except that it *was*, she realised when she was finally able to finish her descent into the entrance hall, where not Napoleon's forces had descended, but instead, her family.

'Spencer? Mama?' she said, blinking at the gathered horde, confusion overtaking everything else.

The congregation froze, turning to her, as her eyes flitted over the rest of them, mingling among harried-looking servants—half the latter with their livery buttoned as if in the dark, which it likely was, considering the clock was chiming the hour of *two*.

I've only been abed an hour.

It wasn't just Spencer and her mother either, descending upon the townhouse as though for some party. Genevieve, Elizabeth, Elizabeth's governess Juliana, the Earl and Countess of Thornhallow and their young daughter Halcyon—somehow still sleeping despite the tumult—Freddie, Mena, even their dog Hawk was here.

And the McKennas.

'What are you all doing here?' she asked weakly, frowning. 'You're meant to be in Scotland. What's happened? Genevieve, is something wrong?'

A surge of panic took over her heart at the thought—she could see no other reason they would risk her travelling in her condition.

'Everything is fine with me and the babe,' Genevieve

smiled reassuringly, stepping forth, whilst the others threw each other sheepish looks. 'We're sorry to have woken you, only as you can see our arrival was mistimed, and there's been a mix-up with Freddie and Mena's things.'

'Hello, Mary,' Freddie chimed in from the back, as though they were all meeting as agreed in a most civilised manner.

Party indeed.

'Hello, Freddie,' she answered reflexively, before shaking her head, and herself, back to her senses. 'None of you have answered. Why are you here?'

There were those sheepish looks between them all again, and Mary was about to stomp her foot in protest when finally her mother stepped forth from the group, looking harried, and tired—natural, considering—but also disconcertingly worried and remorseful.

Older.

'We've come for you, Mary,' she said gravely, and Mary froze, more uncomprehending than ever. It must've shown, for then her mother crossed the distance separating them. 'There's much to be said,' she breathed gently, and Mary's frown deepened as the remorse in her mother's gaze did. 'And we will speak in greater length in the morning. For now, all you need know is that we are here for *you*, Mary.'

'I don't understand,' Mary argued, even though her heart told her she did. Except, if what her heart thought was true…it might just break her. 'I'm perfectly well, I don't know what you've heard to cause you to come here—'

'You're far from perfectly well,' her mother said sadly.

Mary clenched her jaw, fighting the rush of emotion.

Fighting the urge to dissolve into tears, fall into her mother's arms, tell her *everything*, trust her again, and ask her to fix it so she didn't hurt so much any more.

Mama holding my hand as Papa was buried.

Mama holding me tightly as we cried together after she found me the night of the house party.

Mama, Spencer, and I twining arms and bounding off together to ensure his future with Genevieve...

Glancing now to her brother, she watched him step forth, and hoped he would say something which…

Makes more sense, easier to accept than this...care.

'We heard of everything that's happened,' Spencer said instead, and Mary shook her head.

They couldn't have.

'How?'

'Susie,' Mena offered quietly.

Of course. Traitor.

But that told her that *everything* in this instance merely meant her…*disappointment.* Which was…for the best, no matter what the actual disappointment she felt a pang of argued.

Them knowing...would change nothing, only complicate it.

'We're here to help you set things right,' Spencer continued. 'As you did for all of us.'

'Then you've all made a wasted journey,' Mary countered harshly, clearing her throat, her heart, everything of emotion. She simply…*couldn't.* 'Things are as they should be, which I told Susie, by the way, not that she listened, apparently. Good night.'

And with that, ignoring their murmurs and protests, she swept back to her room, locking it to prevent anyone following, stuffed herself back under the covers, shut her eyes tightly, and…

Wept until daybreak, each and every tear she hadn't wept for…

Luca. Myself. Everything.

Chapter Thirty-One

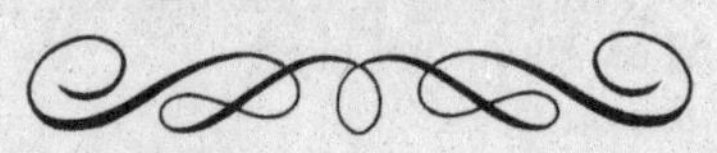

'I'll have a tray this morning, Jacqueline,' Mary groaned as the woman swept open the curtains. She shut her eyes against the bright light, turned over, and burrowed deeper into the nest she'd created. It wasn't her habit to be a lie-abed, however considering last night's…hubbub, and those hours she'd spent…crying like a useless chit, she wasn't exactly well-enough rested to face the day—let alone whatever awaited her downstairs.

I shudder to imagine.

'Forgive me, my lady,' Jacqueline murmured tentatively, and Mary turned, squinting against the light to find the woman wringing her hands, staring down at the rug. 'Her Ladyship, your mother, has instructed you are to breakfast downstairs.'

Of course she has.

Barely a few hours in this house and already Mama was making dictates. Though Mary sorely wished to, she knew no amount of resistance, or raging, would sway Jacqueline—or anyone else—to obey her rather than her mother.

In fact, she could very well imagine Mama sending Spencer and Freddie up to fetch her bodily and *accompany* her to breakfast.

'Fine,' she mumbled, dragging herself from bed against her will. 'Let's get on with it then.'

Trying not to think too hard on any of it, Mary completed her ablutions, and let Jaqueline do her work.

Thankfully it wasn't difficult—not thinking too hard—for not only was she well versed in that now, those days since she'd cast Luca from her life seeming years, she was also…

So very tired.

Far beyond lack of sleep—though that was a blessed gift, as it numbed her mind—she felt tired, deep in her bones. Past weary. Past…much.

In quick measure she was dressed, and as ready as she'd ever be, and taking a deep breath, she made her way to the dining room. So much noise already, which suggested, unfortunately, there were many already within.

Not many; all, she corrected, stepping inside the sun-flooded room, fit to burst with all those within, including the Reids, Freddie, and Mena—most perplexing considering both couples had London homes of their own, and she doubted they'd merely returned for breakfast.

Lord, save me there is a garrison of them; though at least the McKennas are absent from whatever strange duty this is.

'Good morning,' she said, nodding her head once, for if not she'd look like a loose-necked doll, bobbing her head at each of them.

All murmured some version of the greeting, their previously loud chatter falling into quiet tittering.

Rolling her eyes, she went to the sideboard and fixed herself a plate, before settling in the last available seat between Elizabeth and Spencer.

Without a word, someone poured her tea, and she kept her eyes affixed on her plate, mindfully cutting tiny bites as silence invaded the room. Still, she refused to indulge them, determined to have her peace, one way or another. After a few moments, there was muttering and movement, and Julianna took Elizabeth, along with young Halcyon, out, shutting the door behind her.

Damn.

Determined to face whatever was coming head-on, Mary gently set down her cutlery—though it echoed in the thick silence—took up her tea, sipped it, and let her eyes dance across the faces around her, trying to evaluate who her best bet was.

Certainly not Reid—scowling and stoic as always.

Nor Rebecca—his beloved countess—she's likely here supporting Spencer.

Genevieve...no she's examining her plate.

Spencer... Mama... I'd rather not.

Mena? Also examining her plate.

Freddie, then.

Though there was unsettling concern in his gaze, he was right across from her, and looked discomfited. Freddie didn't do well with emotion, and he was also her oldest friend, therefore…

More likely to take my side.

'This is ludicrous,' she said lightly, shaking her head, silently begging Freddie to agree. 'I'm not sure what Susie told you…' *What could she, considering she knows nothing...* 'However, I'm perfectly well, as I told you last night. I was perhaps a *little* out of sorts the last time I visited Nichols House, but then one cannot always be smiling, and carefree. I've had a most busy Season—'

'You're always smiling and carefree, Mary,' Freddie said gravely, leaving her speechless. 'The only times any of us have witnessed you otherwise…something has happened. I'm sorry… We used to speak, so often… We were there for each other, and I've been…preoccupied of late. We all have been. We should've been here, but we're here now, to support you.'

There goes that plan, then.

'So dramatic, Freddie. I suffered a disappointment,' she said flatly. If they were determined to have her admit… *something*, then *fine*. 'It happens. I'm a grown woman. I'll survive.'

'Will you?' Mena chimed in, raising her gaze to Mary's as she took her husband's hand. 'When you came with me to save Freddie, you said you knew he loved me by the way he looked at me. You weren't wrong. I saw the way Luca looked at you; how you looked at him.'

Rolling her eyes rather than letting Mena's words pierce her heart, Mary hardened for the attack.

'Just because you found the love of your life, all of you,' she added, raising a brow at the others, including Spencer. 'Doesn't mean that's what Luca was to me. I was momentarily swept away during my affair with him—for yes, shocking though that may be, that's all it was. Now, would you desist from poking your noses into my business, and go about your own lives.'

And I'll go murder Susie for bringing you here.

Mary set down her cup and made to rise, thinking she'd done well indeed, when her mother spoke.

'Sit down, Mary,' she commanded, in a tone Mary—no matter her feelings towards her mother—couldn't but obey. 'We didn't traipse down from Scotland—with Genevieve expecting—for this.' Clenching her jaw, Mary found herself staring at her plate. 'I know I've failed you,' the Dowager continued, gentler, but still not brooking any argument. 'You, and your brother. However, I will not again. When your brother said we'd heard of everything that happened, he meant *everything*.'

Mary's wide eyes flew to her mother's, and she found tears pooling there.

No...impossible... Susie didn't know, not about Lady Claeyton...how...?

Shaking her head, she meant to deny it, but her mother nodded. Mary turned to Spencer, to find him looking both guilty and heartbroken, then she looked at the others and felt…sick.

Impossible... How could they know it all?

Even if they did, that would mean...

'You told them?' Mary croaked, emotion clogging her throat despite her best efforts, turning back to her mother. 'What happened…? How could you? You had *no* right; it wasn't your story to tell—'

'But it was mine. Ours,' came another voice, and Mary whirled around to find Frances standing at the door.

Susie was beside her, holding her arm, looking uncomfortable, but Mary barely saw her for Frances. For the other woman looked like she was facing a firing squad, though her head was held high, and suddenly, Mary understood.

'You told Viscountess Claeyton,' she breathed. 'Everything… For how long?'

'Ten years,' Frances admitted. 'I hated you, Mary. For so long, it's all I had. Resentment, and bitterness. So when she came to me, and asked my help… I didn't care whose mother she was. Only that she could knock you from your glass castle. Make you suffer as I had. I thought… I'd feel better for it,' she laughed bitterly, swiping tears from her cheeks as Susie tightened her hold. 'Of course I didn't. Not when I received your note, crying off the wedding, and not when the old woman came to crow about her victory. I felt the wretch I am. So I…went to Susie. You'd spoken of Nichols House often enough, and I knew I needed help… trying to repair what I'd broken. One day, perhaps, you, and the Almighty, will forgive me. Until that day, I will atone in any way I can.'

Silence invaded the room yet again, and Mary felt more nauseated than ever.

As though she were on a scrap of wood, tumbling through high seas during a storm. She'd thought…she'd felt it all. Before. Years ago. Days ago. She'd been wrong.

Nothing compared to this…raging tempest of confusion, hurt, betrayal, disgust, anger, disappointment… She wanted to rage, scream at them, march over there and slap Frances, shake them all from their silent watch, demand what right *any* of them had…

She wanted to shake her fist at the Heavens and demand an answer as to *why*, with all the power she'd held, *all these years*, with everything she'd done to prevent such terrible emotions taking over, they still were, but instead she merely turned in her seat, and forced herself to breathe as she stared at a patch of expertly polished wood.

Blood rushed through her ears as she tried…to make sense of it. To make a plan, to do something other than just sit there and stare whilst she heard, vaguely, Susie and Frances come sit.

Nothing came.

'If you know everything,' she managed to say after…a long while, her voice hollow, and bitter. 'Then you know there's nothing to be done.' Glancing up at her mother, she dared her to disagree. 'There comes a time when one must accept defeat, and so I have. I've been bested, and I paid the price. I won't risk destroying others so that I may, perhaps, enjoy a moment of…something.'

Mary made it to *upstanding* before her mother again froze her in place.

'For someone so infinitely clever, you are being dull this morning, Mary.' Again, her eyes widened, and her mouth too, like some gaping fish. 'It really is vexing you would not only underestimate your friends, but that you would underestimate me. We mightn't have known *everything* when we left Yew Park House—for you should know as soon as Susie's letter reached us, we departed—still, we didn't merely *charge* down here without a plan, knowing how desperately stubborn you are.'

Mary blinked, and her mother shook her head; the notion as ludicrous as the Norman Invasion occurring in 1466.

'We'd asked Susie to meet us in Hertford, so that we might…agree on how to approach you. When we arrived… Frances was there too, and we learnt…the rest, and *obviously* made a plan to deal with Claeyton. The question that *you* have to answer right now, Mary, is will you be brave enough to do what is necessary to win back the man you love?'

'To what end?' Mary bit back, a plan of attack finally spurring her on, past *feeling*. 'So that I, much like a vapid princess in a fairy story, may have a beautiful happily ever after? What do you think will happen to us, all of us, if Luca takes me back, and *all's well that ends well*?'

She looked around at them like the clodpolls they were.

'What remains of our family's good standing will be *ruined*. Our power will be diminished beyond repair! Do you forget, *any of you*, what it took to ensure we weren't cast away? When Spencer stood by the two of you,' she spat at Reid and Rebecca. 'Do you know what it took to have Mellors transported? To have him punished at all? To have you welcomed back into Society—you, the Disappeared Earl, and his *housekeeper*?'

No one answered, and on she went.

'And you, brother mine? Surely, you cannot have forgotten what it took Mother and I to keep doors open to you and Genevieve. I told you the day you went after her, I would face Society's scorn rather than see you unhappy, but I lied. I knew we could control it, or I would've told you to leave her. Have none of you any idea of what I've done all these years, to shield you, protect you, and keep us in enough good standing so that we may continue working towards the betterment of this land? Have you any idea of what I've done to ensure we were safe?'

Still, they remained silent, though they did all look her in the eye, and that bothered her, that they weren't cowing.

'And you, my dearest mother, you come here, and pretend to know me, and say all will be well, but how can it? How can I trust you after you lied to Spencer and me, for over thirty years? I *do* hate you, despite what I said when *your* truth was revealed. I *am* angry. You were the last person in the world I trusted, and everything I did, was to become like you, and then you betrayed me. Do you think me finding love, marrying Luca, will make everything right? Fix all the wrongs any of us have done? Will it assuage your guilt? Repair all that was broken by your hand? I'm the last one standing, keeping it all together, keeping *myself* together, doing what *you* taught me, and you come here and tell me to throw that all away? I have sacrificed all that I am, and I will not yield now!' she screamed, only then, in the resounding silence which followed, aware of the fact.

That she'd been screaming like some harpy, and that unwanted tears had been streaming down her own cheeks.

Sucking in deep breaths, she tried desperately to regain her composure, though the longer the silence went on, the less she felt…

Vindicated. Right.

The more she felt…ashamed. *Wrong.*

Yet also…*better,* for having expunged that poison from her heart.

'You say the words you spoke when I nearly lost Genevieve…' Spencer said quietly, rising and taking a step towards her, and God help her, she didn't have it in her to move away. 'Were a lie. I don't believe that, Mary. I don't believe you supported me, *us*, merely because you knew you could weather the storm. All these years, you've supported your friends, strangers even—for don't think for one moment I don't know what you did for those women prey to the same men as you and your friends, or to the man Rebecca was, and countless others—because it was *expected*. Best for you, for *our*, standing. You did so much quietly, secretly, for no other reason than you are, at heart, a kind and loving woman.'

Mary shook her head, more tears falling, her mind refusing to admit it even as her heart screamed he was right.

That perhaps, after all, her brother *did* know her.

'I think you're scared, Mary. Rightly, of losing everything you thought important. All of us at this table have been where you are now. And perhaps, you will—*we will*—lose all of that. Only it pales in comparison to the happiness, and fulfilment, you might have. Our family will survive—no matter the scandal. Our name may be tarnished, doors may close, and some things may become harder to achieve. But we won't be lost—for we have friends, and each other. We will fight, as we always have, to do what's right, and that's all any of us can ever do.'

Spencer stood but a hair's breadth from her now, and gently, he chucked her under the chin, forcing her to look at him.

Against her will, she did, his eyes their true mother's, reflections of her own, but for one thing.

They hold so much love.

'The day you told me to go after Genevieve,' he whispered. 'You also said that were there ever someone for you, you would wish them to risk as much for you as I did for her. It seems however, the challenge has been issued to you. Know, that if you decide to take the risk, you won't be alone. You've never been alone.'

Mary's heart twisted with his words, and she searched his eyes, begging him to take it back.

All of it.

Only he didn't.

She yet again looked around the room, hoping to find some support, someone to say, *you're right Mary, we understand, go live your miserable life*, only she didn't.

Freddie's eyes darkened with resolve, and before he even opened his mouth, she knew what he would say.

The same words he spoke to Spencer.

The words I spoke to him so he would grasp happiness with Mena.

'I thought you had more mettle,' he challenged softly, a wry smile at the corner of his lips.

I never did.

Yet somehow, standing there, all of them watching, waiting, and silently supporting her… She felt as if she might just.

There's so much to make right.

But it seems, I'm not alone.

'So…what's this grand plan of yours, then?'

Their plan was…ambitious, and well underway already, as she learned when they all retired to the drawing room to speak of it. At its core, it wasn't a plan at all, but an extension of what they'd already done for her. *Stood up, and proved that I'm not alone*. It was simple, actually, though there was no assurance it would succeed in reuniting her with Luca.

That would be up to him, and him alone.

The plan, however, would succeed regardless of his choice in a greater way, which Mary would be proud to be part of; no matter if she ended this chapter of her tale alone. Of sorts. That notion—that she wasn't alone—was one she was only just learning to accept, though if she repeated it often enough, perhaps someday she would truly believe it. Seeing them all gathered in the drawing room once they'd finished explaining had helped.

Once they had finished their...exposition, Mary knew she had...apologies to make. Longer talks too, with each of them, but those could wait. Most of them. First, she had to apologise, for her hurtful words, and...behaviour.

So she did, cornering each of them before they left the room. Most of them shrugged her apology away saying they *understood,* and were sorry themselves for not having...been there for her. A few of them—well, all barring Reid—hugged her, Spencer the longest. Frances... Frances escaped before Mary could speak to her. Slowly, they all disappeared, until Mary was left with the hardest of all.

Mama.

'I'm sorry, for what I said earlier, Mama,' she said weakly.

It wasn't the most eloquent beginning, but it was the only one.

Her mother patted the sofa, and Mary went to sit with her.

'You spoke the truth of your feelings, Mary, for the first time I think,' the Dowager said sadly. 'I'm grateful for it, no matter how it hurt. I understand your hatred, your anger. It isn't wrong—only if you hold on to it. I thought, like you, for so long... That I *was* doing what was right. That my sacrifices were for the greater good. Unfortunately, I made mistakes. I tried so hard to mould you, and your brother, into what I thought you had to be...even knowing it was wrong. All I ever wanted, was for you to be safe. I tried...'

Closing her eyes, the Dowager took a breath, and Mary tentatively placed her hand on hers.

Nodding, her mother pushed back tears, then finally reopened her eyes, clasping Mary's hand tightly.

'I never forgave myself for what happened to you,' she whispered. 'Only, I never realised...just how long before that *I* had hurt you. Making you into this perfect, unsustainable creature, who could never find happiness. I told you to move on, *relentlessly*, taught you to bury it deep—for that's what I did when life's hardships threatened to fell me. Even all you felt when you discovered the truth of Muire… I wanted to believe it could be so easy, that you could accept it, forgive me as you pretended to, and that isn't right either. I should've known, and seen, what it did to you, only I couldn't. I know that everything which has passed between us cannot be repaired in a day. I know it will take time for you to trust me again. But by God, I will see you be happy. That's all I wish for you now. I'll always regret the lessons I taught you—'

'They kept me safe, Mama. They made me strong. *You* made me strong.'

'And I also made you value the wrong things,' the Dowager countered gently. 'I couldn't see it, not until your brother broke free, and chose what I couldn't. What I never thought possible, nor important. That which I know now is all that is truly worth fighting for.'

Mary nodded, and gazed unseeing across the room.

It was nearly time. Mary stared at her reflection in the glass—the same glass which still stood in her room at the townhouse now.

The night of her first ball after her come out. A pale cream gown. Brightness, determination, hope, excitement, and yes, trepidation in her gaze. She was ready, only she wasn't. Neither her hands nor her breathing steady.

Mama appeared over her shoulder. Mary tried...to look ready.

A silk-lined box. A pearl and silver set Mama had worn her first Season—just as her grandmother had.

She looked up at Mama, and saw...

What she hadn't that night—seeing only the pride, and resolve.

She saw the love which had always been there. She'd felt it in Mama's touch as she helped Mary put the set on.

She felt it...always. Even when she didn't think she did. Even when she thought there was no love at all.

It was always there.

'Even if Luca won't have me,' Mary said quietly, the memory…along with everything else, granting her the peace she'd sought, but would've been unable to find, had they all not come for her. 'I will be happy. That we've found a way to each other again. The road will be long, for all of us, but I shall walk it gladly.'

'As will I.'

They sat there some time, enjoying being together, as they hadn't ever before.

Mary sent out a silent prayer of thanks to Luca, wherever he was, for had he not illuminated her world with his love, she might've never found all she'd lost.

The love already in my life.

Chapter Thirty-Two

The night of the Duchess of Fanshawe's Spring Ball arrived, and Luca had never been gladder for any Society event. Though the past weeks had been...surprisingly pleasant, *considering*, he would be relieved to finally leave it all behind. To spend some pleasant months with Deirdre and his family, properly grieving the loss of his love, and most of all, making plans for the future.

He was glad to be going somewhere they could just *be*. Not act, not have to mingle, smile, laugh, and play the game. It hadn't bothered him so before, but then Society hadn't taken...everything from him.

Not everything. You still have Mamma, Sofia, and Deirdre.

Deirdre, who'd been *his* rock, and without whom he might've emerged from this experience...a very different man. He was changed, yes, but Deirdre had made it her mission to ensure he didn't lose himself; and he would be eternally grateful for that.

And everything else.

He was quite certain Deirdre had also ensured the number of occasions they found themselves attending the same event as Mary was...low. He wasn't sure how, but considering they'd only attended the same gathering *once* in the past weeks—an exhibition of new inventions, two days ago—the likelihood was that it wasn't Fate or Mistress Chance saving him from seeing Mary, but Deirdre. Considering how he'd felt seeing Mary, he was again grateful to the lady for her intervention.

Luca hadn't expected the first time he saw Mary again to be easy. He expected it to hurt; to be filled with regret, and longing. So he was. What he hadn't expected however, was…the pull. The invisible force, beckoning him to her. He'd hoped, the weeks having been…more easily navigated than expected, that the ties between himself and Mary would've been broken. He would never cease to care for her, but he'd hoped his body might not…still feel as if their souls were tied.

And he hadn't expected worry for her to still fill his heart—he should've, it was a consequence of love—but the worry he felt as he glanced at her at every discreet opportunity made moving on…difficult. Oh, Mary was smiling, and charming, as always, only…it wasn't the same. Not even the same as when she'd put her mask back on, when she'd broken…everything. She wasn't the Mary from before—his or Society's—but subdued. As if she'd been broken too, or ill, and was healing.

If the truth of them had come out, he might've thought she was suffering the consequences, but no one it seemed had uncovered what they'd been about to do; he suspected she had much to do with that, and was grateful to her for it. Perhaps she'd been broken by her choice, as he had, but it didn't feel…entirely right. Not that Luca could explain it.

Not that it's any of your business.

No, it wasn't. And he had to keep reminding himself of that. He'd have to remind himself of that tonight—another reason he was…anxious was that he knew Mary would be in attendance, along with her family. Her family, who, along with her friends, had descended back into town—a surprise, considering the Marchioness's condition—though no one had yet seen them at any *public* events. Whyever it was they *were* here; it didn't matter. Again, *not Luca's business.* Though he could admit, to himself…he was glad they were here. That Mary wasn't alone; despite her feelings, and reservations towards her family, their presence… reassured him. He hoped in time, perhaps, she could…find a way to them fully again.

In time. As with many things.

So, yes, the past weeks had been…endurable, though he was looking forward to spending time with his own family and friend somewhere tranquil. They were leaving tomorrow—not *first thing*, as the ball would no doubt end late, or early, depending on how one viewed it—and would collect Mamma and Sofia before stopping at an inn a few miles from Downsham for the night. Depending on the roads, and everyone's feelings, they should be in Norfolk in a few days.

With all its greenery and brisk seaside air.

For now, however, it's glittering wealth and stuffy ballrooms.

Checking himself one last time in the mirror, he nodded, then, after one last look and prayer to the little goddess on the mantel, he made his way to Deirdre's.

'You look splendid, my lady,' Luca bowed, before offering his arm as she descended the last steps into the hall. It was the truth, though there was something more to her beauty tonight than the excellent dressmaking at work on her forest-green velvet gown. More to it than the masterful work of her maid in arranging her hair; or even the exquisite emerald set she sported. This evening, Deirdre seemed…

As excited as a chit going to her first ball, yet as mysterious as a well-seasoned seductress.

'I don't think I've ever seen you quite so…well, you're

different, and it suits you,' he said, leading her over to Henrikson and the others so they could finish their work. 'Is it the prospect of the seaside that has you looking so well? For I doubt it's the ball. I know you enjoy it, but you have attended many times, so I shouldn't think there's anything noteworthy about this evening.'

'Thank you. I think it's the ending of this chapter which has me in…hopeful spirits,' she smiled. 'Now, let us be off. We cannot be wasting this beauty of ours here all night,' she said, winking as he took her arm and led her out to the carriage.

They settled inside, Luca helping to arrange her skirts, and then they were off on what would be a very short journey, which they could've walked in less time—between the line of carriages awaiting entry and so on—but God forbid. Or rather, *Society* forbid.

They travelled in pleasant, comfortable silence for a while, until Luca realised, it had been a longer while than usual. Or perhaps that was only his mind playing tricks.

No, it isn't, he realised, pulling back the curtain and glancing outside to discover though they were near their destination, they weren't travelling *in the direction of it.* Letting the curtain fall back, he turned to Deirdre, frowning, a question on the tip of his tongue, which was silenced by her expression.

She looked…as he imagined an ancient goddess, or sorceress might—the knowledge of the ages in her gaze and a reassuring smile full of hope on her lips.

'You need time to read this,' she explained—though it explained nothing—pulling a letter from her reticule and handing it to him. His heart stilted as he recognised the handwriting. *Mary.* 'And you need time to make a decision.'

'I don't understand,' he said weakly, holding the letter carefully, as though it might bite. He felt a sudden surge of anger, at…whatever it was. 'What is this?'

'I had some visitors earlier this week. Though I was… reluctant at first, to indulge them, and their requests, they… made a good case. Read the letter, Luca,' she told him seriously, brooking no argument. 'Whatever you decide, I will stand with you.'

With a final nod, she turned, pulled back her own curtain, and gazed out of the window.

His hands trembling slightly—*shaking thoroughly*—he settled back against the squabs, took a deep breath, and opened the letter.

Luca. My love.

His hand tightened, crumpling the paper slightly, but he forced in a breath, pushing through the rush of tender, bitter emotion.

Yes, I presume to call you thus, for you are, and ever shall be. If any morsel of the love you felt for me remains, I beg you forgive me that, and read on.

Pausing yet again, he allowed some of the tenderness to creep in, washing away some of the bitterness; listening as his heart bid him to keep reading. Somehow, he knew, the words on this page would change his life yet again.

I have sent this letter to you via Lady Granville, as she was the only one I could trust to...convince you to give me a chance, and read this.

Some might call it cowardice, saying all I must—or rather, some portion of it—in a letter, and not facing you myself. Perhaps there is cowardice in my choice, however, I made the decision to write as I wanted you to be free to rip it up, to be unkind, to curse me, or whatever you might, that you wouldn't have had I stood before you. There is so much to say...and not enough pen and ink in the world to say it.

I am sorry.

I would write those words a thousand times over, and still it would not be enough.

You were right. I do love you, with all I am, and even if...this letter does nothing more, I pray it will do that. Convince you that your love was enough. Has been, would have been, will be, enough for me. You were enough.

Forcing in another breath, Luca swiped at a tear before it could fall and mar the paper.

Forgive me, for all I did to you. The callous, cruel words I spoke. How I hurt you by uttering them, but most of all for not trusting you. For now I must tell you, something did happen to make me...cast you away. And I know... I see now... I should've given you the truth, trusted that you, and others, could help me find a way from beneath the waves drowning me. Only I could not. I felt alone, trapped, and powerless, while the names, lives, livelihoods, and families of others were at stake.

Something…clicked inside Luca, cogs, falling into time, into place. Deep down, he'd known there was *something*, and now, he knew he'd been right all along. About who Mary truly was, and that revelation, or acknowledgement, reignited the flame of hope in his breast.

I do not say this to explain away what I did, nor excuse it, and though I ask your forgiveness—though

I beg and hope for it—I know there is a chance you will not be able to give it. Know that I understand.

If you can find it in yourself to forgive me, then read on. If not, consider this the end of my letter, which I will close with the words, I love you.

If you think you have it in your heart to not only forgive, but also, love me, and give me another chance, even if only to be your friend again—though I will never deserve it—I would ask you to accompany Lady Granville to the ball.

She will explain all that has happened before you arrive, and I will be waiting for you there, hope in my heart. Hope that my fear, my doubts, have not cost us everything; though I will understand if you make the choice to refuse me.

If I do not see you again, know, Luca, that I wish you the best of everything life has to offer. A life of joy, adventure, and yes, love. A better love than that which I showed you. You are a kind, beautiful soul, and my dearest wish is that the wounds I inflicted upon you heal someday.

I love you.

I am sorry.

I love you.

Yours, always,

Mary

Tears fell onto the paper then, before he had a chance to lovingly fold it and place it by his heart.

The swell of emotion was…inexplicable. Overwhelming. All the love he'd known he could never rid himself of, loose and free again, and though he knew there was still a long road ahead, of healing, forgiveness, and trials, he also knew…

I would never choose anything else than to give our love another chance.

He was grinning when he turned back to Deirdre, like a child excited for their first snow, and she smiled back, broadly, with as much happiness in her eyes as he had in his heart.

'Thank you, Deirdre.'

'You have nothing to thank me for. So. A few more turns about these streets whilst I explain the rest to you, and then I suppose we shall be heading to the ball?'

'Yes,' he breathed.

A thousand times, yes.

Chapter Thirty-Three

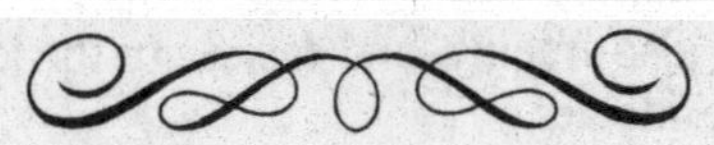

From a very young age, Mary had been taught how to, if not cure nerves, then conceal them. Those lessons had served her well over the years, though tonight she couldn't seem to implement them, resulting in her being a sweaty, jittery, fidgeting mess. The knowledge of *all* they would be doing here tonight helped soothe her, but she couldn't stop thinking…

What if he doesn't come?

Luca would have every right to deny her another chance, to move on and find happiness with another, or on his own; it was her inability to trust that had broken what they'd had, yet…

The hope you kindled inside me will not die, Luca.

'They'll be here,' Spencer whispered, answering her unspoken thoughts.

Over the past week, they'd been able to find…a closeness, an openness, which they hadn't ever had, and it felt… *glorious*, to have her brother with her.

Again. As never before. Especially tonight.

Yes, tonight, he'd been…a silent sentinel, accompanying her on her obligatory rounds as the others made sure everything was in place, then keeping her company as they waited in a quiet corner of the ballroom; waiting for the time to come. There were two ways this could go—and waiting to know which was…*maddening*.

This evening had been much as the past week had been; a whirlwind, interspersed with moments of calm, reflection, and learning. Mary hadn't had much to do—the plans her family and friends had made well underway, or being seen to by themselves, so that she only had to deal with… telling everyone the truth. Which had been as hard as it sounded, but also freeing, and easier, for the love of those who stood beside her.

Genevieve appeared at Mary's left, slightly breathless, and Mary looked over, her heart threatening to just…beat straight out of her. But then Genevieve smiled, nodding, and a centring calm washed over her.

He's here.

'They're here,' Genevieve confirmed. Mary forced herself not to seek Luca, nor any of the others of his party—Lady Granville, Signora Guaro, nor Sofia—lest she…lose her nerve. They were here; that's all that mattered. *He's given me another chance. He loves me still.* 'Everything is in place. The Duchess of Fanshawe has cornered Lady Claeyton just there,' she said, waving her fan discreetly towards the opposing corner of the room. Yet again, Mary silently thanked the Duchess for…*everything*. Supporting them…allowing this… *Being so...unexpected.* 'As soon as you're ready, Mary.'

Mary nodded, pushing back all she felt—hope, joy, nerves—so she could focus on the task ahead.

What I do now isn't solely for myself.

'Go, Mary,' Spencer ordered, kissing her cheek.

One last look at her brother, full of gratitude and love, and she was gone.

Weaving through the masses, stopping for no one, she made her way quickly to Viscountess Claeyton's side.

The Duchess made a quick retreat once she spotted

Mary, so abruptly that Lady Claeyton didn't even have time to process who had left, and who had appeared at her side.

'Lady Claeyton,' she greeted with a perfunctory nod, surveying the room—ensuring she focused on the faces of her family and friends so as not to be distracted—checking that everyone was where they were meant to be.

'Lady Mary,' the woman said, with some measure of surprise, though she did a commendable job of concealing it. 'To what do I owe this pleasure? Not more empty threats, I hope,' she smiled, lowering her voice as she recovered her wretchedness.

'No threats tonight, Lady Claeyton,' Mary smiled sweetly, taking the woman's arm, folding it into her own. Surprise and confusion lit the Viscountess's eyes, and Mary used her advantage to lead the woman to the edge of the crowd, where it met the dance floor. 'Though I do have something to show you.'

The first notes of a waltz rang out above the buzz of the packed room, and Mary released the woman's arm as familiar figures took to the floor amidst the throng of other couples.

Mama and Luca.

Spencer and Signora Guaro.

Freddie and Sofia.

Reid and Lady Granville.

The sight of them, swirling and swaying, lifted her heart, and she smiled.

'You think this display will deter me, girl?' Lady Claeyton mocked, and Mary's smile widened.

'No, madam. I would beg you, however, to look about the room,' she said, glancing at the edges of the crowd herself, where women, known and unknown, came to stand at the forefront, each, like Mary, her friends, and family, with a yellow rose pinned to their chest. *So many of them...* 'Some of these ladies you might recognise. Frances. The Duchess of Barden, with her husband, of course. The Marchioness of Winternell, and the Marquess, beside her. Our sisters, hurt by your son and his friends.'

Lady Claeyton stiffened, and made to turn away, but Mary put a hand at her back, preventing her from fleeing.

'As for the others… You should know them, considering what you threatened them with, so I beg you, look well now, and commit their faces to memory. Many couldn't be here this evening, though they are in spirit. Not for *me*, but for themselves. For each other. To show you that we are not afraid. Not any more. Our stories, are our own, whether you, or someone else takes it upon themselves to tell them. We know our own truths, and we know that we are not alone.'

Mary looked over at the Viscountess, feeling…

Free. More powerful than ever before.

Only it was a different kind of power. A mighty, righteous one; not one born of deceit, manipulation, and lies. One which came from truth, fellowship, and honour.

And love, most of all. Every manner of it.

She saw the defeat in the woman's eyes, her fury slowly melting away, her clenched jaw slacking with every passing second, though she stood painstakingly straight.

'I should think this will be your last public appearance, Lady Claeyton,' she said flatly, casting her gaze from the woman she no longer hated, nor even pitied. *For whom I feel nothing.* 'I hope your retirement to the country will be full of reflection and repentance. Now, if you'll excuse me, I have an appointment I cannot be late for.'

Luca had known what to expect from this apparently expertly planned-out evening. He'd been told what would happen when he made his choice to…seize his destiny, just as apparently Sofia and Mamma would be by Mena Walton if and when Deirdre's carriage was seen taking a particular turn towards the Duchess of Fanshawe's home.

Had he made a different choice, they would've all merely returned to Deirdre's, before setting out for Norfolk in the morning. It was so…meticulous, and carefully planned, it felt like something from a tale of spies and rogues rather than…

The tale of love it is.

Mamma and Sofia were solemn and serious when they all met in the front hall of the Fanshawe house—well past time for the greeting line—as was the woman he recognised as the Countess of Thornhallow—Mena having transferred custody of his family to her, not being one for… crowds—a moment before Deirdre made the introduction.

There was no time to speak of…anything—though Luca knew there would be, after tonight—for in a flash they were all shuffling into the ballroom hurriedly to take their places. Sofia squeezed his hand, offering him a reassuring and supportive smile, whilst Deirdre stroked his cheek gently, before leading his family off to wherever they were meant to be. Then, the Countess of Thornhallow led him through the crowd, nodding politely, but patently ignoring anyone who sought to engage her, to where the Dowager Marchioness of Clairborne awaited.

Small and beautiful, with sharp eyes and features, the Dowager was an intimidating woman who emanated power and grace, though Luca had no time to *be* properly intimidated, think on how this woman would be family soon—nor even to be introduced.

'There you are, Signor Guaro,' the Dowager said, as though they were the oldest of friends, whilst the Countess faded back into the crowd, and the first notes of the waltz sounded high and clear. 'I thought for a moment I might need to find myself another partner,' she said meaningfully.

'I wouldn't dream of missing this dance,' he replied, bowing, before taking her hand and leading her to the floor.

Out of the corner of his eye, he saw Sofia, Mamma, and Deirdre pairing up, though he focused his attention on the woman in his arms as he led her gracefully across the floor, tittering and excited voices underscoring the music.

His heart was pounding—with excitement, fear, and hope—and truth be told, if he'd had any more time to *think* of what was happening tonight, he might've been liable to trip over his own feet and make a mess of it. Thankfully he didn't, managing to lead his partner with ease and grace. He wouldn't make a mess; he wouldn't distract from those who were to be the true focus of this evening.

Glancing around, sure of his own footing and position, he saw them slowly emerge from a mostly unsuspecting crowd, the yellow roses on their chests glowing like victory torches.

All of them stood together now, quietly defiant—not merely of one woman who threatened them, but of any other pitiable fool who ever dreamed to. They stood in full view of Society, of the world—unsuspecting though it may be—telling it they would remain in the shadows, in forced silence, no longer. He felt…proud to be part of this moment, however apparently unassuming.

You, your family, and friends did this, amore.

You brought all these women together; reminded them they were never alone either.

'Thank you,' the Dowager said gently, distracting, but focusing him all at once. 'For bringing my daughter back to me.'

Emotion clogged his throat—from the surrounding scene, and the Dowager's words—and he nodded.

'I'm glad she found her way back to you. All of you. But it wasn't me, Your Ladyship. I only walked the path with her, she chose it.'

'It will be an honour to have you as part of our family now, Luca.'

Gently, she brought them to a standstill, some of the other couples having to quickly redirect—not that he saw any of them.

Mary.

'May I cut in?' his love asked, positively glowing.

A brilliant light amongst the blur around them, and not because of the pale blue silk she wore, though it, and the diamonds at her throat and ears, glittered and gleamed brightly in the light of the chandeliers.

No, she shone, for she was free. Not of shadows and pain, but of their hold. She was…entirely herself. The little goddess had finished reconstructing her true visage, and it left him speechless.

Reflexively, he bowed slightly as the Dowager disengaged herself and left, then again as Mary stepped forth into the circle of his arms.

Taking their positions, Luca revelled not only the feel of her, but in the love that shone brightly in her eyes.

'Luca…'

'Later, *amore*,' he said quietly, pulling her much closer than propriety allowed. 'We have a lifetime for all that. Right now, let's dance. And perhaps give them all something to gossip about.'

The most exceptional sunrise in the history of the world couldn't match the beauty, nor promise of her smile, and he swept her away across the floor.

Before long, all attempts at proper waltzing positions were abandoned, and Mary was nestled tightly against his chest, right where she belonged. Eventually, the music faded away, everyone departing the floor but them.

Then, Mary gave Society something to gossip about when they finally stopped swaying. She reached up and kissed him. Desperately, passionately; that same promise of love, hope, and courage in her touch. Luca responded in kind, and it wasn't until her brother interrupted them with a light tap on his shoulder that they finally left the dance floor.

Though not the ball—as desperately as he and Mary may wish to; they had a lifetime for that too. No, they spent all night, until the first rays of morning, *enjoying* themselves. Speaking with their friends—old and new—their families, and celebrating the end of one chapter.

The beginning of another.

Epilogue

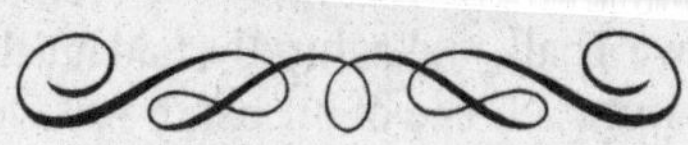

London, one month later

'She's very small... And wrinkly,' Mary noted, looking at the strange creature, all bundled up and quiet —*now*, though she hadn't been mere hours before—in her arms, swaying slightly as she'd been instructed by her mother and Mrs McKenna.

Mary had held babies before, but never one so *new*, and had she not felt Luca's presence at her back, she might've felt slightly more terrified about dropping her new niece.

'Though she already has an impressive head of curls—I cannot tell whether that is from our side or yours, Genevieve.'

Mary chanced taking her eyes off Justine Muire Eleanor Clairborne—born June the fifteenth 1832, at the hour of eleven—for a moment, to glance over at her sister, currently resting in the fresh bed, surrounded by their family.

Spencer had Elizabeth on his lap, sitting against the headboard beside his wife, whilst Mama and Mrs McKenna sat in chairs by Genevieve's other side. The others—Freddie, Mena, Reid, Rebecca, Mr McKenna, even Sofia and Signora Guaro—were all gathered nearby, awaiting their own turns to hold and greet the new arrival.

They had debated returning to Yew Park House, or even Clairborne House, for the birth, before deciding they were perfectly fine in town, and another voyage may not be advisable for Genevieve. Especially considering Spencer and Mama's—and Mary's own—alarmingly high anxiety over the birth.

So they remained, and had a most wonderful time.

Society had been scandalised by the events of the Duchess of Fanshawe's ball, and naturally, had much to say about Mary's inadvisable choice of husband—*though not nearly as inadvisable as the woman her brother chose*—but no one truly paid it any heed, and in the end, ruin did not befall them.

Once Luca and Mary were wed—at St Gregory's, attended by their closest friends and family, a mere week after the ball—then moved into their own townhouse some two streets away from that of the Clairborne family, Society... moved on. Found much more interesting things to be scandalised by. Oh, some in that world decided the Clairborne family—and Guaro family—were not people with whom one should be acquainted. But for every acquaintance that snubbed or rebuked them, there were five strangers waiting to be introduced.

The world was a big place, full of countless strangers waiting to become friends. Full of adventures waiting to be had; full of new things to be discovered. Something Mary had always known, but refused to see, too busy clinging to what she'd held important before she'd seen...all the rest, illuminated by love. Now, she was looking forward to what the rest of life held.

This past month had been one of healing, and long-overdue conversations. With her mother, the McKennas, Spencer, Genevieve, Freddie...all of them. With Luca, and his family. With Susie, and even the other women who'd come to London to stand together. With Frances too, though unfortunately, it would be a long time before her friend truly forgave herself and began to heal further. She was on the right path though, and Mary knew Susie had become a regular visitor to Fenton Hill.

So yes, this past month had been one of change, and grounding. Now, she and Luca—and the others, in their own ways—were looking to the future, and making plans. Luca still wasn't entirely sure what he wished to do with his life—but they had time. He had time, to figure it out. One plan they had agreed on was to travel. Once Justine was slightly older, her family and friends would return to Scotland, with Signora Guaro and Sofia—while Mary and Luca hopped aboard one of Freddie's ships and crossed the Channel to explore the Continent. First, they would meet with Simone and her partner in France, then continue on to Italy.

Lady Granville would potentially join them for some portion of the expedition, having expressed a wish to return to Italy—though she was wary of intruding on the newlyweds' time, which, they assured her, she wouldn't be. Lady Granville—*Deirdre*, as Mary had been instructed to call her—was not only Luca's dearest friend, but she'd become a good one to Mary too, and everyone knew just how instrumental she'd been in facilitating the match. Whatever the lady decided, they would see in time.

We'll see so much in time. I look forward to meeting every challenge, every adventure, every moment, with Luca by my side.

Mary looked back down at Justine, just as the sun peeked through the rainclouds, and marvelled at how the little girl's hair shone like pure gold.

'Yours, I would guess,' Genevieve said, tired, but in good health and supremely good spirits. 'Elizabeth barely had a stitch of hair when she was born.'

'*Mamaaaaan*.'

The room chuckled, and Justine stirred.

Wincing, Mary increased her swaying, whilst Luca rubbed his hands gently across her shoulders, prompting her to relax.

'I suppose I should give someone else a turn,' she said after a while, just…basking there.

Turning, she waited for someone to step forth; someone who ended up being McKenna.

Grandfather.

Kissing Justine's forehead, she gently passed her niece over to meet her great-grandfather, who took his charge into his big arms with reverence and awe.

Then, leaning back against Luca, who wrapped his own arms around her, she basked some more in the love and light that filled the room.

'*Ti amo*,' Luca whispered, kissing her cheek.

'*Anch'io ti amo*,' she told him, turning to gaze up into those dark eyes. Eyes which had prompted her from the first to unveil herself; and which would for ever hold her captive, reminding her who she truly was. 'I love you, too, Luca.'

What a life we shall have, you and I.

What a life of dreaming, hope, love, and...

Whatever else we wish it to.

* * * * *

If you enjoyed this story, make sure to read Lotte R. James's latest romance

The Viscount's Daring Miss

And why not to check out her Gentlemen of Mystery miniseries?

The Housekeeper of Thornhallow Hall
The Marquess of Yew Park House
The Gentleman of Holly Street